MW00758097

Enjoy!
Elaine Levine

War Bringer

A Red Team Novel by

Elaine Levine

This book is a work of fiction. Names, characters, businesses, places, events, and incidents are either the products of the author's imagination or used in a fictitious manner. Any resemblance to actual persons, living or dead, or actual events is purely coincidental.

All rights reserved. Except as permitted under the U.S. Copyright Act of 1976, no part of this publication may be reproduced, distributed or transmitted in any form or by any means, or stored in a database or retrieval system, without the prior written permission of the publisher. To obtain permission to excerpt portions of the text, please contact the author at elevine@elainelevine.com

Published by Elaine Levine
Copyright © 2016 Elaine Levine
Cover art by Hot Damn Designs
Cover image featuring Ken Davila © Luis Rafael Photos
Last Updated: 05/01/2016
Proofing by Carol Agnew
Editing by Editing720

All rights reserved.

Print Edition
ISBN-13: 978-1533048653
ISBN-10: 1533048657

A NOTE FROM THE AUTHOR

We begin *War Bringer* at the point where *Assassin's Promise* left off. To maximize your enjoyment of this serialized story, I highly recommend reading the series in order, starting with *The Edge of Courage* and including the Red Team wedding novellas, before beginning this book!

As a fun extra, I've included at the back of this book a chapter of Abbie Zander's book, *Dangerous Secrets*—the first story in her amazing Callahan Brothers series. If you enjoy sampling stories from authors I admire, drop me a note so I know to do this with future books!

—Elaine

OTHER BOOKS BY ELAINE LEVINE

~Red Team Series~
(This series must be read in order)
1 The Edge of Courage (2012)
2 Shattered Valor (2012)
3 Honor Unraveled (2013)
3.5 Kit & Ivy: A Red Team Wedding Novella (2014)
4 Twisted Mercy (2014)
4.5 Ty & Eden: A Red Team Wedding Novella (2015)
5 Assassin's Promise (2015)
6 War Bringer (2016)

~ Men of Defiance Series ~
(This series may be read in any order)
1 Rachel and the Hired Gun (2009)
2 Audrey and the Maverick (2010)
3 Leah and the Bounty Hunter (2011)
4 Logan's Outlaw (2012)
5 Agnes and the Renegade (2014)

DEDICATION

For Barry, who never lets my brand of crazy delay dinner.

ACKNOWLEDGMENTS

Many thanks to my team of beta readers. I can't tell you how much I appreciate your fitting my emergency reading requests into your packed schedules!

A special shout-out goes to my readers who made this story and this entire series possible simply through your encouragement. Your frequent reminders that I'm not on this journey alone mean everything to me!

WHEN WE LAST VISITED THE RED TEAM...

Here's a refresher for those of you who have read the previous books in the Red Team series. Skip these spoilers and go read the previous stories if you haven't yet! This is where we left our heroes...

*** * * * SPOILER ALERT! * * * ***

- Greer and Remi uncovered the Friendship Community's involvement in King's biowarfare experiments with smallpox.

- Greer and Remi have decided to pursue their relationship.

- Greer learned what happened to Sally, the girl who tried to kill Kit in *Honor Unraveled*.

- Mandy and Ivy are pregnant.

- Rocco and Mandy have hired Wynn Ratcliff as a teacher/babysitter for Zavi.

- Rocco is still struggling with his PTSD.

- Someone—was it Greer? Ty? Owen? King?—killed Senator Whiddon.

- Kit asked Val to look into Ivy's new waitress, Ace Myers, who has a mysterious background.

- It's September, and the team is in their fourth month of investigation.

- Fiona was kidnapped at the end of *Assassin's Promise*.

And now, we continue with Kelan Shiozski and Fiona Addison's story in *War Bringer*...

CHAPTER ONE

How much loss one person could survive wasn't something Fiona Addison ever wanted to learn. But learn it, she did.

Her sophomore year at Colorado State University began with the fatal car accidents that took her mom and friend and ended with her stepdad's death. She lost everything...and found her heart in the wreckage of her life.

His name was Kelan Shiozski.

A former member of the elite Red Team special operations unit in the Army, he was part of the private security team that exposed the terrorists her stepdad had been working for.

Kelan had been there for her when her life had imploded, an anchor in a world that no longer made sense. Fiona drew a deep breath. Just thinking of him made her feel safe.

She was on her way up to the team's headquarters to spend her birthday weekend with him. Her skin tingled at the thought of finally moving their relationship to the next level—a thing he'd refused to do until she was twenty-one.

The remote highway she drove between Colorado and Wyoming was especially scenic on a late summer evening like this, with the sun casting orange light over green hills and granite outcroppings. Her excitement for the weekend sharpened her senses; colors were brighter, scents richer. God, she couldn't wait to be with Kelan.

She checked her mirrors. A couple of white vans were quickly approaching in the left lane, going a lot faster than the speed limit that she was already exceeding.

She looked forward again as the first one passed her. The second one slowed down and moved over to her lane. Weird that there were two white vans so close together. Could be they worked for the same company and were in a hurry to end their workday.

She grinned. She was in a hurry to get up to Kelan, so she could understand the need for speed.

The first van moved into her lane then hit his brakes. Maybe it realized how fast it was going. There weren't a lot of cops on this road, but if any were lying in wait, they'd pull these guys over in an instant.

The van behind her got closer. The one in front of her slowed even more. She watched in confusion and growing fear as they got dangerously close to her, realizing too late that they were trying to run her off the road. She hit her brakes, but that was a big mistake, as her slower speed let them maneuver in closer. She tried to change lanes, but her car jolted as they blocked her in.

* * *

Waiting for Fiona to turn twenty-one made Kelan Shiozski feel as if he wore his skin inside out. But that wait was at an end; they would be celebrating her birthday this weekend.

It was time to talk about the claiming ceremony. He wasn't in a hurry for the ceremony… Well, yeah, he kind of was. He was ready for them to be together forever.

He checked his watch again. Fiona had planned to leave Colorado a little later than usual today. She'd been good about varying her schedule, her route home, being alert and aware. This evening, she'd stayed in town to get her homework finished so that she could give him her complete focus for three full days.

He didn't like her being so far away during the week, but it was working. So far. He especially loved that her school week ended Thursday afternoons, since she didn't have classes on Fridays this semester.

He made another turn about the room, trying to keep his mind from thinking about locking the two of them in his room for the next few days.

A weekend was not going to be long enough, but it was a start. He'd already made it clear to Kit that he was off the clock. He was going to take Fiona over to the site he'd selected for their claiming ceremony. It would be a good time and place to explain to her what the ceremony was all about.

The guys were gathering in the living room, though it was a while yet until supper. Plenty of time still for Fiona to join them. The team had had a big break at the Friendship Community, blowing King's biowarfare lab wide open. Felt as if things were turning in their favor at last.

His phone rang. He saw Fiona's number and instantly got a hard-on. "Hi, babe. What's up?"

"Kelan?" Her voice was breathless. *"No. No. Stop it! Kelan, help me—"*

Static came across the line. Kelan froze. "Fiona? Fiona?"

"Fiona's not your worry anymore," said a man. *"She's heading to her true home. If you know what's good for her…and you, you'll forget you ever knew her."*

Kelan straightened and frowned. "Who is this?"

The line went dead.

Shock froze Kelan as he stared down at his cell phone. None of the guys in the room moved either. He felt as if he were watching himself from a safe distance, someplace soft and numb, where he couldn't feel the blood leaving his heart in an undertow of fear.

He looked at Greer. "They have Fiona."

Greer hurried over, phone in hand. "Fee's phone shows her moving south on Highway 287, back toward Colorado."

Kelan pocketed his cell and went into the hall,

heading for the garage. He grabbed a set of keys to one of the team's SUVs and had the door to the garage open when Kit stopped him. Kelan shrugged free and jogged down the steps into the garage.

"Hang on, Kelan," Kit said. "Fee could be God knows where by the time you make it down to where she is now. We don't know what we're dealing with, if she's bait to get to you, to us."

Kelan glared at him. "I know my woman's been taken by our enemies. I know she's headed south. And I know I'm hitting the road. Send me updates when you have them." He looked at Kit just before getting into the SUV. "And if I'm bait, they can have me."

Kit's lips were pressed tightly against his teeth. "Angel, take shotgun," he snapped.

* * *

Kelan navigated onto the narrow mountain road that Wyoming called a highway and sped toward Laramie, where he'd be able to pick up the road Fiona's captors were on.

Angel monitored her progress on his phone. Kelan looked over every few minutes, watching the red dot blink in and out. It was a lifeline for him; as long as it beat, she was still alive, still traceable.

Five minutes later, it stopped moving. "What happened?" Kelan barked.

Angel changed the screen to get more detail about

the location. "They probably tossed her phone. Looks about twenty minutes outside of Fort Collins." He glanced over at Kelan. "It's just her phone, man. I'm sure she's okay. They wouldn't take her just to kill her. She's leverage for something—she has value to them. For now, at least."

Kelan met his eyes. His hands tightened on the wheel as he faced forward again. There were only a few ways to get to Laramie from Fort Collins, where her university was, and only a single route from Laramie up into the Medicine Bows, where the team headquarters was. He should have met her. He should have picked her up. There was so much distance between them. It had been his greatest fear something like this might happen.

That it might have happened even if she'd switched to the University of Wyoming instead of continuing at Colorado State University was cold comfort at the moment.

He should have hired a bodyguard. At the very least, a chauffeur.

But even that was no guarantee of her safety. A chauffeur could have been compromised or killed. The truth was there was no level of security that could have ensured her safety against someone intent on harming or abducting her.

Because of him and the work the team did.

He should have insisted she sit out a semester or two until things settled down in the mission.

"This wasn't your fault, bro," Angel said quietly.

"She was mine to protect. It is my fault."

Angel pointed to a barren stretch of road between two low hills. Fiona's Acadia was parked on the opposite wayside. They were on the same highway she'd taken to come up to Wyoming; she hadn't even made it a half hour out of town when they'd grabbed her.

Kelan pulled off the road. They crossed the street to her vehicle. The dirt in the wayside had been undisturbed since the rainstorm a few days earlier, letting them clearly see the tracks her SUV made, along with those from other vehicles that pulled in front of and behind her. They probably forced her from the road, sandwiched between their cars.

"There's another set of tire tracks over there," Angel said, pointing back the way they'd come. "The tracks look as fresh as these, but who knows if they're connected." He crossed over, then came back, tracking the dusty footprints. He looked at Kelan. "They come from this side."

Kelan glanced in both directions down the long road. He followed the two sets of large hiking-boot prints, seeing no smaller footprints that would have indicated Fiona crossed the road on her own volition. Maybe they carried her. Or an accomplice might have taken her phone south to dispose of it, while the other vehicles took her north. Who knew where she was.

He closed his eyes and mentally searched for her energy. He was certain she was still alive; he could feel her fear. She hadn't used her emergency necklace yet—or the secondary security bracelet he'd given her. Maybe she couldn't. Or maybe she was waiting for a safe moment. He hoped whoever had her hadn't taken them.

"Let's go get her phone," Kelan said, certain that was all they'd find.

"Want me to drive her car?"

"No. I will." He had the second key for her car always with him. Stupidly, it made him feel closer to her when she was away at school.

A few minutes down the road, they pulled over again at the point where her phone was still pinging. The highway's shoulder and wayside spilled down a steep slope and into open rangeland. None of the earth looked disturbed. There were no tire marks, but also no footprints to indicate an improvised explosive had been set or the way to her phone was otherwise booby-trapped.

He and Angel used their phones to find hers. Kelan picked it up with a plastic bag he brought from the car. He wanted to activate her screen and see the last few calls she'd made, but Greer would need to process it for fingerprints first. Besides, they had her call logs.

Cars from the road whizzed by in waves of noise. Kelan stood in the hot evening wind on the tinder-dry hillside. Had Fiona been followed all the way from their condo? Had there been other people waiting for her in different spots along her route up to the team headquarters to ensure they caught her in their net? If she was followed, had she known it?

Shit, the fear she must have felt—must still be feeling.

Angel put a hand on his shoulder. "We'll find her."

He shook his head and asked, "Why Fiona? Why not me or you or any of the other guys?"

Angel considered his question. "Most likely she was the easiest target. They could snag her a fair distance from Blade's, giving them time to get away with her."

* * *

Kelan marched into Blade's, leaving Fiona's vehicle in the garage for Max and Greer to process. Angel left the SUV parked out front for quick access should a lead present itself.

The women were gathered in the hallway. Their anxious faces stopped him and Angel. "Is there any news?" Mandy asked.

"No."

"Kelan, we're so sorry," Ivy said as she slipped a hand around Mandy's waist, both of them watching him with big, worried eyes.

He clenched his jaw, tamping down his emotions as he nodded. He looked from Mandy and Ivy to everyone else. Hope, Remi, and Eden. The Jacksons. The kids, Zavi and Casey. The team's family had grown. That his Fiona had been taken was a wound in his soul. But the truth was that he would have felt the same if they'd lost any of their dependents.

He went down the hallway, heading for the elevator to the weapons room. He heard Angel telling the group to stay on the property for the next few days until they knew what they were dealing with.

Kelan waited for Angel, then they both went down to the bunker. Max and Greer paused in their work, looking up at him as he entered the ops room. Their calm, intent expressions told him what he needed to know: there was no new information on Fiona or her abductors.

Kelan handed Fiona's phone to Max and tossed Greer the memory card from her dash cam, glad no one wasted words on empty hopes for Fiona's welfare. "Tell me what we know," he quietly ordered as he entered the conference room.

"There's no new chatter. No ransom calls. Nada from Jafaar," Kit said.

Greer pulled up the video from Fiona's car. "Here it is."

Kelan's heart banged with fear and hope as he waited for the images to open on the big smart screen. Angel dimmed the lights. Greer forwarded the recording to the end, bypassing the footage of Fiona leaving the parking garage and heading out of town. They could go through that portion later.

Kelan's hands clenched as he watched Fiona's abduction. As they'd seen from the tracks, two vans had sandwiched her Acadia, forcing her off the road and onto the wayside. She tried to get her car free of the others, but she was squeezed between them. Her abductors, three of them, were dressed head to toe in black long-sleeved tees and jeans, with black baseball caps. One had a gun. The camera didn't get a look at their faces.

Their vehicles were missing license plates. Another white van was stopped on the other side of the road. Fiona's SUV bounced, probably when one of her captors broke her window. There was some kind of off-camera struggle, then her vehicle went still. Her captors must have carried her across the road at that point. The cameras only picked up a little of their movement before two of the three men returned to their vans and drove off. She wasn't with the men who returned to the two vans.

The whole event took less than ninety seconds.

As soon as it was over, the room scrambled to action. Greer restarted the video from the beginning, looking for evidence that those vans might have been captured on traffic cams anywhere along Fiona's journey from Fort Collins. Blade checked with State Patrol to see if anyone had been stopped for missing license plates or other erratic behavior. Angel and Val called up highway cams along the route Fiona took.

Kelan walked into the weapons room and unlocked one of the long-gun cabinets. He took out an M16 and set it on the center island. From the handgun cabinet, he retrieved two Berettas. He selected a KA-BAR and its holster from the knife drawer, paused, then also took an ankle-holstered KA-BAR.

Images of Fiona flashed through his mind—her unruly cap of dark blond curls, which were so goddamned soft, and blue eyes the color of forget-me-nots.

"What are you doing?" Kit asked.

Kelan blinked those thoughts away—along with the barbs they held—and rubbed the heel of his palm against his heart, where they still stuck. He didn't look up.

"Preparing for the war I'm bringing to whoever has Fiona."

"You know you're not a lone wolf, right?"

Kelan did look up at that, meeting Kit's hard eyes. "You know it's not your heart in the hands of our enemies, right?"

"She's one of us, Kelan. She is my heart."

Kelan spread a cleaning mat on the island, then began disassembling the M16. "I'm going to kill them." He looked at Kit from beneath his brows. "Every fucking last one of them."

Kit shook his head. "Ah, no. You'll stay in formation and take the orders you're given, like everyone else on the team, feel me?"

"Then I quit."

"Not today you don't, bro. Keep it together. This is bound to get worse before it gets better. Fiona is now our number one priority."

"Kelan," Owen said as he joined them in the

weapons room. "You have the full resources of this team and my entire company. Whatever you need, whatever we have to do, we'll do. Inside or outside of the law."

Kelan met Owen's eyes and held his gaze for a long moment. At last he nodded, then resumed cleaning his weapons.

He'd failed Fiona. He would find her, secure her, and leave a long, bloody gash in the body of the enemy while he did it.

CHAPTER TWO

Fiona felt something hard and cold beneath her cheek. She took stock of her senses and her environment without moving or making a sound. Her hands were bound behind her. The metal of her security bracelet pressed into her wrist. She moved slightly, relieved they hadn't taken her security necklace either.

She was on the floor of a cargo van, one clearly in motion. Where were they going? How long had she been unconscious? Her legs weren't bound. She tried to open her eyes, but all she saw was black. And at that, she panicked. Sitting up fast, she felt pain explode in her head. She couldn't remember being hit. Had they drugged her?

She sucked in a deep breath and caught a mouthful of fabric. A black cloth covered her head. She was nauseated and had to focus all of her energy on not vomiting for a moment. Taking slow, deep breaths through her nose, she waited for her stomach and head to calm down.

Kelan had probably found her car by now—and

its dash cam video. He would find her. He'd tear the whole world apart looking for her.

She just had to stay alive long enough for him to do it. She shut her eyes and conjured up his image, taking comfort from his strength, his silent power. His eyes were so dark, they were almost black. His hair shimmered like liquid tar, but in the sun, you could see the burnt umber highlights in it.

She remembered the faint sandalwood scent he had. Sandalwood and sunshine. So much better than the stink of the hood covering her face.

The road they were on was straight and smooth. In the time since she'd awakened, they hadn't stopped at lights or intersections. Probably a highway, then. Where were they? How long had she been out?

After a while, Fiona thought of a way to get out of the van and get her hood removed and her hands untied.

"Hey!" she shouted, uncertain if anyone was in the back with her or if they could hear her in the front. "Hey, someone!"

"What?" a man answered. His voice was muffled, as if he spoke through a partition.

"I need to use a restroom."

The man cursed. She could hear him say something to someone else. A phone call was made.

"You need to hold it for a while."

"I can't. I'm going to pee in your van if we hit another pot hole."

The men argued up front. The van started to slow

down. The terrain got rough as they pulled off the road, then stopped. Fiona's heart started a fast rumble. If they were anywhere near civilization, she could make a break for it.

Someone opened the back doors, and she was yanked roughly out of the van. It wasn't dark yet—she could see late evening sun filter through her black hood.

Another vehicle stopped behind them. Whoever was in the second car had to see her bound and hooded. Relief flooded her system at the thought of a potential ally—until she remembered there had been two vehicles that originally pulled her over.

One of the men dragged her around the corner of the van and started to unfasten her jeans.

"What are you doing?" She kicked at him and tried to get away, but another set of beefy arms blocked her.

"You said you had to pee."

"I do, but not like this." She sucked in a rough gasp and got a mouthful of hood. "Not with an audience."

"She's not going anywhere. There's nowhere for her to go," one of the men said as he untied her hands.

"And the hood. I can't see anything with it on."

Rough hands fumbled with the strings behind her neck, then dragged the bag off her head. She looked up at two men in black ski masks. The day was a hot one. Sweat was beading above their dark brows.

16

"Get to it."

"I need privacy."

One of the men shoved her back against the side of the van. "You don't get to ask for anything, bitch."

"Careful with her! Just let her do her thing so we can get out of here."

Fiona looked back at the men still in the second van, both of whom were watching her. "They have to go, too. I can't pee with anyone watching me." She looked over to the empty prairie hills—they were way out east somewhere. "Where would I run to anyway?"

The lead guy shook his head, then waved the other men over. As a group, they went around the front of the first van. Fiona pressed her alert necklace and jogged to the end of the second van. She waited, listening for a car coming in either direction. The first she heard was headed toward them on the opposite side of the highway.

She ran across two lanes of traffic and was halfway across the median before the men spotted her. She was waving madly toward the truck heading her way at seventy-five miles an hour. Three of the men crossed toward her. Already the car was slowing down.

Oh, heck. She hadn't thought this through. The men had guns—she was endangering anyone who stopped. But if she didn't try something, she would end up dead herself.

The lead guy didn't bother chasing her. He shouted toward her. "You weren't the only one we took today. We got the boss' kid in the second van. Come back over here or I'll shoot her. We only wanted her for insurance. Thought we'd need her to keep you in line."

Fiona lowered her arms. *Oh. God. No. Not Casey.* Fiona wasn't even aware there were tears on her cheeks until she felt wind cool the heated streams on her skin. "I don't believe you."

The man shrugged, then started toward the back of the second van. The truck Fiona had been waving down came near, slowed, then stopped.

"You need some help, miss?" the middle-aged cowboy in the driver seat asked.

Fiona wiped her cheeks. She looked back at the guys standing by the vans and in the median. *Casey. They had Casey.* Maybe it was a lie, but she had no doubt if she walked around the other side of the truck and got inside, they'd shoot the man and get her out anyway. She looked at her would-be rescuer, deciding there was still a way to pull some value out of this encounter. "Have you seen Kelan?"

"Who?"

"My boyfriend. Kelan. Have you seen him?" Of course the guy hadn't. That wasn't the point. The stranger she acted, the more likely this guy would be to report her erratic behavior to the cops. The team would get wind of it, and they would know it was her.

"No, I haven't. I don't know what you're on, lady, but playing chicken in traffic like this is gonna get you and someone else killed."

"I just need to find Kelan. I need Kelan. Please."

"I'm gonna call the cops, miss."

"Please do. And never mind. Kelan said you'd get it. It was just a stupid college prank. Tell Kelan you saw me, okay?"

She turned and walked toward the men in the median, trying to keep herself between them and the pickup driver. Her rescuer waved an angry hand at her as he started off down the highway. Other cars passed, each of them slowing.

"I want to see Casey," she demanded when she reached the vans.

"Sure." He took her behind the second van. Before she could say another thing, a big hand clamped a thick fabric to her nose and mouth. A sharp scent pierced her nostrils and stung her throat seconds before she dropped to the ground.

* * *

Rocco looked at the glass teacup Yusef's wife had made him. He'd come down to their hotel in Cheyenne to see if his informant had heard anything about Fiona's kidnapping.

He sipped the sweet blend and exchanged pleasantries with his host, both of them speaking in Pashto. Funny how clear his mind was when he was acting as anyone but himself.

When their cups were empty, both men set them on the brass tray between them. "I am grateful that you are visiting me this evening," Yusef said, opening their business discussion.

"As am I. It has come to my firm's attention that Abdul Baseer al Jahni's representative, Jafaar Majid, may have made some commitments he cannot keep, ones which expose my client needlessly to the eyes of the American government."

Yusef's eyes widened. "What has he done?"

"One of the federal agents who has been tracking my client's work too closely has had his girlfriend abducted. Was not a smart move. I like to watch them, but not stir them up. Abdul will not be happy with this turn of events."

Yusef got to his feet and began pacing around the small living room, one hand tightly squeezing the other. "That is not good."

"No, it is not. I am trying to ascertain Jafaar's level of involvement. I don't want it to come back on Abdul."

"He has not spoken to me about this. Why would he do such a thing, Khalid?"

Rocco smiled benignly. "One of many questions that beg an answer. Is he still in the area?"

"Yes." Yusef frowned as if trying to remember details Jafaar had told him. "He was going to be in Denver for a time. I do not know what he is doing there."

Rocco stood and gave a slight bow as he prepared to take his leave. "Thank you for the tea. It was most excellent." They exchanged the traditional farewells, then Rocco left.

* * *

Kelan glanced around at the unkempt facade of the motel Kit had selected as the base for their search for Fiona. The place was a dive, but had the benefit of being right off the highway where her security necklace had finally pinged. He and Angel had just come back from checking out that area. Another waste of time. No way of knowing if the people who'd taken her had sent a decoy out east for a long drive with her necklace just to throw them off. Max and Greer had been keeping an eye on the cameras along the border between Colorado and Kansas. So far, no white vans had left the state. Of course, they may well have ditched them by now and transferred her to a different vehicle.

Kit and Val pulled up next to them. He hoped the bossman had some news, anything. Kit shook his head. Angel stayed with the SUVs while the three of them checked in.

The motel owner sent them surreptitious looks as he checked them in. "You guys ball players?" he asked.

Yeah, like this was an obvious place for majors— or even minors—to kick back. Wasn't anywhere near a ball field.

Val chuckled, answering for the group, which was good because his or Kit's response would have alarmed the little man. "Well, yeah. How'd you know? Is it that obvious?"

"Your size kinda gave it away."

Another deep chuckle from Val. "Right? It does its own advertising."

Kelan knew the proprietor was not on Val's wavelength.

"What team do you play for?" he asked as he handed them their key cards.

"Well, ours, of course." Val laughed. "Too many benies to swap for the other side." His inimitable vapid chatter caused the proprietor to fall silent as he unscrambled Val's meaning, letting them leave the lobby without more questions.

Kelan dropped his bag on the first double bed in the room he and Val were sharing. Kit and Angel had the adjoining room. He sat on the bed and started unlacing his boots, craving a shower and some quiet so that he could think. He could hear the guys discussing their dinner order in the other room. Would have to be fast food—was the only thing open in the middle of the night.

A phone rang. "Go, Greer." Kit and Angel walked into their room.

"A man called in a report to the Colorado State Patrol about a woman who waved him down on Highway 70 east of Denver. He said she was crying and acting odd. He saw two white vans on the opposite side of the road. Didn't see license plate numbers, but said there were several men with her. When he asked the girl if she needed help, she said no and apologized

for flagging him down, that it was just a college joke. He didn't buy it, but either way, thought the cops ought to know about it. The girl matches Fiona's description. They said she kept rambling about someone named Kelan."

Kelan felt the muscles in his entire body tighten. She'd been where he and Angel just were. So whoever took her hadn't separated her from her necklace—at that point, anyway. "When was that, Greer?"

"About two hours ago."

"So about the time her necklace started pinging," Kelan said.

"Yeah. We've been watching for those vans to cross the border. They haven't yet. We have the State Patrol looking for them. Max is on his way to visit Pete. And Rocco just got back from Cheyenne. He found out from Yusef that Jafaar is supposedly in Denver. And this next thing may not have anything to do with Fiona, but it's something else."

Kelan and Angel exchanged looks.

Greer continued, *"Lobo says there's some buzz going through the sex traffickers about a big transaction happening. In Denver. This weekend. It's not his investigation, so his boss isn't sharing deets. Owen is pulling some strings to get more info."*

Kelan's heart dropped. Thousands of people in the U.S. alone disappeared without a trace each year, many of them sucked into the sex-trafficking trade. And those were people without the enemies he had. Fiona could be anywhere in the world by now.

"If any of this has something to do with Fiona," Greer said, *"and we don't know that it does, why her? They gotta*

know they're starting a war by taking one of our own."

"Maybe they anticipated exactly how we'd react," Blade said, his voice a little farther from the phone. *"Fiona's abduction has made us shift gears, take our eyes off other aspects of King's operation. It's brilliant, really."*

Kelan had to bite back his visceral response to Blade. It wasn't fucking brilliant, but he had to admit it was a good strategy.

"So what are we missing?" Angel asked. "What's the bastard up to that he's covering by shifting the clamshells?"

Kit shook his head. "Greer, if Owen's successful at getting more info out of the FBI, dig into whatever he gets, see what you can find from the backend that might help us tonight. The rest of you see what the players from Bladen's ledger and Greer's spider chart are up to. Find the patterns," Kit ordered.

Kelan put his weapons on the dresser, then stripped to his black boxer briefs. He was on his way to the shower when Kit came back into the room.

"Hey," Kit said. "We ordered you a Caesar salad with double chicken."

"I'm not hungry."

Kit wasn't happy with that response.

"What I need isn't food," Kelan said before Kit argued. "It's quiet so that I can sit and listen."

"If you think you can face what we're heading toward weakened from not eating, then you might as well go on back to Blade's, feel me?"

Kelan nodded. "I'll eat."

He went for the shower, wondering if Fiona was being fed. Had she been given water? Was she in pain? Afraid? He needed the silence so that he could feel her.

Why, *why* had they taken her? Was it a coincidence they'd nabbed her on her birthday weekend?

CHAPTER THREE

Max stood in Pete's apartment over the White Kingdom Brotherhood's clubhouse. Of course the WKB prez wasn't alone. Two women were in bed with him, naked and wasted like he was. None of them even knew he was there. He hauled Pete up over his shoulder and took him outside. The clubhouse had shut down a while ago. The September night was cold, so the guys had scattered to crash wherever they could find a warm bed.

Feral was the only one awake and keeping an eye out for the WKB's president. That kid would take a bullet for his club. Too bad his club didn't give a good goddamn about him.

Feral was standing by the bed of the truck Max had hot-wired. "Jesus, Mads. That's the fucking president. What're you doing?"

"Taking him for a little convo." He met the kid's eyes. "You gotta problem with that?"

"You gonna kill him?" Feral asked.

"Not yet."

"What's goin' on, Mad Dog?"

"A war, Feral."

Feral rubbed his nose, shuffling his weight from one foot to the next. "Whatever. A war." He shrugged.

Max looked at him and wondered if he'd ever known a world not at war. There'd been very little peace in the kid's life—living with the WKB was like being in a constant war zone of sorts.

"You know I'm on your side," Feral said.

"You don't even know what my side is."

"I know you're solid. S'all I need to know."

Max met his look then nodded. Pete wasn't getting any lighter. He dumped him in the back of the truck. "Don't worry about Pete. I'll leave him the truck so he can drive back."

Feral nodded, sniffled, then shoved his hands in his jeans pockets.

Max drove Pete to the overlook where he and Hope had shared a beer. Selena had parked one of the team's SUVs a little farther down the road. She helped Max get Pete strung up on the large outcropping overlooking the ravine. The cool air and cold granite helped Pete begin to rouse from his nightly blackout.

Max nodded at Sel, giving her the signal to wait out of sight. He cracked open a plastic bottle and dribbled water over Pete's face. Took half the bottle, but Pete finally gasped. When he opened his eyes and looked around, his hands scrabbled for a hold on the rough surface of the rock.

"Relax, Pete. You're not going to fall." He paused then added, "As long as you don't move too much."

Pete sent a fast look around them. "How did I get here?"

"I brought you here. Wanted to have an uninterrupted chat with you."

"Couldn't we have talked at the apartment?"

"Not my favorite place."

"And this is?"

Max looked down at the ravine. "It's one of them."

"What are we talking about?"

"About my friend's girlfriend who was kidnapped a few hours ago."

"How would I know anything about that?"

Max shrugged. "You're more plugged in than I am."

"I'll ask around. Come see me tomorrow. Who's your friend?"

"He's one of the Feds down the street." Actually, they were private defense contractors, but that was one and the same to the WKB.

"Why would I care what happens to a Fed? You forget who I am?"

Max smiled and shook his head. "I haven't forgotten our agreement either." Max had promised to give Pete fair warning when the government was coming for him—time enough to OD so he wouldn't have to face prison. "I need info."

He settled near Pete on the big boulder. "My

friend loves his girl like you love your smack. It's killing him not having her." He looked out into the black ravine. "Our women and kids are not part of the mix. You know no man fucks with the other's family. Whoever did this broke the code. Tell me what you know."

"I know Senator Whiddon bit the dust."

"Yeah. Tell me something I don't know."

"You guys do it?"

Max shook his head. "No."

"I hear his suicide note was full of interesting info."

"It was."

"Am I in it?"

"No."

Pete leaned his head back against the hard stone behind them. "Jafaar's been odd lately. Said he was doing a special project for King. Thought it meant he was working with one of the Mexican gangs to move his heroin. Maybe he had something to do with what happened to your friend's girl."

"Maybe. One thing's for sure. I'm going to find who's involved. And when I do, they'll be wearing their tongue for a tie. What's the word from Lion?"

"Haven't heard a thing about him or from him. King keeps things compartmentalized."

"Who's guarding the tunnels?"

"Couple of our officers. They got 'shoot first and ask questions later' orders."

"I hope King doesn't mind empty vaults."

"What're you sayin'?"

"If I wanted my eggs protected, I wouldn't put foxes in the coop."

He stood and started to climb back up the rocky ledge.

"Wait! What about me?"

Max gave Pete a lopsided smile. "Turn around and climb up. I'm leaving you the truck. It's still running. Guess you have about a quarter of a tank left before you got a long walk home."

* * *

Fiona woke in an unfamiliar room. The bare walls looked as if they'd last seen new paint about a century ago. Bars were on the window, dimming what light the filthy panes allowed in. Daylight. How long had she been unconscious? Had they drugged her?

It wasn't a very large space she was in. There was a room divider midway that didn't quite reach to the ceiling. She moved, relieved to discover she was no longer restrained. Her hand went to her neck, feeling for the team's security necklace. It was gone, as was the security bracelet Kelan gave her. And the garnet earrings he'd surprised her with after her first week at school. Her feet were cold…and bare. At least she still had her clothes on.

She sat up and the world began to spin around her. She groaned and braced her head in her hands.

The floors creaked as three young women

30

crowded the opening of her alcove. "She's awake!" one of them announced.

She tried to speak, but her voice was drier than a dirt road. "Water, please," was all she could manage to say.

The youngest of the girls left then came back with a plastic cup full of tap water. Fiona guzzled it down as she looked at the four women staring at her. Their expressions ranged from tension to boredom.

Who were they, and where was she?

"What is this place?" she asked them.

"Typical," the bored girl huffed. "They never know."

The girl standing next to her was barely more helpful. "It's a place your old self would never know and your new self will wanna forget."

Fiona frowned at that cryptic announcement.

The bored girl rolled her eyes. "You're in a cathouse, honey. Out in the middle of Colorado's big, empty nowhere."

Two dogs started to bark outside. The youngest girl jumped. Her eyes got big, then glazed over. The dogs ran from one side of the house around to the front, snarling at something.

Fiona went to the window, but whatever was happening was on the other side of the house. There was a mechanical sound like a garage door opening. The dogs were going crazy.

"Do yourself a favor," the bored girl said as the group left her room. "Stay put in here and don't make a sound." She shook her head. "No matter what you hear."

Someone came into the house. "Haley, girl, I'm early today. Couldn't wait," a man announced. "You don't look happy to see me." There was some shuffling of feet. One of the girls was being shoved into the alcove next to Fiona's. "Don't matter. Seems whatever you do works for me."

Fiona's heart started to beat hard. There was a scuffle. A bed creaked. She heard the man's heavy breathing, then the bed creaked in time with his grunts.

Fiona covered her mouth with her hand. It seemed to go on and on. No one screamed. No one fought. *You're in a cathouse, honey,* the girl had said. Were they prostitutes? None of them looked even as old as she was.

They had to get out of here. She looked up at the bars on the windows. Maybe there were other windows that weren't barred. Or the front or back doors. Maybe they had a phone here—she could call Kelan. God, he had to be worried sick by now.

Fiona slipped silently to the ground to hunch against the wall, afraid any more movement would make the floorboards creak. Someone turned on a radio, covering the sound of the girl's whimpers.

Fiona knew she was a coward, shaking in this corner as she passively witnessed another woman being raped. She thought of her training with Angel. He always said if avoidance was an option, take it. But would Selena huddle here and do nothing?

No, she wouldn't.

But she wouldn't have to. She knew how to gut a man while he still stood.

After a bit, the man finished. He said something to the girl that Fiona didn't quite hear. There was the soft sound of clothes being adjusted, then he made his way through the house. Fiona heard a door being closed, then the garage door opening. The dogs outside started to bark.

Fiona stayed locked in place, uncertain if it was safe to move about. She heard the girl get up and go into the bathroom. After a few minutes, Fiona got to her feet then moved silently to the edge of the partition. She peeked around the other side. Everything was straight in the girl's room. The bed was made up neatly, the blankets tucked in tight, like the bunks down in the bunker of Ty's house.

Fiona looked at the bars blocking the window in that room. God, if there was a fire, how would they get out?

She left the bedroom and went into the main room. The house was tiny. It had only the two bedrooms, both of which had been partitioned into two sleeping quarters, the bathroom, and a bigger room that had a couch at one end and the kitchen at the other, with a table in between.

The other girls were in the kitchen; the one who was bored before was stirring something in a pot on the stove. Smelled like SpaghettiOs. For breakfast.

The girl looked over at Fiona. "You got a name?"

"I'm Fiona."

"I'm Bess." She pointed her spoon at the other girl and said her name. Fiona didn't see the youngest of the group, and when she realized what that meant, her stomach threatened a revolt.

"What just happened?" Fiona asked.

"What do you think?" Bess answered without looking up from the stove.

Fiona pointed to the bathroom door. "She can't be more than fifteen."

"So? Geez, what a precious world you must have come from."

"Why didn't you stop it? Why didn't all of us stop it? It was one man. We could have taken him."

"Why? So we get rid of one. What do we do with the forty others that come by after him?"

The youngest came out of the bathroom, pale-faced and tear-stained. She crossed her arms and didn't look at anyone.

"That's Haley," Bess said after giving the girl a brusque once-over.

Fiona frowned. "I'm not staying here for this."

"Where you gonna go?" the other girl asked.

"I have friends who will come right now to get us. Let me use a phone."

"No phone here."

"A computer, then. I can email them."

"They'll be shot if they come for you."

Fiona smiled. Her friends weren't the usual kind.

"No, they won't."

"Look, we got nowhere to go," the girl seated at the table said.

"Then come with me. I'll find you someplace to go. I'll get you help."

"You even try, they'll kill you. And us," Bess said.

"Who will?" Fiona asked. The girl at the table shrugged and gave her a blank look. Bess stabbed at the boiling pasta. Haley never looked up.

"Well, then, answer me this. I had earrings and a bracelet on when they took me." She didn't want to accuse the girls of stealing them, but she desperately needed to know if she'd had them when she got here...if they were still here somewhere. "Did they fall off when they brought me in?"

"Never saw them," Bess said from the stove. Her back was to the room. She didn't see Haley's gaze shoot over to Fiona.

"Okay. So, I guess I'm outta here." Fiona turned on her bare heel and started for the front door. The windows that were in the main room were also barred. Hopefully, one of the doors was unlocked.

Haley ran ahead of her and blocked the door. "You can't go out there."

"Why?"

"The dogs."

Fiona smiled. "They are just dogs. Probably, they've been mistreated and are touchy. They're not going to hurt me."

Haley shook her head, her brown eyes big. "They'll

kill you. They were trained to kill us."

Fiona looked from Haley to the other girls. Their faces were tense. Well, whatever. She'd worked with Eden, helping her train some of the dogs she had at the kennel at Ty's. She knew how to be calm and assertive with dogs.

"Let her go," Bess ordered. "It's her funeral."

"I'll send back help," Fiona told the girls.

"Don't bother," Bess said.

Fiona frowned. "This is no way to live."

"It's better than living on the streets," the girl at the table said. "Here at least we have food."

Fiona looked at the two open SpaghettiOs cans. She remembered feeling sorry for herself after Alan died, having no family, no home. No one. But she did have family. People who loved her and cared for her. She had her friend Mandy, then the whole team, and Eden and Ivy and Casey and Zavi. And Kelan. Tears filled her eyes. They had to be worried sick. Kelan especially.

She gave Haley a reassuring smile as she gently pushed her aside. "I will send help. I promise."

She turned the doorknob, and was glad it wasn't locked. She opened it. The dogs were not out front. Maybe they wouldn't even know she was outside. She glanced around the yard, looking for a gate. It was off to the side, by the drive. All she had to do was get from the front door to the gate—and through it— before the dogs caught up to her.

She couldn't tell from where she stood if the gate

was locked. If the dogs really were crazed beasts, she took a significant risk trying to leave without knowing if the gate was kept locked.

She closed the door quietly so as not to rouse the dogs. "Is the gate locked?" she asked the girls behind her.

Bess shrugged. "Never tried opening it."

"It probably is. We're completely locked in here," the girl at the table said.

Fiona didn't look at Haley, who was watching her with enormous eyes. Fiona crossed the room to the backside of the house. There was a small alcove off the kitchen. A glass door with iron bars taunted at the freedom beyond. The window was filthy, smudged by years of accumulated dust and wear.

One of the dogs saw her at the door and ran up the steps, snarling. She could just see its big teeth flashing through the grime on the window. When his big body slammed against the window, she was instantly grateful for the bars that kept him from coming through the glass.

Nevertheless, she tested the doorknob. It was locked.

She returned to the kitchen through the short, jumbled laundry room. The girl at the table was eating her canned pasta. Bess leaned against the counter, a bowl in hand.

Fiona went to the garage door. It was made of steel and was also locked with a deadbolt.

The only way in or out for them was through the

front door…and into a yard that may or may not have a locked gate. Haley hadn't moved from her post by the front door. Fiona looked at the girls. Bess appeared mildly irritated, the others utterly hopeless.

"Give me a knife," Fiona said to Bess.

The girl shook her head, then opened a drawer and took out a standard dinner knife.

"No, I mean a real knife."

"Don't have any."

Fiona didn't accept that answer. She went over to the drawers and started pulling them out, looking for any kind of sharp knife, hopefully longer than a paring knife. Bess hadn't lied. Fiona sent her a dark look then checked the cabinets. There was a large iron skillet. It would have to do. She could use it as a club or a shield.

No one tried to stop her. She paused in front of Haley. The girl reached out to grab her forearm. "Don't do this. Please, don't do this. They will tear you apart."

Fiona didn't give in to that hysteria, though she fully believed the girl was right. "I need your help."

"No." Haley vigorously shook her head.

"Go to the back door and keep their attention." Fiona took her arm and led her across the room. "Make noise. Keep them occupied. Buy me some time to get to the gate—and back if it's locked."

"And then what?" Bess asked. "You get out and leave us?"

"No. I get out and open that garage door. We all

leave."

"It's a bad idea," Bess said.

"You got a better one?"

Bess met her gaze. Her eyes were hard. Fiona hurried to the front door. Bess followed her. She looked at the girl who seemed to be a leader of the others, wondering if she would sabotage Fiona's escape plan by summoning the hellhounds. She had no choice but to give it a try.

A car came down the road. Fiona couldn't see it for the cornfield between the house and street.

"Showtime, girls. Slurp your food down and get in your places," Bess ordered. "You"—she pointed at Fiona—"get back in your half of Haley's room and keep your trap shut. No one's supposed to touch you, but who knows if they can resist fresh meat."

Fiona looked at Haley. Her eyes were glazed over. Once again, she quietly retreated to her space. "We can fight them," Fiona whispered as she entered their room.

Haley had withdrawn deep into her mind. She didn't respond. Whatever fight she had was long gone. Once again, Fiona had no choice but to crouch in the corner of her room. Men came continuously over the next few hours. The other girls giggled and made jokes with their johns, but Haley was always silent.

It was late afternoon before Fiona could venture out of her hiding space. She went to the back door to see what the dogs were doing. She couldn't see them, so she banged on the door. Instantly, they began barking and lunging at the glass.

"What are you doing?" Bess asked.

"I'm getting out of here"—she looked at the two girls who were in the living room—"with or without your help."

Haley came to stand at the door to her room. Bess frowned as she looked at her. "Wait," Bess said to Fiona. "Wait."

Fiona and Haley both looked at Bess. She went into the laundry room and rummaged through something Fiona couldn't see. When she returned, she held out Fiona's security bracelet.

"Is this one of those security bracelets?" Bess asked.

Tears flooded Fiona's eyes as she took the bracelet. "Yes." Her hands were shaking as she pressed the activation button hidden near the clasp. Her knees went weak. She crumpled to the ground, crying as she smiled up at the girls. Her relief was so great, she couldn't summon anger that Bess had lied to her.

"Everything's going to be fine now."

CHAPTER FOUR

Kelan's phone buzzed with an alert—the one he'd been waiting for. "It's Fiona. I gave her a secondary security device—a bracelet." He sent the coordinates to the team. They gathered their weapons and hurried out of their motel rooms.

"I'm driving," Val said as he unlocked one of the SUVs. Kelan didn't argue.

"What are we looking at, Kelan?" Kit asked over their comm units as both vehicles cut through traffic.

Kelan used the vehicle's Wi-Fi to check the coordinates sent by the bracelet. He expanded the satellite image the security app brought up. "It's a farmhouse in the middle of a cornfield. About forty miles east of here. It's got some outbuildings, but no other houses or large structures for at least a klick in either direction. The signal's coming from the house."

They drove east, passing the industrial fringe of Denver, urban and suburban neighborhoods, then hit the farms and miles of crops—onions, beets, beans, and corn, some of which had been harvested, some still waiting. All of it looked peaceful in the crisp

September afternoon.

The fields where their target was had not been harvested. Tall spires of drying corn hid just about everything. Worse than merely limiting visibility, it gave an enemy perfect cover. He exchanged looks with Val, all of his senses firing a warning.

They couldn't wait for backup. Not even an hour had passed since Fiona's ping. This was the first break they'd had in the nearly twenty hours since she'd been taken. Val pulled onto the narrow dirt road, with Kit close behind him. After a short drive, an area opened in the cornfield, revealing an old farmhouse, a yard, and some other supporting farm structures. Kit drove around behind the house, then turned around and parked.

A high chain-link fence surrounded the front and what Kelan could see of the side of the house. The eight-foot fence was topped by an inward sloping course of barbed wire. The place looked like a prison.

When Kelan got out of the SUV, he saw two dogs leaping and barking at something in the house. He could just make out a figure at the door. He thought it might be female. She was banging at the glass and shouting. Was it Fiona? Adrenaline burned his veins…and it wasn't the only thing burning. A thin line of smoke seeped around the door, but the girl couldn't come out because of the dogs.

"Val, there's a fire inside! I'll get the dogs. You get them out!" Kelan drew his weapon then opened the gate and whistled for the dogs. They paused in their vicious assault on the doorway and looked back at him, then rushed down the steps toward him. Totally expecting an attack, he was surprised when they sat at his feet and looked up at him.

The girl opened the door and shouted for him to get them out of there.

Everything happened so fast. He ordered the dogs to heel and took them out of the gate. At the trunk of his SUV, he retrieved a rope and tied them to the far corner of the fence.

Val was already inside the house with a fire extinguisher. Two girls hurried outside, coughing, sucking in fresh air, and coughing again.

"One...more...girl," one of the girls said. "Inside. One. More."

Angel tossed Kelan the fire extinguisher from their SUV then took over the care of the girls, leading them away from the dogs toward the SUV Kit had parked at the side of the house.

Kelan hurried inside the house. *One more.* Was it Fiona? Val was working on a pile of rags that still smoldered. The smoke burned Kelan's eyes. He rushed through the tiny house. The two bedrooms had been divided into four cribs, each with a narrow bed and nightstand. The first three he checked were empty.

In the corner of the last was a small, huddled shadow. Unsure if it was a pile of dirty linens or a human, he rushed toward it and saw it stretch up as it sucked in a bit of air from a shattered, barred window.

He scooped her up, knowing instantly from the feel of her that she wasn't Fiona. The girl tried to scream, but her lungs were too filled with smoke to make more than a hissing sound. She clawed at him and fought, but as he raced her outside, she started to scream, "No! Nonononono."

"Easy, baby. I gotcha. The dogs are tied up."

She wrapped her arms around his neck and clung to him. Kelan handed her over to Angel and went back inside.

Val had the fire extinguished, but it still smoldered. He'd kicked the back door open to let the thick cloud of smoke dissipate. "The doors and windows were locked and barred. Their only way out was through the dogs, who would have mauled them."

Kelan looked out the front door to the dogs lying down by the corner of the yard. "Someone wanted them dead."

Kelan's boot crunched on something on the floor. He bent and picked it up. A mangled bit of metal—it was all that was left of Fiona's bracelet. He went outside. The girls were sitting under the back hatch. Angel had found two blankets, which he wrapped around the girls.

"Where is she?" he asked them as he held up the bracelet. "Fiona. What happened to her?"

The youngest of the girls, the one he'd carried from the house, pulled the blanket corner from her face. "Are you him? Her boyfriend? She said you would come."

He nodded. "Where is she?"

"They took her."

"Who took her?"

The girl shook her head. Hers were the saddest eyes he'd ever seen. He'd seen that look in Afghanistan, in territories that kept passing between allied and Taliban control. Savaged though she'd been, he could tell the pain in her eyes was for him and Fiona.

"I don't know them," she said. "Fiona fought, but there were too many of them. They hit Bess and set the fire when we tried to keep them from taking her."

"Describe them." He could hear emergency vehicles in the far distance. The girl started to cough. Angel handed her and the others bottles of water.

One of the other girls looked at him. "They were white. They wore ski masks. It happened so fast. We were too focused on the fire to notice much else. Thank you for coming. She said you would."

The fire engine was first on the scene. Kit and Val went to talk to the firefighters, hoping to keep the house as intact as possible so they could collect evidence. An ambulance arrived and the paramedics started working on the girls.

Kelan stepped away to phone Max. "What do we know about the owner of this house?"

Max told him the guy's name. *"He's been on the watch list of several agencies. Among other criminal activities he's associated with, he's suspected of being a kingpin in Denver's sex-trafficking industry, but they haven't been able to pin anything on him."*

"Until now."

"And maybe not now. The house has been leased for the last two years by a Fred Perkins."

"Text me the addresses."

"There's a flag on the owner's info, but I'm sending you the renter's. Oh, and Lobo's on his way over."

"He's just pulling in now. I'm out," Kelan disconnected the call.

Angel came over, slipping his phone into his pocket. "Blade's coming down with Eden. She wants custody of the dogs."

Kelan shook his head. "Not a good idea. You saw them when we first pulled up. They've been trained to attack females."

"I told her about them. She said if she doesn't take them, they'll be euthanized—for doing what they've been trained to do. You know how she feels about that." Angel grinned.

Lobo didn't come alone. Several other Feds and a couple of cop cars pulled in behind him. So much for keeping this quiet. It was looking like a RICO bust. He just hoped reporters didn't show up soon.

Kit talked to Lobo about getting the girls some protection while they were at the hospital and whatever shelter they ended up at. Kelan told them about the owner and tenant of the house. "I want to talk to the owner."

"No," Lobo nixed that. "You'll jeopardize a case

that's been three years in the making. I don't want our informants and agents compromised. There are a lot more women at stake than just yours. And it's not my case. I can't make that call."

Kelan's smile was no smile at all. "You're moving too slowly. Your methodical process nearly cost these girls their lives. It's time to shake things up. Warn your people I'm coming in. Do what you have to do, but don't be in my way."

Kit stepped between the two of them before the situation could escalate. "Go visit Perkins," he ordered Kelan. "See what info you can get out of him. He's closer to this and likely to know more anyway."

* * *

The house Fred Perkins lived in was a typical mid-last-century home in a neighborhood that had only started being revitalized. They went up the steps just as the guy was walking out the door. He stopped short. "Who are you?"

"The guys who just saved your cathouse from burning down," Kelan growled.

The man immediately tried to get back inside, but Kelan and Val were right with him. All three of them stepped into the foyer as a woman was hurrying down the stairs, two kids close on her heels. She was dressed in a suit, and the kids were lugging backpacks, as if it was any other normal morning.

"Honey, take the kids upstairs," Perkins ordered,

like a fucking stand-up family man trying to protect his family.

She did as he requested. He waited until she was completely upstairs, then turned and walked into the living room. The TV was on. "So what's this about a fire? And how does it involve me?"

"Three girls almost burned to death," Val continued. "They were locked inside when the house you're renting was set on fire."

"You want to tell us why you're trafficking underage girls there?" Kelan asked.

The man's mouth opened and his eyes bugged in a look of shock. He held his hands out, palms down as he gestured for them to keep their voices quiet.

"Did you think the taint of your business wouldn't soil your family?" Kelan asked. "Or are they in on your lucrative dealings?"

"It's not lucrative. It's not anything. I don't have anything to do with it."

"And yet you don't deny your name's on the lease…"

"It isn't what you think."

"I saw the girls dying in that house. One is probably not even fifteen." Kelan tilted his head. "How old's your oldest? Just a couple years younger than that? You're in a shitload of trouble, Perkins. How about you start talking?"

"Oh, God."

"Yeah, we're gonna need more than that," Val said.

"I was afraid this would happen." The man wrung his hands and started to pace. "I have a gambling problem."

"You have a helluva bigger problem than that."

He sent a look toward the stairs. "My wife knows about my gambling. I tried to quit. I had quit, for a long time, but a couple of years ago, we went through a bad patch. She left, and I thought I'd lose myself in a few rounds of poker. The good rounds—high-stakes, backroom kind. I thought if I could just make some quick money, I could buy us a vacation, and we could work things out. Well, I lost money. A lot of it.

"When I couldn't pay it back, they threatened my family. One day, when I was here alone, they came for me. They drove me out to a house and told me I had three choices. Pay them back immediately, get a bullet in my head, or agree to put my name on a lease. If I chose the last, we'd be even. They swore I'd never hear from them again—and I wouldn't have to pay the rent. They just wanted my name."

"Who are these men?"

"I don't know. I had never seen them before. Nor since."

"What did they look like?" The plaintive wail of a siren began in the distance.

Perkins shook his head. "It was two years ago. I was panicking. I don't remember what they looked like."

Kelan pulled his lips back from his teeth. The siren was getting closer. He was almost out of time. "These men took my woman. They're dragging her into the sex-trafficking underworld. How would you like it if your wife was taken and your young daughter fed into the system?"

"The only name I have is the bookie's who set the games up. But I heard he's dead." He gave them the name. "I don't know who took his spot."

"Where was this game?" Val asked.

The man gave him an address.

The wife came back down the stairs. "You leave my husband alone. I called the cops. They're going to be here in seconds."

Kelan looked over at her. "They were already on their way."

She sent a worried look toward her husband.

"I swear I had nothing to do with this."

Val opened the door as the cops came across the porch.

Kelan looked over at Mrs. Perkins, who was watching the cops search her husband, then cuff him as they read him his rights. He wondered if she knew more than she let on. How could she not know what her husband was caught up in? Despite his protestations of innocence, did he avail himself of his captive sex outlet when he wished?

At that thought, Kelan pivoted on his heel, heading back into the room to lay into the guy, until Val grabbed his shirt and dragged him outside.

"He's going to jail. He's destroyed his family. A broken nose isn't going to make anything measurably worse for him. And you don't need to get arrested while we're looking for Fiona. Save it for the rest of the bad guys."

* * *

Rocco was in the bunker, analyzing the social media threads of their main people of interest, when his phone buzzed. Max stepped out of the ops room and pointed to him. "It's Jafaar. You're on, Khalid."

Rocco put his phone on speaker.

"Peace be upon you, Khalid," Jafaar said in Arabic.

"And upon you, peace, Jafaar," Rocco returned.

"I am calling with felicitous news. One of our important allies is celebrating the wedding of his daughter this weekend. Only his closest friends and allies have been invited to attend. My boss and your client, Abdul Baseer al Jahni, has been selected to represent his region. As his only agent in this country, I will be standing in for him at this momentous event. Each representative is allowed to bring a guest. I choose you. As my friend and in your capacity overseeing the security of his foreign affairs, it is correct that you join me. I regret not being able to give you much advance notice, but I suspect King did not give anyone much, due to his need for security."

The hair lifted on Rocco's neck. He flashed a look at Max and saw that it had the same effect on him.

"I am honored that you asked me. I will be pleased to attend with you. And it will provide me with an opportunity to review the security infrastructure he has in place. I'm sure I'm not the only one attending the event who is interested in ensuring King has taken adequate precautions to ensure the privacy of you and all his guests."

"I will call and set up that walk-through."

"Where and when is the ceremony to be held?"

"Meet me at Yusef's hotel at noon tomorrow. We will travel to King's private quarters together. There are two events: the initiation tomorrow night and the wedding Sunday morning."

"Very well. But know that if King refuses to allow us to inspect his security procedures, I must counsel al Jahni to decline his participation."

"Indeed, as he should."

"I will need the exact meeting coordinates in advance."

"I do not have them. We are to park at a rendezvous point, where we will follow one of King's vehicles for the remainder of our journey."

"So be it. I will see you tomorrow, my friend."

"Allah keep you safe," Jafaar said. The line went dead.

Greer strolled into the conference room.

"What the fuck was that about?" Max growled.

"You up to this, Rocco?" Greer asked.

"Yeah. I am."

Max nodded. "I'm calling Kit."

"Bolanger here."

"Rocco got a call from Jafaar. Have a listen." Max

replayed the call for Kit.

"Well, damn. What the fuck was all that cryptic shit? What initiation was he referring to?" Kit asked. *"And who's King's daughter?"*

"Your guess is as good as mine," Rocco answered.

"Son of a bitch," Greer snapped. "You don't think it's Fee, do you?"

Kit sighed. *"Don't think we can rule that out."* Silence. *"Rocco, you good to do this?"*

"I am."

There was another pause at Kit's end. *"Look, I don't know if these two things are connected, but Lobo just said that several international power players who've been on their watch list are heading to Denver. It raised flags because there are no known meetings or summits happening here this weekend."*

"Maybe they're coming out for some R&R," Greer suggested.

"Not this group. They're heads of shadow banks, oil magnates, and top governmental leaders and advisors to leaders in several different countries. This group isn't on friendly terms most of the time."

"Jafaar said he was representing al Jahni at this event. Made it sound like there would be other geo-reps there," Rocco pointed out.

"All right. Rocco, I want you to take Selena as your date. Greer—get Rocco and Selena outfitted so that they can patch us in when they can. Blade will tail you in Rocco's truck. When Jafaar gets into Colorado, Angel can join the parade. Maybe this is the break we needed. I'll update Kelan on this. I'm out."

CHAPTER FIVE

When Kelan and Val got back to the motel, Kit and Angel were already there. Twenty-three hours had passed since Fiona was taken. They'd come so close to getting her back that afternoon. Barely an hour had passed between when she first summoned them via her bracelet alert and when they got there, but in that time she'd been moved again, and the girls she'd been with were almost killed.

It tore him up that the FBI had enough data on sex traffickers in the area to know that there was buzz about a big transaction, but they refused to share that info with the team.

"What's the word on that renter?" Kit asked.

"He was arrested. Sounds like he was just leasing out his name. He got roped into putting it on a lease in exchange for having some gambling debt forgiven. I sent Greer the guy's bookie's name."

Kit nodded. "Good."

"Not really," Val said. "The guy died a year ago. Max and Greer are checking to see what's known of his network, if he associated with any sex traffickers."

"Owen got us some intel on the likely players in whatever big event is going down this weekend."

Val frowned. "How'd he get it?"

Kit shook his head. "One thing you learn about Owen is to never ask those questions. Let's just roll with it. Whatever's happening is going down this weekend." Kit looked at Kelan. "Khalid got an invite from Jafaar to go to a wedding celebration for King's daughter."

Kelan frowned. "Is Fiona his daughter?"

"We don't know yet. Jafaar either didn't know where the wedding was happening or was withholding that info. Rocco and Selena are going to meet him tomorrow afternoon. Greer is going to follow them. In the meantime, we have to check out whatever the big transaction is that's going down this evening."

Their phones buzzed. Max had sent a list of five targets. "Angel and I will take the first three. Kelan, you and Val take the last two. I don't know if this big transaction is related to Fee or not, but I sure don't like coincidences. My gut says the two big events this weekend are connected."

Kelan was glad they had something to work on. Also, it was a relief to know that whoever had taken Fiona was keeping her in town—if she was part of either event. He wondered again why her captors had driven out east on the highway. Maybe that was where their hidey-hole was.

"Which one first?" Val asked. "Biker bar or strip club?"

"Biker bar."

* * *

Both establishments were on the east side of town. Four different rows of bikes out front, guarded by hang-arounds, said the bar was open to multiple clubs. Val parked their SUV in the side lot. A few of the guys out front gave them hairy-eyeball looks as they approached the entrance.

Kelan yanked open one of the double doors. The bar was dark inside. Took his eyes a second to adjust to the shift in light. A big, bald guy in a sleeveless tee and leather cuts stepped in front of them.

"Private bar," he barked.

"We have an invite from King," Kelan said.

"Whoever that is," the guy scoffed, as if he really didn't know.

One of his friends came over and stood in front of Val. "You know, I'm thinking two of these guys are not like the others," he said to his pal.

Val's brows lowered as he looked himself over. He and Kelan were wearing their standard operational attire: cargos, tees, boots. He looked at Kelan. "Are they dissing our clothes?"

"Naw," Kelan said with a shake of his head, his eyes locked on the guy in front of him. "He's just announcing his education stopped at the Muppet level. Use small words with him."

The guy Kelan insulted roared and lunged for

Val's neck, which started his friend on the offensive. Kelan punched his forehead once, twice, moving him back a few feet. When he came forward again, Kelan swirled and delivered a kick in his chest that knocked the wind out of him and dropped him on the spot.

Val threw a punch that spun his attacker around. Kelan blocked a right hook from another guy who came at him, and countered with an uppercut to his jaw. A couple more punches and Kelan's opponent fell back against a table on top of a card game just as Val dropped his to the floor.

"I've told you clothes don't make the man, Val."

Four more guys got up to replace the three they'd dropped.

"Enough!" the bartender shouted. "Either sit your asses down and have a beer, or get the fuck out of my bar."

Val nodded at Kelan. "That's more like the welcome I expected."

The bartender put bottles down in front of both of them. "You guys cops?"

Kelan took a sip. "Nope."

"Feds?"

"Nope."

"What's your interest in King?"

"Heard he bought a girl," Kelan said. He hadn't exactly heard that, but putting two and two together, he made the assumption.

"So?"

"I want to buy her back."

The bartender laughed. "That ain't gonna happen."

"My money's as good as his."

"Nothing's as good as his. Going up against him is a fast way to end up dead."

"How about you let me worry about me."

"Yeah, how 'bout it?" A new guy joined their convo, leaning an elbow on the bar. Kelan noticed the bartender took a step back. Maybe he was talking to a shot caller, at last. "There's still time to squeeze one more competitor in tonight." His gaze shifted from the bartender to Kelan. "There's one way you can get in on the action."

"What's that?" Kelan asked.

"Get on her delivery team. Or compete to be on her delivery team, anyway."

"This girl have a name? Or did King just grab someone off the streets?"

"Oh, she's got a name. Princess Fiona. She's his kid."

Kelan felt the room go still, or maybe it was just that his senses blanked out for a second. So Fiona was King's daughter. *Fiona's not your worry anymore. She's heading to her true home*, her kidnapper had said.

"So how do I get on her delivery team?" Kelan asked.

"There's a competition for the honor. The winner presents her to King and becomes her bodyguard."

Kelan took a long pull from his beer. "I'm in."

"*We're* in," Val corrected.

The guy smiled and shook his head. "Only one of you goes."

"Then I go," Val said.

Kelan's eyes narrowed. "She belongs to me. It's my privilege and duty to fight for her."

"It's a rigged game, K. Let me take the fall—that way, you survive to have a life with her. When she's free."

"I'm going."

"*Fuck. Me,*" Max growled over their comm units. "*Neither of you is doing jack shit. Kit and Angel are on their way. String it out until they get there.*"

"Where is this competition happening?" Kelan asked.

The guy leaning on the bar smiled. "An undisclosed location." He looked at his watch. "It's a time-sensitive offer that's quickly expiring. The competition begins in an hour, and we still have to transport the princess."

Kelan stood. "Let's do it."

"Where can I pick him up afterward?" Val asked.

"No need. If the winner beats three guys, Princess Fiona owns him—you'll never see him again. If he loses, he'll be dead, and you'll never see him again. So say your goodbyes now. Leave your wallet, phone, and weapons here." The guy looked at Kelan. "And if you're wearing any other communication or transmitting devices, get rid of them." He nodded to the bartender, who took his phone out of his pocket and texted someone.

Kelan started disarming. He removed his earpiece and set it on the bar. He met Val's solemn eyes; they both knew it was going to be up to him to reach out to the team when he could, because it was highly likely they weren't going to be able to follow him to where Fiona was.

He shook hands with Val. Something pressed into his palm. Val's earpiece. He glanced at the bar where his own comm unit still lay.

"Let's go," the guy said.

Kelan didn't move. He watched Val take his things and walk out of the bar. He wasn't leaving Val at the mercy of the gang bangers. "We'll go as soon as I see him pull away."

When Val's SUV left the parking lot, Kelan followed the guy out the back way into an alley. A black Mercedes with matching black tinted windows was waiting for them. The driver got out and came around the backside of the car. He removed something from the trunk—a wand to check for transmitting devices. Kelan had already checked that the earpiece was off. The wand didn't detect it.

They got in the car and went a few miles to an industrial complex long past its prime. The driver stopped outside the steps leading to a side door. "There's an entrance fee you have to pay."

"Aaannd that's something you should have said before having me leave my wallet behind."

The guy laughed. "Money ain't gonna buy you a spot in the competition. Go inside. You'll know what you have to do."

* * *

Kelan moved up the stairs to the entrance, surprised he was not challenged. He left the comm unit off in case someone inside wanded him again. The guy who brought him here took off. Kelan paused to listen at the rusting steel door, but could hear nothing from inside. He tried the door. It was unlocked. He pushed it open.

She was here. He knew it in a way that had nothing to do with logic. He could *feel* her.

The cavernous space was filled with empty air and industrial pillars. The lack of windows would have made the space relentlessly black, except for the one drop light that illuminated a table deep inside the room. Something was on the table. No, not something—someone.

Fiona.

They'd changed her somehow. Given her long golden curls—was it a wig? The gold-and-cream-colored fabric she wore shimmered slightly; perhaps it caught the whisper of air let in by the open door.

She was halfway inside the room, bait for him or someone. He couldn't charge toward her without expecting an attack. She was completely still, her hands folded over her midsection. He couldn't see restraints, and she was too damned far away to check her breathing.

He looked around the perimeter of the space. There were doors at either end. He moved deeper into the room, prepared for the shitstorm his presence would trigger.

He lowered his gaze to the floor, letting his senses roll outward from him as he scanned the space.

When he stepped forward, he held the same vibration as the steel floor, pillars, and walls, moving soundlessly toward where the other half of his soul was lying so utterly still. The long sleeves and long skirt of her dress spilled over the edges of the table. Her skin was as pale as the fabric she wore. Her brows and lashes had been darkened. Her cheeks were artificially colored. Her lips were battlefield red.

She was his Fiona, and yet she wasn't. She was different. She was made up as if for a viewing. Like a corpse. Or an actress on a stage.

Time and distance seemed to distort; the closer he came the farther she appeared. He wondered if he were hallucinating.

She looked peaceful. Eternally so.

But not everything was as it seemed. Shallow breaths moved her chest.

Before he could get close enough to touch her, two men entered the room from the doors at either end. He didn't look at them. Instead he kept his gaze on her and observed them from his peripheral vision. They were dressed all in black and moved like shadow warriors. They had a significant advantage over him…they weren't emotionally involved with the woman on the table. But he was, and instead of letting that distract him, he had to use it to give him focus and fuel his fight.

Kelan moved a few steps to the side. He didn't want to get very far from Fiona, but he didn't want her injured in the coming fight, either. He watched the two men, judging from their movements how they would fight. He could tell they were experienced fighters from the way they squared their bodies, spreading their shoulders and legs to enhance their mobility.

When the first guy threw a punch, Kelan grabbed his wrist and pulled his body in close so he could slam his knee into the guy's diaphragm. He bent over reflexively, sucking back the air he'd lost. Kelan took advantage of the moment, and braced himself on the guy's back, then levered his feet up the other guy's chest to wrap them around his neck, tumbling them both to the ground. The second guy fought to get free, but Kelan ended him with a quick twist to his neck. He didn't know what the night held for him, but leaving either of these two alive so that they could come after him again was not an option.

The first guy was on his feet again, and he was pissed. Kelan waited for his next move, but was distracted to see someone else coming out of the far door. How many would he have to fight before he could get Fiona free?

Kelan tried to slip between the newcomer and Fiona, but the first guy stopped him. They exchanged a few punches, but when the newest guy started to roll Fiona's table away, Kelan had to finish the fight fast. He did a roundhouse kick to the guy's chest. He stumbled backward, and as he righted himself, he pulled out a switchblade.

Fiona was being rushed from the room. It was taking too long to deal with this guy. Kelan pretended he was focused on what was happening with Fiona, letting the guy lunge toward him. At the last moment, Kelan caught his wrist, turned it back toward his attacker, and thrust it into his chest.

No one else challenged him, so he was free to race after Fiona. He slammed through the doors she'd just been taken through. The room was a black void. Before the door shut behind him, he noticed another door on the opposite side. He checked it, but it was locked.

"Hello, Mr. Shiozski."

How did they know him? Where had they taken Fiona?

"I've been waiting for you."

"Why?" He remembered his comm unit and turned it on, but wasn't sure Max could hear him in the metal box he was in.

"Because you are the War Bringer we've been told was coming."

Kelan went still. He thought of the tattoo he had on his right arm. He'd gotten that ink before he went into the Army. It was the skull of a Lakota warrior. A red bandana was tied around his forehead, holding back his hair. On the other side of the skull were the words, in big block letters, War Bringer. Kelan had designed it as an appeal for the protection of his ancestors against the enemies he would encounter. Its meaning was personal for him, yet this disembodied voice was talking about it as if it had meaning of another sort.

He wasn't going to let that oddity distract him from his purpose. "Where's Fiona?"

"You shall have her, soon, if you are successful in the competition."

"Who are you?"

"No one of importance."

"Why did you take Fiona?"

"It was her destiny."

Great. These were the fruitcakes that had the other half of his soul. "All right. You've had your fun. Game's over."

"No. In fact, it's just beginning. Fiona is in the next room. Go to her."

The door opposite him opened, showing another long, narrow room. Fiona lay on a pallet on the floor, in a thin blue beam of light. The whole room was padded in white fabric, like something out of an asylum. As soon as Kelan stepped through the door, a panel slid shut behind him. The room moved then paused. He heard heavy doors close on the other side of the steel panel, then the room rocked as if in motion.

It wasn't a room at all, but the trailer of a big semi.

Kelan walked over to Fiona. A thick acrylic panel separated the two portions of trailer, blocking him. He sat down, folding his legs as he assumed a traditional yoga pose, facing her. He took the earpiece out of his pocket, put it in his ear, and lowered his face, letting his hair and posture obscure him from any cameras that might be watching him. "Max, you read me?"

No answer.

"Max, come in."

Nothing.

Either the comm unit was broken or the truck was blocking the signal. He'd leave the earpiece in until they stopped at their destination. Hopefully, it wasn't so far that it would be out of range.

He looked over at Fiona's prone body. He hadn't noticed before, but the silk gown she wore was nearly sheer. He could see the dark shapes of her nipples.

As he watched her, she started to rouse. She pushed herself to a sitting position. Her now long blond hair spilled about her face. She brushed some of it out of her face, then held it and looked at it, frowning.

She glanced his way, then tilted her head as if she couldn't believe what she was seeing. "Kelan!"

She scrambled toward him, but the long gown she wore inhibited her progress. She huffed a ragged breath, then gathered the fabric away from her legs and crawled over to the clear panel that separated them. She flattened her hand against it. He raised his hand to cover hers. Maybe, if they held still, their palms would heat the acrylic, and it would be as if they were actually touching.

"I can't believe I'm seeing you," she said, her voice muffled by the dense panel between them. "Is it really you? Or is it another dream? I don't know if I'm awake or asleep even now."

"It's really me, Mahasani."

She nodded. Tears slipped down her face. "How long…how long has it been?"

"A day."

"It feels like a lifetime. Kelan—they said they had Casey, too. Is she also missing?"

He shook his head. "She's safe at Blade's. They lied to you."

"Thank God." She looked up then around at their container. "Where are we?"

"In an eighteen-wheeler, headed somewhere."

"Why? Why is this happening?"

Kelan shook his head. "I don't know. One of our captors said a whole bunch of stuff about destiny." He didn't tell her one of them had said she was King's daughter. Princess Fiona. He nodded toward a bruise on her cheek. "They hurt you."

"I fought them when they tried to take me. Then again at the house out on the plains." She closed her eyes as the memories flooded her mind. "Kelan, there are girls being held there against their will. Minors being used as sex slaves."

His fingertips pressed into the glass. "Not

anymore. We got there just after you were taken." He also didn't tell her the bastards had tried to burn the little house down, occupants and all. "The girls have been taken to the hospital. They'll be cared for in shelters."

"They aren't criminals."

"I know."

"What's going to happen to us?"

"We'll find out soon. Stay calm. Do what they say."

"What if they separate us?"

"I will find you. I will always find you, Fiona. Let's see what they're up to."

"I'm afraid."

He nodded. "I'll get you out as soon as I can."

Her blue eyes met his. He could see the tremble in her chin, even through the thick panel. "I love you," she whispered.

"I will not fail you, Mahasani." Words that he knew, as soon as he'd spoken them, were a lie. He'd already failed her by letting her get taken in the first place.

CHAPTER SIX

The truck pulled to a rough stop. Kelan got to his feet. There was no door on Fiona's half of the truck, so they were going to have to come through him to get to her. He braced his feet and waited.

A panel in the door slid open. "Put your hands through," someone ordered.

Kelan stayed put.

"There are six of us out here. You don't think you're a match for us, do you?"

He didn't answer. He had a more defensible position inside the rig than he would out in a wide-open space. And with him out of the truck, they could get to Fiona. After some debate amongst themselves, along with a cryptic comment about needing to get him into "the arena," the steel panel at the back of the semi slid open.

Two men jumped inside. Kelan prepared for their attack. The one on his left jabbed straight at his chest. Kelan blocked that thrust then slammed his boot sideways on the guy's calf, breaking his knee. As the second guy slammed Kelan back against the wall, two more men jumped into the truck, one with a cattle prod, one with a dogcatcher's loop. Kelan couldn't dislodge the guy holding him pinned to the wall, so instead of fighting for release, he jammed the guy's head against the steel wall with his elbow.

While they fought, the man with the cattle prod managed to zap Kelan's side. The pain stunned him temporarily, long enough for the man with the dogcatcher loop to slip that wire over his neck and pull tight. Kelan turned his attention to the wire, giving them a chance to slap a pair of cuffs on his hands. When he still struggled, the man with the dogcatcher loop tightened it until he hit his knees. A couple of the other men went inside and unlocked the big acrylic panel, letting it swivel open. They rushed in and grabbed Fiona.

She tried to resist, but her strength was no match for theirs. As they walked her past him to the truck opening, Kelan jabbed his elbow into the groin of the man holding the cattle prod. Yanking the prod from his hand, he used it to zap the man holding the choke wire about his neck.

He freed himself from the wire loop then tossed that man out of the truck, into a new fighter. He kicked yet another oncoming fighter in the head, then leapt out of the truck. A whole new circle of fighters stepped into formation around him.

Someone clapped. The man wore a black beanie and dark sunglasses, even though night had fallen. Kelan watched behind the guy as Fiona was taken inside a large steel building. The man leaned close and whispered to Kelan, "Save your strength for the competition. If you win, you will have a night with the princess." He shrugged. "If you lose, someone else will have a night with her."

Kelan recognized his voice—it was the same as the one on the speaker before he got into the truck.

The guy stepped back and glanced at one of the men circled around them. "Take him into the arena."

"He won't go."

"Oh, he'll go. And without resistance. Uncuff him."

"Are you crazy? Have you seen what he did here?" The guard held his hand out, indicating the prone and groaning men.

The man in the sunglasses turned to the guard. "Do you challenge me?"

The guard made a rapid attitude adjustment. Was he King? Kelan stared at him as the handcuffs were removed. Freed, he took two long steps toward him before two men blocked him.

"Good. Good." The man smiled again. "You still have some fight in you."

Kelan never changed his expression. All this chitchat was keeping him from Fiona. He turned away and started toward the structure where they'd taken her. The circle of men made an opening for him to pass through. The man in the beanie fell in step beside him.

Kelan looked around as they went to the arena,

taking stock of his whereabouts so that he could bring the team back here. There were no other buildings he could see besides the big steel arena. The place looked like it got a lot of use. A thick row of cedar shrubs surrounded the area, and a cluster of huge cottonwoods provided the building and dirt parking area with a windbreak in winter and dense shade in the summer.

* * *

Fiona was wobbly on her feet. They must have drugged her. The last thing she remembered was being taken from the cathouse. They'd done something to her hair. She was wearing an unfamiliar gown that clung to her body and was so fine a silk that it was almost translucent. The men walking on either side of her cut a wide swath through the crowd. She didn't see any women anywhere.

She glanced back to check what was happening with Kelan. He'd gotten off the truck and was standing inside a circle of men. She couldn't see his face, but she knew he watched her. And then, without ceremony, she was yanked inside the steel building. Lights were scarce. Four bare bulbs hung on long wires, illuminating four sets of bleachers. One larger set of spotlights hung down over an empty area in the center of the bleachers. It had no ropes or stages, just the bare, compacted dirt floor.

There were too many men for the bleachers to

accommodate, so they stood in the aisles between them. The noise was a shock to her ears after the silence of her drug-induced sleep. And the smell was noxious. Horse dung, unwashed male bodies…and something else, a scent she couldn't quite identify. Excitement, maybe. Did that have an odor, she wondered? Fear did, and its stink was in there, too.

The ground between the bleachers was loose dirt. It was hard for her to walk on it in the stilettos she wore. She looked at her feet and caught sight again of her nearly invisible clothes. Why had they put her in this terrible outfit? Dreading what was coming, she lifted her head and wore the frostiest expression she could muster.

The men led her down to the center of the arena, then around to the middle of one of the bleachers, where a huge, throne-like chair sat in front of the bottom row.

"Princess," one of the men said, indicating she should sit in the chair.

Fiona's brows went up. "Princess?"

They said nothing more to her, just took up positions on either side of the chair. Fiona sat, if for no other reason than it blocked most of the audience from staring at her body through her barely there clothing.

A man walked past her. He looked at her, marking her with his eyes as his. She let her gaze focus on something behind him, cutting him from her attention. Kelan followed him. Like the other man, he wore only a pair of black boxer briefs. His feet were bare. He had bruises on his chest, on his face, a cut on his lip. His high cheekbones made the hollows in his cheeks look stark. When his eyes met hers, they were stoic. She could tell he was in pain.

What was going on? How had her world turned so upside down?

He paused in front of her then knelt. The entire arena went silent as he bowed his head. His black hair spilled forward. Tears welled in her eyes. She caught his face and whispered, "Kelan, what's happening?"

He leaned his forehead to hers. "It's some kind of role-playing game. I don't know anything about it, what the rules are, how one wins. Just go with it. Buy us some time."

"Why do you have to fight again? You're already injured."

His eyes hardened, and in them she saw the echoes of his warrior ancestors. "I will fight for you forever."

She blinked her tears away. One of the men next to her was becoming restless. She noticed a red bandana hanging from his pocket. "Wait," she ordered Kelan, then reached over and took the bandana. She looked into Kelan's eyes as she tied it around his black hair. She pulled him close so that she could kiss his brow. "Finish this for us so that we can go home."

Kelan nodded and stood, then walked into the center of the fighting floor. An announcer stepped into the middle of the arena. He held up his hands.

There was no microphone, but the acoustics in the building let his bare voice carry.

"This event has been nearly twenty-one years in the making! King's very own daughter is coming home at last. The fighter who wins tonight's challenge will earn the right to deliver her to King—and to be her bodyguard and her champion.

"Now, listen up! This is no free-for-all. Each contestant will fight until he has defeated three others. The first to do so wins the challenge." He looked at the two men, then went over and lifted Kelan's right arm. "Fair notice to all who think to attempt it. This is no ordinary man; he is the War Bringer. And the princess has already chosen him."

Fiona forced herself to watch Kelan in the ring as if she was accustomed to such violence. But she wasn't; she felt the pain of every punch or kick that he took or delivered. It was surreal when he finally got the other guy down and snapped his neck.

She'd just watched him kill a man.

The next guy brought a knife to the floor. It took five long minutes for Kelan to help him fall on it, ending that round.

The third guy carried two swords. He tossed one to Kelan. Fiona gripped the arms of her seat. The swords were long and wide and looked hellishly heavy. Fighting with them was a specialized and archaic skill set. Kelan was tired. His footing wasn't as steady as it had been with the first challenger. At least the bandana she'd given him kept the sweat from his eyes.

At one point, he had to duck a forward thrust. He went down in a crouch and stayed there, his wide back bared to his opponent. As the man ran in to finish the fight, Kelan unwound, slicing the heavy blade across the guy's stomach, then running it up his body, through his chin and out the back of his head.

Fiona wanted to vomit at the blood that spilled from him. A chant started in the stadium. Faint at first, then growing louder. "War Bringer! War Bringer!"

And then a fourth man came forward to challenge Kelan.

Fiona couldn't take any more. She started to rise, but one of the men posted beside her chair pushed her back down. "No!" She shoved herself free of his grip and rushed to the stage, slipping between Kelan and his latest opponent as the last victim was dragged offstage.

"No, Fiona," Kelan growled as he pulled her behind him.

The announcer hurried into the arena. Fiona stepped around Kelan. "He has met your terms. Three fights. Three wins. This is over."

The announcer held up his hands, silencing the roaring crowd. Before he could speak, the fourth contender thrust a knife into his back. The look of shock and pain seared itself in Fiona's mind. Kelan stepped in front of her and forced her back.

The fourth guy laughed. "Fuck the rules. King

wants a champion for his daughter who will stop at nothing."

Kelan still held the bloodied sword from his last battle. He was so intensely focused on his new opponent that he didn't see the crowd begin to stir...or hear the siren wailing in the far distance.

A siren! Fiona had never been so happy to hear that sound. It meant a return to reality very soon. But what were the cops going to say about the four dead men, three of whom Kelan had killed?

They had to get out of there.

She wasn't the only one with that thought. Before Kelan and his newest challenger could begin their fight, men swarmed the floor. She and Kelan were hurried to a door where an SUV awaited. They were rushed inside. The windows were so heavily tinted that they could see nothing out of them. A black divider separated them from the front seat.

Fiona was shaking. She tried to open the door, but it was locked. What now? Where were they being taken? How were they going to get out of this?

* * *

Val pulled the back doors of the semitruck open. It was empty, but what a strange setup inside. A thick acrylic window separated two portions of the cargo area. The larger one was covered in pristine white padding. The back portion nearest the doors was left in its raw state.

Kit shined a flashlight into the cargo hold. "What the fuck?"

Angel held up one of the team's comm units. "Found his earpiece. It was lodged in the bumper."

"Max, what do we know about his tractor trailer?" Kit asked via his comm unit.

The truck was reported missing two weeks ago. The tags were stolen a day ago. We can process it for fingerprints, but that's about all the info we're going to get from it.

Kit shook his head. "Great. So now we've got two missing people."

Val jumped down from the truck. "Kelan kept the earpiece I gave him off until it pinged ten miles from here. Either he couldn't safely turn it on, or he was in the truck and the signal wasn't getting picked up. Let's go see what there is where the signal first came online."

Kit called the truck in to Lobo for processing, then they made the drive out east, deep into the prairie. The original ping had come from what looked like a big steel horse arena. There were no vehicles in the parking area, but it was clear that there had been a lot of them there recently.

"Max, what other buildings are near here?" Kit asked.

Nothing. Not for a good two miles in any direction. That building is the only thing in that whole section.

The door wasn't locked. Angel and Val entered from the front, Kit from the back. As soon as they cleared the building and knew it was empty, they flipped the lights on. Stadium rows stood like aluminum skeletons in the dusty arena floor.

"Kelan was here," Angel said, holding up his abandoned clothes and boots.

"Shit, look at this," Val said in the center of the stadium seating. "A fucking throne. Was King here?"

Kit was looking around the compacted dirt…and all the blood that stained it. He frowned. "I don't know, but I got a bad feeling about how much time those two have left. If any. We need to find them, fast."

CHAPTER SEVEN

Kelan wore only his boxer briefs. They'd left in such a hurry that he hadn't been able to grab his clothes. He'd lost his earpiece during the fight in the truck. Hopefully, it hadn't broken. If the guys could pick up its signal, they'd be after them quickly.

He reached over and squeezed Fiona's hand. He couldn't make out much of her features, but he could tell that she turned to him. He didn't smile, because it didn't seem appropriate given where they were, and she would see it anyway.

He'd seen a blanket folded on the back seat when he got in. He grabbed it and put it around her, getting her to fold her legs so that her feet were tucked in. She leaned against him. He kissed her forehead, pulling in her scent. She didn't smell like her usual strawberries, but some foreign soap he didn't recognize. Beneath it all, he could still catch her essence in the mix, and he focused on that. It was unimaginably fine having her in his arms, even if they were still snagged in their captor's crazy world.

They drove far out into the country. The roads in

this part of rural Colorado were divided into square sections two miles by two miles. When they'd left the arena, they were headed south. The driver took occasional turns off then back on the same road, either to confuse Kelan or to dodge anyone following them.

At last, they pulled off the road onto a driveway more gravelly than the dirt road. The vehicle stopped, but no one got out. After a moment, they pulled forward a short distance, then stopped again. Kelan felt the vehicle jerk, then had a distinct feeling they were descending...down, down, down.

The air in the cab of the SUV stopped smelling like newly harvested fields and started smelling like recycled air, as if from inside a building.

When their descent ended, the driver pulled forward and turned into what had to be a parking spot. He shut the engine off.

Fiona's hand tightened on his. If they were to die, if there was no way to get out of this, they would die together. It was the only comforting thought he could summon at the moment.

The two men in the front of the SUV got out and opened their doors. "Get out and come with us."

The guards separated them, each taking an arm, and guided them across a parking garage. They entered an elevator and again descended. How many floors, Kelan couldn't determine because each level had a name not a number.

Their handlers' disposition changed as the group

stepped out of the elevator. They didn't jerk, pull, or prod them anymore. Now their hold was light on their arms. Kelan sent a look around the place, awed by its elegance. The floor was polished marble topped with a red runner that went the whole length of the hall. Tall marble columns stood like sentinels every fifteen feet. Between each column was either a long banner with a slogan supporting the principles of a new world order or a sculpture or a painting. Except for the banners, the whole place looked like a museum that might be found in any large city.

"Where are we?" Kelan asked.

"King's Warren."

And that was about as helpful as anything the rabbit might have said to Alice when she fell into his burrow. They walked through a few corridors, went down some stairs, turned into another hallway, and soon came to a stop. His guard unlocked a door and led them inside.

Kelan looked around the extravagant room. "What is this place?"

The light-brown-haired man removed his sunglasses and sent a look around the room, too. "King had this made for you." His blue-gray eyes cut toward Kelan. "Well, for the princess and the War Bringer, anyway." He dismissed the two other guards. When they were gone, he looked right at Kelan. "You have one night. I will come for you in the morning. Be ready." He gave Kelan a hard look. "I cannot save her. Only you can."

"Who are you? Are you King?"

The man went through the door without answering any questions. Kelan stared at the door as he heard the lock catch. That guy was too young to be King. Besides, King made everyone believe he was omnipotent. King could save Fiona if he wanted to— he wouldn't have said Kelan was the only one who could.

He turned slightly and glanced at her. They had one night—one that was already well progressed. One night to figure out a way out of here and get her to safety.

She stood in the center of the room, in the middle of a blue- and cream-toned oriental carpet. The blanket from the SUV was still wrapped about her shoulders. She took a few steps around the room, looking at the furnishings and decor. He followed her, as troubled by what he saw as she was.

The room was a suite of luxurious appointments. The ceiling was twenty feet high and filled, corner to corner, with a mural of clouds in a deep blue sky surrounded by lush gardens. All around the edges, naked couples were copulating while winged cherubs flew about the edges of the garden observing them.

Fiona looked up, then away. Color blossomed on her face.

The bed's canopy was suspended from the ceiling in the middle of one wall; its long panels of white silk hung to the floor. All of the furnishings in the room were of an Empire style with slim, delicate proportions and ornate decorations. The exposed woodwork was a mix of fine woods. The walls and fabrics of the cushions were pale yellow, cream, and gold. The room was big enough for him and delicate enough for her.

Tall windows led to what looked like a moonlit garden. Kelan walked over to check it out. He went up a couple of steps to the huge double glass doors and opened them. A breeze came inside, humid and smelling of roses and peat moss. Somewhere in the garden was a water feature; he could hear it. The ceiling in that space was dotted with little lights that twinkled like stars.

The two rooms were beautiful, elegant, and as fake as a theme park ride.

Kelan pulled Fiona into his arms, sighing at the feel of her so close. He'd never let himself give up hope of holding her again during the hellish hours that had just passed, but the fear of never being here with her like this again had stalked him.

She looked up at him. "Kelan...I don't think this is some role-playing game. Three men died fighting you. They would have gladly killed you, too. And the way they were chanting the words on your tattoo. Why would they do that?"

He'd killed more than three yesterday, but that wasn't a detail she needed to know. "King is a sick bastard. I think we shouldn't be surprised by the depth of his depravity."

"They said I'm his daughter."

84

Kelan studied her face, trying to interpret her reaction to that. "Doesn't mean it's true."

"I don't understand any of this."

"Nor do I, but then we aren't operating with the same deck of cards King is. We may never understand his game."

* * *

Fiona stepped away from Kelan and made another circuit around the room. There were two closets, each the size of her room at Ty's house, both full of clothes, shoes, and other accessories. To whom did they belong? Did whoever it was know she and Kelan were using their suite? But that man had said it was a suite King had built for them.

A nuptials suite.

The large bathroom between the closets was big enough for two people to move around in simultaneously. It had a two-person shower with a dozen showerheads and a big two-person soaker tub in white alabaster marble. The tiles on the floor and walls were tumbled marble, and the vanities were more of the crisp white alabaster. The linens matched the colors of the other room.

Kelan shadowed her around the spacious suite. There was a sofa with scroll arms and smooth yellow damask fabric. Off to one side of the sitting area was a desk of burled walnut with painted black and gold legs.

She walked to the open doors off the garden. The bottom half of her gown, the part not covered by her blanket, blew and billowed around and between her legs.

"I'm not King's daughter."

Kelan stepped up behind her and slipped his arms around hers. "How do you know?"

"I don't feel any connection to him as a father. If he was responsible for my abduction and tonight's fight, he repulses me." She felt Kelan nod behind her. She turned in his arms and put her hands on his bare chest. "What are we doing here? What is this place?"

"More questions I cannot answer."

She touched the edge of his eyebrow. "He made you fight man after man. What if you have a concussion?"

He smiled. "Maybe I have cracked my head. I'm standing here with you, and I can't believe it." He touched her face, his fingers brushing a tender spot. "Did they hurt you?"

She wrapped her hand around his wrist. "You mean, am I still a virgin?"

"No. I mean did they hurt you? I know they scared the hell out of you, but did they beat you?"

"I don't know. I wasn't always conscious. They used chloroform on me." She looked at the crease of her inner arm. "And once they injected me with something. I don't what it was. I don't know if I have a disease now." She rubbed her arms in disgust.

"What happened after the shot?"

"I don't remember. I passed out."

"Maybe they only tranquilized you. When we can, we'll get you checked out. By the way, that trick you pulled on the highway was brilliant."

Her eyes widened. "Did you hear about that?"

"We did. We were just hours behind you. So damn close."

"They had guns. I was afraid they would shoot the man who stopped to help, so I made up that story."

"You are smart and brave." He took her hand and led her down the stairs. "How about a shower? Would it help you feel better?"

It would, actually. She nodded.

He led her over to the sofa. "Sit here for a minute. I want to check these rooms out, then I'll help you."

"In the shower?" She couldn't help the path her thoughts took, and where they went was written all over her face.

"To bathe only. We have too much to discuss before we can become intimate."

She smiled up at him and leaned in to hug him again. A long sigh eased from her. When she straightened, already she felt revived.

"I need to use the bathroom, while you do your thing."

"Hold the shower for me."

She bit the inside of her lower lip. "I will."

She stepped into the bathroom and closed the door, both nervous and excited about what was coming. She'd never showered with a man. Really, she didn't make it a habit to get naked in front of anyone. She was probably the only twenty-one-year-old virgin left at her university. Her friends had spent the last week teasing and lecturing and offering to educate her.

It was odd that her mom had made such a big deal about her staying a virgin until she found her forever man. In her teen years, Fiona had thought her mom was outrageously old-fashioned. But then things had just worked out that she never considered being intimate with anyone until she met Danny in her sophomore year at the university.

They didn't date, though he wanted to. He was cute and funny. With him, she was leaning toward giving in to her curiosity about sex, but all that ended the week both he and her mom had died in separate traffic accidents.

After that, staying a virgin felt like a connection to her mom that she didn't want to break. Now, she was glad she waited. Having Kelan as her first lover would be a gift to herself that she would carry with her always.

Of course, she would be lying if she said she wasn't nervous about their first time. She hoped it wouldn't be awkward. She shouldn't have listened to her friends' stories of their first times.

The thing that really made her edgy was the claiming ceremony Kelan kept mentioning. It was a big deal to him, yet she had no idea what it was or what to expect from it. She'd even Googled it, but couldn't find anything that sounded like what Kelan had mentioned.

Fiona used one of the private toilets. When she washed her hands, she was still preoccupied with her thoughts. Would Kelan find her attractive? Would he change his mind about her being his other half—his Mahasani?

She lifted her eyes to the mirror and gasped. The face staring back at her was hideous. She touched her wet fingers to her cheek, smearing the heavy makeup. What was this? She never did her face like this, with thick foundation that was too pale, pink cheeks that looked like they might glow, globs of mascara, brows too dark for her complexion, and red lipstick that colored the skin around her lips.

She bent over the sink and started to wash it off, then took another look at herself. It hadn't budged. Oh, God. Kelan had seen her like this. She looked hellish, like a made-up zombie.

She grabbed a bar of soap and a washcloth and started scrubbing at her face. The soap stung her eyes. Now, not only was the heavy stuff mushed around her face, but her eyes were red-rimmed, too.

She glanced at the door, glad that she had closed it…but it wasn't closed anymore. Kelan stood there, a horrified look on his face.

Fiona hid behind the washcloth and cried. "I can't get it off."

He hurried over to her and pulled her away from the mirror, holding her while she cried. "I shouldn't have let you come in here like this. Alone."

"What did they do to me? My hair. My face. My clothes."

"I think they wanted you to be seen by the crowd."

"I look like a corpse."

He chuckled at that, which helped ease her chest a little. "Yeah. But it's not permanent."

"The soap isn't getting it off."

"No. You need an oil of some sort." He started to poke through the cabinets and drawers. She peeked at him over the cloth.

"How do you know about stuff like this?"

He held up a jar of coconut oil and smiled at her. "Because I've worn face paint a time or two. For ceremonies." He pushed her hands down and tilted her face up. "Close your eyes."

When she complied, he scooped some of the coconut oil out and held it to her forehead, waiting for the heat of her skin and his fingers to melt it enough that he could smooth it around her brows, her eyes, her lips. His touch was so soothing, she felt herself begin to relax just a little.

He took her washcloth and held it under the warm tap, then gently wiped the hellish goop away. "Now look."

She sent him a worried glance then faced the mirror. She was herself again. She looked up at him standing behind her in the mirror, so dark with his silky black hair and dark, solemn eyes. He watched her tensely.

She smiled at him. "You worked a miracle." She held up a lock of her artificially long hair. "What about this?"

"If there are scissors, I can cut it, but I'm no stylist. And it doesn't really look bad. For now."

"Do you like my hair longer?"

Kelan's face tightened. "I like your hair how you like it."

"But do you like it longer?"

A rose color darkened his cheeks. "I do like it longer."

Fiona smiled. "Then we'll leave it for now. And maybe I'll grow it out after this."

He slipped his hands into her hair, spreading his fingers over the base of her skull. "I would like that. Ready for that shower?"

She nodded.

"Give me a minute." He disappeared into the opposite toilet and shut the door.

Fiona quickly looked around for a toothbrush. There were several in a drawer still in their original packages. It was heaven to scrub her teeth—she was still doing it, in fact, when Kelan went to the sink to wash his hands.

It felt strangely comfortable standing with him in a shared bathroom, brushing her teeth. He was doing the same. He looked at her in the mirror. His eyes smiled at her. She looked away, shocked at how normal it all seemed.

When she finished with her teeth, she gathered a couple of towels and set them on the warming bars near the shower. She chanced a glance at Kelan. He was standing a few feet away. His eyes were heavy with unspoken words. She froze in place. Was now finally the time they would be together?

CHAPTER EIGHT

Kelan bent over to drop his briefs. Fiona lowered her eyes to give him privacy. He straightened. "Fiona. Look at me."

She lifted her eyes to his, but they moved down his chest to his navel, then up again to take in the broad width of his shoulders. He had very little chest hair. A narrow trail of dark hair led downward from his belly button to his boxer briefs...and the big bulge in them.

"Don't look away." His voice was deep and steady. He pushed his briefs all the way down his legs and kicked them aside. She kept her eyes on his. Watching him, yet resisting her instinctive curiosity to look *there*, set her skin on fire. He didn't move. There was no hurry in his eyes. He simply waited.

The silk gown she wore irritated her erect nipples. A strange heat coiled low between her hips. She blinked. He waited. She looked at his chest and drew a deep breath. Her gaze moved lower, over the rippling muscles covering his ribs, to the dark hair leading down between his hips, then her eyes jumped to *it*.

It was huge. And darker than the rest of his body. It pointed slightly upward and to the left. At its base was a thick patch of dark, coarse hair.

"Does my body please you, Fiona?" His voice was even deeper than usual, as if it was hard for him to breathe and speak simultaneously.

She looked at him and nodded. Her mouth moved with her answer, but the sound never hit the air. She cleared her voice and tried again. "Yes."

"May I see your body?"

Fiona licked her lips then lowered her gaze to the floor. Now was the moment she'd waited for so many months to experience. Now, when she hadn't groomed herself as she would have wanted. She hadn't shaved her legs or underarms in a couple of days. She wasn't clean. Even her hair wasn't her own.

"No."

"Why?"

"I'm not ready." She ventured a look and saw his wounded expression. "I mean, I'm ready. I'm sooo ready. I'm just not put together yet."

He closed the distance between them. Every step he took deepened the drumbeat of her heart. "We're bathing. Nothing more."

"I want more." He was only a foot away. So close, but he wasn't touching her. "I want to be perfect for you."

He didn't smile to alleviate her fears. The corners of his jaw worked. His nostrils flared. He reached for her hand and placed it on his heart. "You don't understand the depth of my feelings for you. It has nothing to do with the shell of you. You are my other skin. Do I doubt my own flesh?" He shook his head. "No. Love is too shallow a word for what I feel. We are part of something bigger than ourselves. Like the earth is nothing without the pull of the moon, and night would never know light without the sun's transformative burn. You and I together are part of the infinite that is. Without you, I am nothing, not even an afterthought of the universe."

Fiona blinked. A tear spilled free. How could she argue with that? Locking her eyes with his, she lowered one shoulder of her loose gown, then took her hand from his heart and lowered the other, slipping the fabric from her body, letting the gown drop to the floor.

She heard his sharp intake of breath. Her eyes flashed his way while his were still moving over her. Tension had etched itself on his face. Thinking something had to be wrong with her, she looked down at herself and noticed the gross makeup that had been all over her face was also on her nipples, and the tawny hair that was neatly patterned in a triangle on her mound had been artificially darkened.

She looked at him in horror, folding her arms over her breasts. "Kelan, it's here, too."

He eased her arms apart. "It's only cosmetic. We'll get it off."

"Why did they do this to me?" God, they—

someone—had touched her while she was naked and unconscious.

"I suspect they wanted to enrage me in that arena so that every time I looked at you, I would see your beauty and what your gown barely covered. Like a spear in the neck of a bull at a bullfight, seeing you exposed and in danger was meant to motivate me to fight."

"It did. You never stopped."

"Nor would I." He stepped over to her sink and grabbed the container of coconut oil.

"Kelan, what if...what if they raped me?"

He looked at her, then set the coconut oil on the bench in the shower and came back to stand before her. She was glad he didn't just brush her fear away.

"Do you have discomfort down there? Are you bleeding? Sore? Is there any odd discharge?"

"Does that happen after sex?"

"Sometimes. You wouldn't normally bleed after consensual sex, but if you were taken against your will..."

She shook her head. "I didn't feel anything—until I was here, with you. I'm achy and...wet."

He smiled. "Good. That's all good. If you didn't feel those things while they had you, I suspect they didn't touch you—other than to prep you for your 'appearance.'" He kissed the side of her forehead. "Let's take that shower and wash this day off us."

He turned the water on. It spilled from a half-dozen steel heads. He held his hand in the water until the temperature was just right and steam began to rise. There were two sides to the big shower, but Kelan shared one with her, letting her stand in the streams of water with him.

She liked the feel of the water and his hands on her, the smile that lifted the edges of his lips, the anticipation in his eyes. When their eyes met, his smile widened.

"Let's get that stuff off you." He reached for the coconut oil. He dipped his fingers into the thick white stuff, melted it between his palms, then rubbed it on her breasts.

Fiona sucked in a sharp breath. Her back arched into him, pressing her nipples against his palms. Once both had been slathered, he held one breast and rubbed his fingers over the sensitive peak. His fingers were warm and sure and strong. When he repeated the process on her other breast, she gripped his biceps. His muscles were so wide that her hands were spread open. He looked down at her. Her lips parted to pull more air.

He bent close to her and kissed her mouth. Her fingers tightened on his arms as he pulled her against his body. His rigid penis pressed against her belly. His tongue entered her mouth. She opened herself to him. Her hands moved up from his arms to lock around his neck as he bent toward her. She stood on her tiptoes, but the inches she gained did little to even out the disparity in their heights. Still, she could feel the entire length of his body against hers, hard where she was soft.

His hands tightened around her. He straightened, lifting her as if she weighed nothing. His mouth worked hers. She moaned, loving the feel of him around her, his tongue in her mouth. She forked her fingers through his wet hair, capturing the base of his skull. He broke the kiss and started it again.

When he stopped, he pulled away just enough for their noses to still touch. His black eyes were edgier than ever as he stared down at her mouth.

She caught his face in her hands, causing him to lift his eyes to hers. "I love you."

He stared at her for long, breathless moments, then kissed her, feverishly, like a man starved for the touch of his woman. "Mahasani, you are my life."

"It's time, Kelan. It's time for us to be together."

He gave her a long and searching look, then lowered his gaze and eased her to her feet. Without words, he dipped into the coconut oil, retrieving a bit he could use on the soft, coarse hair over her mound. His face was fiercely tight and he didn't meet her eyes. He took a washcloth and lathered it with the soap bar. Its nubby texture sent shock waves through the nerves of Fiona's skin as he washed away the oil.

Supporting her with an arm around her waist, he turned the front of her body into the streams of water. He pressed the washcloth between her legs, up against the soft flesh there. Heat zinged everywhere in her body, over her skin, up and down her spine. She leaned against him, pressing her head against his chest. Her fingers dug into his arms. He stroked her soft flesh, up and back, pressing here and there, spreading her legs with his knee.

And then something happened that she'd never experienced. She lost all sense of herself, was floating and exploding, her body coming apart in throbbing waves.

"Kelan!" she cried out. Her body was bucking against his hand, the epicenter of the sensations racking her.

"I've got you. I've got you, Fiona. Let it happen."

She couldn't have stopped it even if she'd known how. When the tremors slowly eased and her mind could focus again, she felt weak and rubbery. "What was that?"

Kelan grinned. She was glad he still had an arm around her. She turned in his arms. "Have you never pleasured yourself before?"

"No. Was that an orgasm?"

"Yes. Want to feel it again?"

"I do. I want to feel all of it, Kelan. All of you."

"We haven't had our claiming ceremony yet."

She caught his face in her hands. "I claim you, Kelan."

His eyes grew somber. "It isn't that simple."

"Do I have to eat worms or a beating heart in the ceremony?"

His eyes scolded her for her humor. "No. It's an intense exchange, not driven by the passion of the moment."

"Good. I trust you to lead me through it."

"You haven't accepted the terms."

"I accept you. Only you. For the rest of my life. Make love to me, Kelan."

His eyes seared hers. His face was like stone, the hollows of his cheeks sharply defined. She reached between their bodies and caught his heavy erection between her palms. He hissed a sharp breath and bared his teeth, but didn't stop her. The skin of his penis was soft and hot and sheathed flesh so rigid it felt like bone.

Fiona looked up at him as she smoothed her hands over the length of him. He spread his legs slightly, bracing his weight as he began to move in her hands. His movements were rhythmic.

"Will this give you an orgasm?"

His nostrils flared. "Yes."

She smiled. "Will you be able to stand through it? I don't think I can hold you up."

A smile flashed across his face. "I can stand on my own."

His intensity fired more of her nerves. She bent down to kiss the tip of him. His hand rested on her shoulder, then dug into her hair and fisted it, forcing her to rise.

"That, I can't take. It will end me."

She didn't understand him. His dark eyes looked down to where she held him, stroked him. The length of him couldn't fit fully in her hands from fingertips to the heels of her palms, but she could cover him by

100

stroking forward and back. He didn't release her hair. His teeth clenched, then his penis jumped in her hands. He threw his head back and groaned, the sound grinding up from his chest. White cream spilled into her hands in hot bursts.

It was fascinating. Scintillating. She'd given him pleasure. Total and complete release. She looked at the evidence of his pleasure in her hands. He took them and rinsed them in the water. He reached for the shampoo, then poured a stream of it into his palm and rubbed his hands together. He tilted her face up so that the soap wouldn't get in her eyes as he massaged it into her scalp, lifting her newly long tresses up into the soapy glob.

As his fingers worked her hair, he leaned down and kissed her. She held his hips in her hands. His body was all lean muscle on lean muscle. His penis was different from before, relaxed but still formidable.

"Keep looking at me, Fiona, and you had better be prepared for the changes you'll see."

"Does it always do that?"

"Only whenever I see you. Or think of you. Or smell something that reminds me of you. Which is just about every waking and sleeping minute."

"Does it hurt?"

He held her face as he tilted her head back to let the water rinse the shampoo away. "Sometimes, if there's no release."

"So waiting wasn't easy for you either."

"No. And we're going back to waiting. I don't have any condoms. We can't risk your getting pregnant while we're here."

"Kelan, I'm on birth control." She bit her lip. They hadn't talked about this, but she'd wanted to be ready for this when he was.

He went still. Water still poured down around them. "What kind? You haven't had any of your things since you were taken. You've missed your pills."

"It's a vaginal ring. It's still there. I checked."

"How does it work?"

"I wear it for three weeks, then not for a week, then start a new one. This is my second month on this program."

"How much longer on this one?"

"Two more weeks."

He touched his hand to her face, over the bruise the makeup had hidden. He nodded, then grinned.

"Kelan, I don't want to wait. We don't know what's going to happen to us, when—or if—we'll get out of here."

CHAPTER NINE

Kelan went still. He knew what she was asking. He pulled her close, loving the feel of her body against his, skin against skin. "Fiona, you deserve a perfect first time. A long, leisurely initiation into intimacy."

"Being in your arms is perfect, Kelan. No matter when or where. But given what's happening, I don't want to wait."

He brought her even closer to him as he bent to kiss her. Her hands were on his arms. Her thigh rubbed against his. Her breasts were pressing in to his ribs.

The kiss broke off, then resumed, over and again, in waves of increasing intensity. Her body was small compared to his. It seemed he could crush her if he held her too tight. She was entirely feminine—the exact opposite of him. How could the entire human race depend on a gender so fragile?

Maybe she wasn't as breakable as she seemed. Maybe her strength came in invisible ways that he couldn't see and would never understand. A mystery he wanted to spend his life unraveling.

He caught her mouth with his. Water poured down their faces, around their lips, into their mouths. "I love you," he whispered.

She smiled against his mouth. "Show me, Kelan. Show me everything."

Kelan lifted her. "Wrap your legs around me." He slipped his hands under her thighs to support her.

His cock rested against her opening. Every time she moved, her body slipped against it. He moved her up farther on his forearms, one hand holding her sweet ass, freeing his other so that he could take hold of himself.

"Fiona—"

She touched his cheek. He could feel her warm breath on his lips. "Go, Kelan. Do it. I'm ready." Her strong legs tightened about his waist, bearing part of her weight.

He clenched his teeth. "I'll go slow." His erection pulsed in his hand. He rubbed its wide head back and forth, stroking the length of her core, from her clit to her opening. Her hips bucked at the intimate touch, then she rocked against him. His hand on her ass tightened, holding her still as he set his head against her opening and pushed in. Just a little. Letting her get used to that pressure.

He pulled out, then did it again, going a little deeper. He was big and she was tight, but oh so slick. He moved inside her. He looked at her as he asked, "How does that feel?"

Her lips were parted. Her eyes were bright and

burning like blue flames. "More, Kelan. Do more."

He eased himself in deeper. Returning his hand to her hip, he guided her movements over him. She was holding his shoulders now, her trim nails digging into the skin there. He pushed in all the way and held still. There was no pain on her face or in her eyes. Only hunger.

"Mahasani, it goes like this now…" He began slowly to withdraw, then push all the way back in, then withdraw. She leaned back a bit so she could look at him. Her neck and chin were flushed red. Her breasts were tipped with tight nipples. Her lips were parted, but nothing coherent came from her mouth, only pants and mewls, which intensified his desire.

Her feet locked at the ankles behind him as she braced herself for greater movement. He held the weight of her body completely in his hands, his legs braced wide. Up and down he moved her body. He was so close. So close. He clenched his teeth on an upward thrust, hoping he could outlast her.

And then she stiffened, cried out, and began to rock against him in uncontrollable gyrations, her inner muscles squeezing him. He thrust into her orgasm, deepening her pleasure, prolonging it as far as he could before his balls tightened and his release shot up his cock and into her in hot, pulsing waves.

Her elbows locked as she pushed away from him. Worried, he checked her face for signs of distress. Her eyes were still unfocused, her pupils huge. Her lips were parted, her lungs working hard to catch up with their exertion. She started to sniffle, then big tears began to stream down her face.

Kelan carried her over to the shower bench, which he straddled. Still embedded deep within her, he sat down and leaned back against the tiled wall. He rubbed her back. She wrapped her arms around his neck and buried her face against his. He could feel and hear her crying.

"I hurt you," he stated without waiting for her to speak.

She shook her head. She was sucking air now.

"Easy, Fiona, my heart. Easy. Tell me what's happening."

She lifted up to look at him. They were still connected intimately. She cupped his cheeks and kissed his eyes. "I am so in love with you, Kelan. For the first time in my life, I feel whole. How could I have lived so long without you?"

He caught her chin in his palm. "Did you enjoy it?"

She laughed. "Did I enjoy it? Kelan"—she looked into his eyes—"it's as if you showed me a new color I'd never seen before. Or let me hear when I was deaf before. You showed me something about my body I'd never experienced."

Kelan huffed a short laugh then relaxed against the wall. "You said you hadn't pleasured yourself before. Why not?"

"I didn't know how."

Kelan grinned. "You could have watched a video."

Rosy color blossomed across her face. "I did. And I tried to do what she was doing, but I didn't know if I was doing it right."

"Did it feel good when you tried?"

"Yes."

His cock jerked to life inside her, widening and expanding in the warm, wet sheath of her. She adjusted her position over him, moving to her knees, stretching upward. Everything in his body tightened as her body tugged at him. He thrust in to her.

"Touch yourself now."

She looked worried. He held still until she complied, and when she did, he saw the passion that rippled across her face and through her entire body. Her brows knitted. He grinned up at her, was still grinning when her crystalline blue eyes, now dark and dilated, met his.

He pressed his thumb over her two fingers, increasing the pressure against her clit. She sucked in a sharp breath, then her hips ground against his, her inner muscles tightening like a fist over his cock. Beckoning...beckoning...but still he held off.

"I was afraid," he whispered, looking up at her. "I wasn't sure we would fit together."

"But we're two halves of a whole."

"We are." He smiled, warmed by her words. He caught her breasts in his hands and held her nipples. He felt the tremor that sent through her body. Leaning forward, he took one in his mouth, flicking it with his tongue as he began to pump inside her.

She moved with him, rocking forward, leaning back, going straight up and down, fast, then slow. And goddamn, just like that, she was perfect at fucking. He smiled as he kissed her neck. He licked her small, feminine voice box. His lips felt for the pulse in her neck and gently pulled at the place where it beat, faster and harder as their bodies thrust against each other.

When her release overcame her again, he was right there with her, hot and hard, and so deep inside her.

He leaned back against the tiled wall, glad that it was cool despite the steam of the shower. He flattened his hand against her stomach, absorbing the soft feel of her from her hips to her breasts.

"I love you." He looked up at her face. "I never want to make you cry again, Fiona. I vow to you that I will put you before me. Your joy before mine. Your welfare before my own. Your dreams before mine. And I will put us, our family, before the team, before my job, before the world."

She leaned forward, still connected to him, and caught his hands in hers. She brought them to her chest, held them in the valley between her breasts. "I vow the same to you. But I know how important what you do is—for me, and ours, and everyone. Sometimes, doing for others first is the best thing. I know that. And I accept that."

He nodded. "I come from a long line of warriors, Fiona." She looked at the ink on his big arm and gently touched it. "Without my work, I'm not sure I know what I am. But if it interferes with us, I will learn a new me."

Her smile was pensive. "How did I ever find you?"

"I told you. We were fated."

She touched his face, moving gently over bruises he'd forgotten he had. "I'm ready for what comes next."

He eased himself from her body and straightened. "We'd best turn off the water before they come to see if we've drowned ourselves."

She nodded. He left her on the bench and turned off the shower, then grabbed a couple of towels from the warming rack. After helping her to her feet, he wrapped one around her shoulders then started to dry her hair with the other.

She tucked the towel around her body, then pulled the other from her head and handed it to him. He wrapped it around his hips. Lifting her face, he gave her a worried look.

"I wish we could safely relax and sleep for the night, but we can't. I don't know what King has in store for us, but I think we should get dressed just in case he doesn't wait until the morning to come for us."

* * *

Their closets opened off the bathroom, so they went their separate ways. Fiona flipped on the light switch, stunned again at the room before her. Whose quarters were they in? She'd heard the guy who brought them here say King had made this suite for them, but that just didn't make sense.

Well, the reality was that none of it mattered...and none of it made sense. She needed something to wear, and there was plenty to pick from. She hoped whomever they belonged to wouldn't mind her using them.

And then that thought made her mad. She wasn't here of her own volition. She'd been kidnapped and was being held against her will. If the owner of these things lived here voluntarily, then, well, it was just too bad that she'd have to share her clothes.

She ran her hand over the blouses hanging in their neat section. There were slacks, dresses, suits, casual wear, formal wear. It was an entire wardrobe. All of them had new tags. All were in her size.

She opened the lingerie drawers and found panties and bras, sexy and tempting corsets and babydolls. Beautiful silk stockings. Other drawers had folded sweaters and upscale casual attire. There were three shelving units of shoes, most of them high heels. Brand new. Every color and design she'd ever admired.

The jewelry dresser was also full of a stunning assortment of rings, bracelets, earrings, and necklaces. Even jeweled hair clips. Some of these were new; some looked like antiques.

She heard a noise at the door to her closet. Kelan was standing there, dressed in a black tee, black cargos, black boots. Had his clothes been a perfect fit and selection for him as well?

"Where did all of this come from?" she asked, giving him a quizzical look. "It's weird, but it's all my size. The shoes too. Even the jewelry, the rings." She frowned. "How would they know that about me?"

Kelan shook his head. "I've memorized the feel of you in my arms, yet even I don't know what size you wear. If I had to guess, you would be the size of a minute, but I don't think that's a real thing."

"Are your clothes a perfect fit for you?"

"No. There was a range of sizes for me to pick from, though." He sat down in one of the two wingback chairs in the middle of her closet. "This wasn't a lucky guess. Someone knows you." He studied Fiona. "One of your friends, maybe."

Fiona remained standing as her expression took on a faraway look. She looked at him, stunned, the blood slowly draining from her face.

"Tell me," he ordered quietly.

She shook her head slowly then folded her arms across her chest. "There's a girl I became friends with this semester. I knew her from last semester. We had some of the same classes. I don't know how or why, but we really hit it off this year. We started doing things together. We went shopping one day after classes in the boutiques in Old Town. She had the salesgirl measure us so we'd know which sizes to look for in the retro dresses." Fiona looked at him. "She wanted to be a designer, so I let her help me build an ensemble from a mix of styles and eras. We were just being silly. It was a fun way to forget the stress of school." She looked at the column of jewelry drawers. "We even tried on rings. She got a complete sense of my tastes and sizes. You don't think she worked for King, do you?"

"Give me her name."

"Stacey Atkins. She lives in an apartment near the campus. She was so normal. She never once did anything that made me suspicious of her."

Kelan got up and came over to her. His big hands settled on her arms.

"She stayed at the library doing homework with me the day they took me. She called them, didn't she?" Tears pooled in her eyes as she realized how tainted her world had become. "Is there no one I can trust anymore?"

"No. You need to assume King owns everyone you encounter. Except me and the team. And the girls at the house."

Fiona leaned her forehead against his chest. "I don't like this world very much."

His arms went around her, tight, then tighter. "We'll work through it. It won't always be like this." He kissed the top of her head. "Get dressed. I'll set our supper out."

Fiona scrambled into underclothes, then a pair of jeans and a sweater. She managed to find a pair of flats, which felt like slippers on her feet. When she joined Kelan in the main room, she noticed he'd propped chairs up under the door to the hallway and the one to the conservatory. And he'd pulled the drapes closed over the windows on that side of the room, too.

On the table, two plates were set side by side. He held her chair out then sat next to her.

"I've done a manual check of the room for bugs. Didn't find any, but it doesn't mean we're safe to talk here." He nodded toward her plate. "Eat what you can."

Fiona was exhausted and had little appetite. She pushed her food around her plate.

"Fiona, a few bites, please. You must have missed several meals before I found you. And I don't know what they have in store for us, but whatever it is, we'll need strength to meet it."

She took a bite of the chicken. There was some sort of wine- and mustard-flavored sauce with mushrooms. She pushed the mushrooms off to one side of her plate and made short work of the chicken and broccoli. Kelan finished before she did. She watched him look around their room.

He leaned close and whispered, "I'm going to see if I can find a way out of here."

CHAPTER TEN

A few minutes later, Kelan had checked out the garden room and their suite, looking for a way of getting out. He shook his head when he came back to where Fiona was sitting at the table. "Let's try to get some sleep. Morning will be here soon."

They got under the covers fully dressed. This was the first time in a long time that Fiona felt as if she could relax, but worry about the morning kept her adrenaline flowing. She snuggled against Kelan's side.

"Tell me about the claiming ceremony," she said.

He adjusted his hold around her shoulders. "Not now. You need to sleep."

"I can't sleep. At least not yet. Your voice calms me."

"It's a topic that must be discussed when we aren't exhausted and have time to properly consider its implications."

Fiona didn't argue. He thought he'd gotten a reprieve, until he realized she was softly weeping against his tee.

Having her in his arms was like holding the rising

sun; her weeping was as devastating as if the sun wept. It made his chest hurt. If telling her about the claiming ceremony would help, he would spend the rest of their time together explaining it.

"I warn you, it is not a short story."

She nodded and sniffled. "The longer the better. It'll take my mind off where we are and what's going to happen next."

"So, it goes like this. My grandfather's grandfather's grandfather lived in Iceland," he began.

She looked up at him. "Your great-great-great-great-grandfather."

He smiled. "I'll just call him my grandfather. To his eyes, Iceland was a land of unimaginable beauty. In the long winters, his favorite colors were everywhere he looked: blue and white. At night, the sky would come alive with shimmering colors of green, pink, and purple. His people said that fairies were practicing the colors they would paint the land come spring. And indeed, when spring came and the land woke up, the fairies always outdid themselves, washing fields and hills and valleys with colors so rich that you didn't just see them—you felt them; you breathed them."

"Is it really that beautiful there?"

Kelan shook his head. "My words don't come close to doing it justice. When I was a kid, my family visited our extended family there every year."

She gently sniffled.

He quickly continued. "The elders in my

grandfather's village felt it would be best if he made a journey around the world so that he could see all of its beauty. He agreed. His journey took him more than a decade. He'd grown from a boy to a man during the time he was gone. He'd seen many wondrous things on his travels. But he had a new yearning that could not be ignored. He longed for a lifemate.

"On his way home, he traveled up through the Dakotas here in the U.S. One day, he came upon a scene unfolding in the woods that would forever change his life—and the lives of all of his descendants. There was a huge black bear whose paw was clamped in the jaws of a trap. A woman was nearby collecting berries. She heard the bear's howl of pain. Instead of running away, she hurried toward him. My grandfather rushed to intercept her, but he was a long way away. She got to the bear before my grandfather could get near her.

"The woman eased closer to the beast. He stood on his hind legs, one of his front paws still caught in the trap, and roared and swiped the long claws of his other paw at her. To my grandfather's shock, the woman began to sing. Her song must have reached the bear's spirit—as it did his own—for the bear sat down and just groaned at her.

"My grandfather stayed hidden in the tree cover, fearing his sudden appearance might further enrage the bear. He had his rifle and was prepared to shoot the beast should the foolish woman try to help him, but he couldn't because she put herself between him and the bear as she moved forward to do the very thing he feared she would.

"She reached the trap. She sang her song as she sprang it free. The steel teeth pulled out of the bear's paw. He stood on his hind legs and roared a terrible sound. She stayed kneeling before him, her head bowed. My grandfather shouldered his rifle and sighted the bear, but before he pulled the trigger, he saw the woman spill her cache of berries out for the bear to eat.

"When he began to eat, the woman stood and walked away. The bear followed her when he was done eating, and my grandfather followed the bear to where the woman was at the river. He watched as she cut long strips of leather from her skirt. She collected various plants, heated them over a campfire, then mixed them with moss. Again she approached the bear, singing the song that was her gift to him. Again he let her near. She wrapped the poultice around his paw and tied it in place with the thongs she'd cut.

"For seven days and seven nights, she treated his paw and brought him fish and berries. When my father woke on the eighth morning, the woman was alone. The bear had gone.

"My grandfather couldn't believe she'd survived tending the bear. He decided to approach her. He had to know her name, had to touch her to see if she was real. Before he could get to her, two white men came forward. They were angry with her for setting the bear free. They fought with her.

"The woman who braved the worst nature had to offer was about to be destroyed by men. My grandfather came out of his hiding place and fought them. The Bear Paw Woman ran away. The men chased after her, but the bear she'd saved chased them and mauled them to death. He turned to my grandfather, stood and roared, clawed the air with his healing paw, then ambled off into the woods.

"My grandfather tracked the Bear Paw Woman to her village. Angry warriors who thought he was one of the men who'd attacked her immediately surrounded him. He was brought before the chief. He couldn't speak much Lakota and the chief couldn't speak much English. A warrior was summoned to translate for them. My grandfather told the chief about the Bear Paw Woman's bravery. He said that he was in love in with her and wanted to marry her, if she was a free woman.

"The chief told my grandfather that the Bear Paw Woman was his daughter and that she had refused to marry any of the braves he presented to her, even when they offered twice the bride price he sought. He summoned the Bear Paw Woman and asked if she had ever seen this man. My grandfather finally got a close look at the woman. Her skin was a soft color of honey, so much warmer than his own white skin. Her eyes were dark and big, so different from his blue ones. Her hair was long and black, shiny like wet tar, unlike his own, which was the color of corn silk. They were night and day, sun and moon, and utterly complete together.

"The chief had been close to forcing her to decide among her suitors. With my grandfather's arrival in the village, and his daughter's reaction to him, he decided to let my grandfather stay with them while he considered the matter.

"My grandfather loved her people. They taught him many skills for hunting and riding a warhorse. He shared with them the stories he'd accumulated in his travels. And he courted the Bear Paw Woman, which ever after was the name she was known by.

"When he finally returned to the chief to request the hand of his daughter, the chief refused him. Both he and the Bear Paw Woman were devastated. Her mother, however, didn't give up hope. She explained to my grandfather why the chief wouldn't give the Bear Paw Woman to him.

"It was because so many white men--trappers, soldiers—had taken women from the village in what they believed were honorable unions, only to later learn the women were abused, mistreated, shunned by white society, and often abandoned. He did not want that fate for his daughter.

"My grandfather gave this concern grave thought. He decided to prove himself to the chief in a way that would set him apart from the lowlifes that had harmed the village daughters before him.

"Ceremonies were important to the Lakota, as they were to my grandfather's people. He decided to architect a ceremony that would incorporate essential elements of the Lakota belief system, as well as integrate the honor of his people."

Kelan adjusted his arms around Fiona. "Do you want me to stop? I can tell you the rest tomorrow."

She looked up at him. "What if we don't have tomorrow?"

He touched her face. "We will have tomorrow."

"I want you to go on."

He nodded. "So my grandfather thought long and hard about how he could prove to the Bear Paw Woman's father that his intentions were pure and true. He considered the pain white men had caused some of the women. And he thought about how the women had no voice, no say in their fate.

"My grandfather, you see, was an artist. He asked the Bear Paw Woman to cut two wide strips of leather that he would eventually wear as gauntlets. She pierced the leather so that the edges could be laced up. He embossed the leather with Celtic images that pleased him.

"He collected scrap pieces of iron that he melted down into eight small brands—four for him, four for her. Both sets were made with designs from his Celtic ancestors.

"When everything was set, he requested a private meeting with the chief and his wife. He and the Bear Paw Woman met in the chief's tipi. My grandfather put the brands in the fire until the ends glowed orange. He explained that each brand represented a vow made from one to the other, one from the body, one from the heart, one from the mind, and one from the spirit.

"The chief was incensed that my grandfather wanted to brand his daughter. My grandfather calmly explained that the brands were not for her but for him. It was for him to bear the burden of their union. They each got to choose the vows they would live by for the rest of their lives. He would wear the permanent reminders of those vows on his forearms. He held up one of the cuffs he had designed and explained that their vows would be covered up so that they remained private between the two of them. He explained that it was his responsibility to see that his wife had everything she needed to keep her vows, and he would do the same for himself.

"In this way, he convinced the chief that his love for Bear Paw Woman was forever. That he would put her first, before himself, before the world. The chief asked him about the rest of his ceremony. After much discussion, the chief helped him incorporate the four primal elements and the four directions into the ceremony.

"This is the ceremony that we follow to this day, where I claim you and you claim me and we are forever united."

Kelan paused, bracing himself for Fiona's response. She lifted her head and looked at him. Tears were in her eyes. She smiled as she reached up to touch his face.

"I love you."

"I love you," he said.

"Was that a true story about Bear Paw Woman?"

He smiled. "It's the story I was told. It's best not to question the elders about such things. But I believe, at the very least, it was true in my grandfather's heart."

"I look forward to our ceremony."

"I do too."

"But I don't want you to be hurt. Couldn't we have the brands tattooed on your forearms instead of searing them?"

"Fiona, I've looked forward to wearing the marks of our union my entire life. Don't rob me of that experience."

"It makes me nervous to think about it. It sounds intimidating."

"It is. It's meant to be a solemn event. When two people join their lives, that can never be based on whim."

"For some, it is."

"Not for me. Not for my people."

Fiona sat up and faced him, her legs folded in front of her. He did the same, and took her hands. "Am I your people?"

"Yes."

"How do you know?"

"Listen to your heart."

Her heart belonged to him. It was all she knew, the only truth she believed in this upside-down world they were in.

"In the claiming ceremony, I prepare a sanctuary for our spiritual joining. It can be in a cave or outside, but it is always where we can touch earth. I paint a sacred circle divided into quarters to represent the four directions: east, west, north, south. In the center is a fire. Near the ceremony site is a stream or pool or lake. In this way, all four elements are also an important part of the ceremony. The spirits of the four directions carry word of our uniting out to all of our ancestors."

Fiona felt tears in her eyes. "It sounds beautiful."

"It is."

"Are there witnesses to our ceremony?"

"Only the four winds and the four elements and all of our ancestors. The heavens, the earth, and everything in between."

She met his steady gaze, already beginning to feel changed by the solemnity of the ceremony.

"In preparation for the ceremony, we'll each come up with four vows we'll give the other."

"What kind of vows?"

"Intentions you set for the rest of your life."

"What if we change? People do, you know."

He smiled. "We will. Nothing that lives remains unchanged. But we will change together."

"Do your people ever fall out of love? Divorce?"

His lips thinned. "Not many. I only know of one couple who failed their vows."

"Who?"

"My brother and his wife."

Her eyes widened. His brother's failing had left its mark on him. "What happened? Did they do the ceremony?"

"They did. But they weren't each other's other half. It didn't take."

That filled her with questions. So many questions. She knew very little about his family, complex and unique as they were. She tucked her curiosity away for a future conversation—she didn't want to distract him from his discussion of their ceremony. "Once you've prepared the site and we have our vows, what happens next?"

"We sit at the fire and exchange our vows."

"I like that." His face seemed tense—perhaps she'd missed something of the process.

"In the fire are the eight brands."

Again she asked, "Why must there be brands? Times have changed. Surely the ceremony can change, too?"

He shook his head. "It's an honor for me to mark our vows in my flesh forever. It's my burden to bear, as is the weight of all of our union. It's my job to give you joy, to protect you, to shelter you."

Tears blurred Fiona's eyes. She reached for Kelan's forearms and dragged her hands down them. "I don't want you to hurt."

"I have waited all my life to bear the marks of my other half."

"Kelan"—she choked on a breath—"why does it

have to be this way?"

"It's the way of my ancestors."

"I've never heard of this among the Lakota."

"It isn't their tradition. It was begun by my grandfather's grandfather's grandfather. I will carry the brands of my vows to you on my right arm, and your vows to me on my left. After our ceremony, you'll bandage my forearms. When we return to Blade's, I'll wear leather cuffs to cover them. No one but you and I will see the scars. Our vows are for us to know and no one else."

She nodded and rubbed her hands over his forearms.

He met her eyes. "The vows we give each other are sacred. The scars are the physical marks of those vows. It's an honor to carry them. It means I'm worthy of my mate, and my mate is worthy of me."

She frowned as she looked at him. "You're so strong. Unafraid."

"I am." He gave a quiet chuckle that flashed his white teeth. "Otherwise, I could not be your other half."

CHAPTER ELEVEN

Ty leaned back against the headboard, his arms folded behind his head. Eden was sleeping soundly next to him. They were safe and comfortable while Kelan and Fiona were in the control of a fiend. The team was taking shifts trying to find them. He should be taking advantage of his four-hour sleep rotation, but worry ate at his nerves.

He rolled out of bed and pulled on a pair of jeans, then stepped out of their bedroom to pace the length of the hall and back, trying to figure out what was keeping him up.

Their work since leaving the Red Team had always seemed personal. From the fact that it brought them all back here to his childhood home, Kit's hometown, and Rocco's home state, to some coincidences he was beginning to think weren't happenstance at all.

King seemed to have his tentacles everywhere. His operation was too far-reaching, too mature to have been built within a single lifetime. How far back did this thing go? Ty's own grandfather had been involved in part of it. Was that even the beginning of

King's operation?

How old was King?

He wondered how deeply involved his mother's family was. Who else on the team had tethers in that hidden world? Was it behind what drove the government to set up Max, securing his indoctrination? Rocco was outside the organization. He'd grown up the only child of a ranch cook. And Kit wasn't involved; he'd grown up a town outcast as the son of an addict, but he was tied to this because of their friendship.

And then there was Greer, who was raised as an assassin by a grandfather mired in spec ops missions. What was it that his grandfather had been a part of? Kelan wasn't involved, though he and his brothers all came from the private security world, as did his parents. Who were they providing security to? Angel was a salt of the earth type, son of Puerto Rican parents, raised in the Bronx. Ty couldn't see a connection there. Nor could he with Selena.

The only two left to consider were Val and Owen. And what did any of them really know about Owen? It was no secret that he and Val were cousins, that Owen had lived most of his teen years with Val's family. What happened to Owen's family that caused the death of his parents? And why did Owen keep secrets from Val, his own cousin, when they were practically brothers? Owen knew the rogue Red Teamer they were after. They were in the first class of Red Teamers together.

And now they'd learned that Fiona and Lion were offspring of the man they hunted.

He leaned against the wall and slipped down to the floor. Propping his wrists on his knees, he stared at the door on the opposite side of the hall, realizing he'd come downstairs.

Someone came out of the den. Greer.

"Blade," Greer said quietly. "Can't sleep?"

Ty shook his head and got to his feet. He grabbed Greer's arm and pulled him through the door to the basement, shutting it behind him. The big space was under construction. They were building out rooms and halls, a kitchenette, bathrooms. Whether the space would be used for team offices or for future classrooms for kids of the team hadn't yet been decided. Construction had been stopped for the moment, given that half the team was off site. The bare wood frames, the smell of freshly sawed wood, and the maze of skeletal walls were comforting; it made the basement look new and foreign and nothing like the space he had been caged in as a kid.

"S'up, Blade?" Greer asked.

"Do you trust me?"

"What kind of question is that?"

"One that needs a straight answer."

"Yes. I trust you. Now that we got that out of the way, can I be in the secret club?"

Ty looked at him. "You're in it already. We all are."

Greer shook his head. "I know your mind works

in cryptic ways, but what the fuck are you talking
about?"

"We're trying to find King, but we're not going
about it the right way."

"Okay. I'll bite. How should we be looking for
King?"

"Start with us."

Greer's brows shot up. "You think one of us is
King?"

"No. But I think we're all tied to him. Somehow.
Even if it's only through the Red Team we've all
served." Blade walked away, pivoted, and came back.

"Why are you even thinking this?"

"The tendrils tying us together. Hope's mom's tie
to the WKB, Lion is King's kid, my involvement
through my mom. Remi's background and her work
with the Friendship Community. What if, somehow,
in some way, we're all connected to King and what
he's doing...and we don't know it, but Owen does."

"You think he's King?"

"No. He's not old enough. He mentioned a while
back there was a rogue Red Teamer, but he's done
nothing to have us track him down."

"Yeah, but Wendell Jacobs hasn't done anything to
cause problems except drop off grid."

"Which ordinarily would have been enough to
have us chase him."

"Maybe Owen figures the shit King's into is a
bigger deal."

"Maybe. Maybe the link is our parents and

grandparents. What do we really know about any of them? Look at the mess my grandfather and mother were into. And your grandfather, raising you like an assassin, and here you are using those skills to fight King. Val grew up with Owen, but even he feels there's something the boss is hiding from him, from us. And how did Selena make it onto the Red Team in the first place?"

"Ah…because she's badass?"

"She's the only female to make it through the training. You know as well as I do she's not the only female badass out there. And we know she didn't do it on her back. Who were her parents connected to? There's a whole network of answers linking us. Maybe, if we can find it, we'll know what King is up to before shit rains down on the team while we're spread too thin to help each other."

Greer regarded him for a silent moment as he processed their convo, then he nodded. "I haven't looked at it from that angle—the inside out. Let me do some analysis. I'll get back to you. Am I keeping this on the down-low?"

"For now, but it's not a secret if anyone asks about it. You have all of our vitae. Dig into it. See where we overlap. Find something new. If my theory holds up, we'll bring it up with the team."

They went back to the main floor. Greer returned to the den, and Ty went back up to the room he shared with Eden. She was still in the same position he'd left her in, still softly breathing.

He stepped into the closet and closed the door. Opening the safe, he took his mom's big jewelry box out and set it on the floor. He had only vague memories of her and the box, but very, very sharp ones of Bladen's anger when he discovered it missing after her death.

Why had it upset him so much? Was it just that a woman—his wife, at that—had defied him? Or did he resent the loss of the fortune that he could have used to buy the allegiance of more pedophiles?

Ty opened the drawers, looking over the jewels, many of which had come to his mom from a long line of wealthy Holts reaching back into the early nineteenth century. The jewelry box wasn't an antique. It had several narrow ring and earring drawers—wider ones for bracelets, side panels for necklaces. And why had Blade's mom begged her friend Allie to keep the box for him? Given what his mom was up against, it put Allie in a dangerous situation. As he opened each of the compartments, the thought came to his mind about the hidden compartment in Bladen's desk where he'd found his ledger.

He was sure his mom would have valued her friend's life over a fortune in jewels.

He went still.

Unless, perhaps, she valued her son's life above all else? Was there a message in the jewelry box for him?

He began to pull out each drawer, tug at the red velvet lining, press and tap and pull each component, searching for anything that might release even the tiniest of hiding spaces. He removed the hinged doors. Nothing. Finally, he retrieved a small-gauge screwdriver and unfastened the top lid. When he slid it off, he found what he was looking for: a narrow pocket between the inner and outer back of the case.

He turned the box upside down and shook it. Nothing came out. Had something once been there? Did Allie remove it? He fetched his phone and pointed its light into the compartment. Something was in there, but down too deep to fish out with his fingers.

He grabbed his KA-BAR and used the blade to drag the paper out. It was a sealed envelope with just one word on the outside: Ty.

He didn't recognize the writing. There'd been so little of his mother's belongings in the papers Bladen had left behind. The things of hers that had survived his stepfather had been to her or about her, but not from her. The envelope hadn't seen the light of day for more than two and a half decades. It was still white and crisp, as if it had been recently penned. He could barely breathe as he opened it.

My Baby TyBurger,

How I wish that I could hug you one more time.

It saddens me to think that you might one day read this note. If you are reading it, you're a grown man now. I suppose I can't still call you TyBurger, though it always made you laugh.

I love you, my son. I had no idea the kind of world I was bringing you into. Well, perhaps by the time I was pregnant with you, I knew.

If you're reading this, then there are things you also must know.

There is an entire reality other than the one most people see. You must be prepared for it. I wasn't, even though my father was mired in it. Now he's dead and I am doomed to my fate—and the knowledge that I will not be there to protect you and see you grow into the man you are now.

Phillip Bladen, my husband, is an evil man. You must sever all ties to him, and protect yourself and those you love from him as well. He is not your father. Cordell Ryker is your dad and the man I fell in love with. But it was too late. I was already married to Phillip.

I did not choose to marry him; I was forced to. My marriage to Phillip was an obligation your grandfather owed to the secret organization he belonged to. Had I refused, he would have been killed, which happened anyway. I wish— well, never mind. The time for empty wishes is long gone.

My father and husband belong to a secret group, which is known as the Omni World Order. It has existed for many centuries across most continents under different names. When I was a teenager, the different groups were renewing and formalizing their structures, reconnecting with each other, growing in power.

They aren't like a religious sect that wants its philosophy to rule all others. Their unifying belief is far simpler. They want power. Period. Power begets power.

Many of the world's richest people belong to the organization and many of the world's ruling families are actors for the OWO. It has its tendrils everywhere.

I learned this from papers I discovered in Phillip's office. He was, apparently, a librarian of some sort for the organization. I took the papers—boxes of them—one day while he was away. I stored them in a vault at a storage facility in Denver. I paid for the use of that vault for fifty years, and left them with instructions about what to do should the prepayment expire or should the vault's contents need to be moved. I've included the information you need to access that vault.

Take the papers, but know that I fear they're cursed. If you're reading this note, then I will have paid with my life to secure these papers from the OWO. I beg your forgiveness for what that has meant for your life.

Ty, it falls to you to finish what I started. Bring these papers out to the wider public. The OWO cannot be allowed to exist.

Be strong, my son. Be fierce. Be brave. Be kind.

Please try to find your father. Cordell is an honorable man. Find him. Give him my love. He will help you.

Your loving mother,
Catherine Holt Bladen

Ty slumped back against one of the columns of drawers in his closet. He read the letter two more times, then set it aside and put the jewelry box back together. He put the jewelry in the box and set the whole thing in the safe. When he came out of the closet, the sky was beginning to brighten.

Eden was sleeping so peacefully—as much as he wanted to shout out about his discovery, he also didn't want to wake her. Kit was out with the team down in Denver. Greer was on duty in the bunker, but everyone else was asleep. There was one person, though, he could wake and share it with.

His dad.

Ty dressed, then stopped long enough to see if the storage company was still in business and still located where it was when his mom took a unit. It was.

He drove over to Mandy's place and parked in front of Ryker's bunkhouse. The little house was dark; this was his dad's day off from the diner, so he was probably sleeping in. Ty knocked on the door then tried the handle. It was locked.

A light came on inside the kitchen, then the door swung open. His dad stood there, looking rumpled and irritated. Ty couldn't help but wonder, for the millionth time, what his life would have been like if he and his mom and dad had been able to live together as a family. Maybe he would have had a whole bunch of siblings. Maybe he would have never had to fear or fight for survival.

And maybe fairies farted pink rainbows.

Either reality was as out of reach as the other.

"We gonna stand here and stare at each other? Or are you comin' in?" His dad's voice rumbled into the quiet morning.

Ty stepped into the kitchen. "I found something." He looked at Ryker. "A letter from Mom. It was in her jewelry box."

His dad frowned. He went into the other room to fetch his glasses, then came back and took the letter. When he finished reading it, there were tears in his eyes. He set his hands on his hips and hung his head for a long minute, then looked up at Ty. "Let's go get those boxes. You think they're still there?"

"Don't know, but I'm feeling a sense of urgency. Go get dressed. I need to show this to Owen. I can't go, Dad, so I'm sending you down for them."

The importance of that errand didn't escape Ryker. He met Ty's eyes then nodded.

"I should be able to get one of the guys to ride shotgun with you. Don't want you to go alone."

Ryker was already heading into his room to dress, but he stopped in the hallway and looked back. "Sounds good. I want to see what's in those boxes, boy."

"I'd like that. Come over to the house when you're ready."

* * *

With Kit in Denver, Ty had to take this directly to Owen. He knocked once. Owen came to the door, wearing his loose cotton pajama bottoms. "Blade."

Ty handed him the letter. Owen stepped out into the sitting room outside his bedroom and closed the door to his room.

"What is this?"

"A note from my mom. Found it in her jewelry box."

Owen turned a light on and read it. He looked at Ty. "This place still in business?"

"Yeah. I checked."

"We're spread pretty thin. May have to wait retrieving the boxes."

"I got a bad feeling about leaving them there. My dad can go for them while I stay with Rocco."

Owen looked at Ty. He nodded. "Send Max with him. We could use an inside scoop right about now."

Ty nodded. "On it."

CHAPTER TWELVE

Kelan heard the bolt click on their door. He and Fiona were already awake. There were no clocks in their suite, so it was impossible to tell what time it was. The lighting in the fake solarium had begun to brighten, but there was no way to know if that was actually timed to occur at dawn.

The men who had brought them to this room last night stepped inside. The light-brown-haired guy waved to him. "Let's go. Quickly."

Kelan took Fiona's hand and hurried over to the door.

"Not her. Just you."

"You said I was the only one who could save her."

"You are, but she can't go with you now. And unless you move fast, you'll be too dead to help her get out of here later."

Kelan wrapped his arm around Fiona and started to push through the door, but the two guards shoved them back.

"We don't have time for this. He's on his way here right now. If you don't come right now, he will kill you. And us."

"We'll hide Kelan," Fiona suggested.

"No. He knows now that the wrong War Bringer stayed the night in here with you." The guy looked at Fiona. "He won't harm you, but he'll kill Kelan."

Fiona stepped free of Kelan's hold. "Go. Hurry. Please, Kelan."

One of the guards straightened. "We're too late. They're almost here."

The lead guy dragged Kelan into the bathroom then into Fiona's closet. He hit a button beside her jewelry cabinet, which popped open. One of the guards stepped into the dark tunnel. Kelan struggled for a last glimpse of Fiona. It was wrong to leave her behind, to face the danger herself.

A sharp twinge hit his shoulder, followed almost instantly with paralyzing heat. He couldn't speak, couldn't fight, couldn't get back to her.

His last thought as his mind went dark was that he'd lost Fiona once again.

* * *

Fiona's heart beat hard and fast. She went back into the main area of her suite, then remembered Kelan's boxer shorts and rushed to grab them out of the bathroom and hide them among the clothes in her closet.

She had just walked over to the sitting area of her room when her door slammed open. A middle-aged blond man and four guards rushed inside.

She studied the man, wondering if he was King…her father. She felt absolutely no connection to him. But just in case he was, she memorized everything she could about him so that she could tell Kelan later. He wasn't very tall—a couple inches short of six feet. His hair was thinning in the front but was still a golden color. His pale blue eyes could have been jovial, but instead were like steel. His pug nose was oddly small for his face. His skin was weathered, folded into lines about his eyes, forehead, and mouth. His teeth were small, yellowish, and straight. The corners of his mouth turned down.

"Where is he?" the man asked.

Fiona lifted her brows. "Who?"

"The pretender."

Fiona clasped her hands in front of her to keep them from shaking. "Um. Maybe this all makes sense to you, but just two days ago, I was a student going to Colorado State University. My worst challenge was grasping the finer nuances of macroeconomics, so forgive me if I'm not following you. What 'pretender'?"

Kelan's words of wisdom from yesterday came to mind: *It's some kind of role-playing game. I don't know anything about it, what the rules are, how one wins. Just go with it. Buy us some time.*

Her favorite class in high school had been her drama studies. She had no idea what was expected of someone who was King's daughter, but it no doubt had to do with being regal and having a sense of entitlement. She could play this role.

Especially if she were acting to save her life.

The man motioned his guards to search the place, then crossed the room to stand in her space. She didn't back down. Perversely, she thought Selena would be proud of her.

"I thought it was a bad idea that you were raised out in the world where you would know nothing of your true identity."

"Perhaps you were right. Who am I really?"

"You are the Princess Fiona."

"I see. And who are you?"

"Mr. Edwards. Where is the imposter War Bringer you brought back with you last night?"

"Imposter? I brought with me? In case you haven't noticed, Mr. Edwards, I am no longer in control of my life—I haven't been since I was kidnapped on my way home from school. I've been given no choice in where I went or what I did. And if I resisted, I was drugged until I complied. So you tell me—who was he?"

Mr. Edwards' eyes narrowed. "Don't be coy with me, girl."

"That's 'princess,' I believe—"

"He's your lover, from the Red Team. The one who's been panting after you since he took you from your stepfather's."

That took her aback. How did he know about that? Had Alan said something to them about her living with the guys? "What makes him an imposter?"

"The true War Bringer is a pure-blooded Arian son, not a mixed-breed mutt like the one who was here. Not only is he from a perfect race, but he will be its leader too. And you will be his bride." The man—was he King or not, Fiona wondered yet again—leveled a hard glare at her. "Marriage to him is the start of the very purpose for which you were conceived."

"What purpose is that?" Fiona asked, half dreading the answer.

"Why, to perpetuate the perfect race of Arian warriors."

"No, thanks. I don't think that's what I want to do with my life. I've been having a hard time figuring it out, but I'm pretty sure that's not it."

Mr. Edwards smiled. "That's not your choice to make, as you so wisely observed earlier."

Two girls came into her room, entering from her closet. They brought a tray of dishes, a sewing box…and a white dress.

"I'll leave you to your breakfast and your fitting." He gave her a hard look. "Get your imposter out of your head. He must be here somewhere. I will find and terminate him like the rat he is."

Fiona watched the man and his guards leave her room through the door to the hallway. The girls made no eye contact with them. Did they fear them?

"Princess—" the older one began.

"Please, call me Fiona or Fee."

The girl nodded. "I'm Ellen. That's Bryn. We've brought your breakfast. Once you've eaten, we'll begin your fitting. Would it be an inconvenience if we stayed here while you ate?"

"No, of course not. I'm sure you brought plenty— I'm happy to share if you're hungry."

"That would not be acceptable." Ellen dipped her head. "Though it was kind of you to offer."

Bryn laid the white gown out on Fiona's bed. It was just like the one she and her friend had seen the time they'd gotten the courage up to go into one of the bridal stores in Fort Collins. The dress had cost thousands of dollars, so Fiona had only admired it from a safe distance. If she still doubted her friend had been playing her, she didn't any longer. That dress was one of a kind. Her friend had to be the one who told King's people about it.

Fiona looked at the duo, wondering how deeply mired they were in this weird world here at King's Warren. They'd come in from the same door that Kelan had been taken through.

"I didn't notice a door in my closet," Fiona said as she went in there. Looking around the room, she still couldn't find an obvious door.

"We used the servants' entrance," Ellen said, following her into the room.

"How?"

"It's best if you don't know."

"Was there anyone in there? Did you pass anyone when you came in?" Had they seen Kelan with the

143

men who took him?

"Only servants use that entrance."

"Did you see a few men in there?"

"No."

Fiona's lips thinned. She had no way of knowing if Ellen was telling the truth. "Can you show me where the latch is?"

"Please, Fiona. You cannot go in there. Mr. Edwards will know I showed you."

"I won't tell him. This suite makes me a little claustrophobic, having only one way in or out. If there's a fire, I'd like to know how to get out when my hall door is locked."

"Are you going to start a fire?"

"No. I just would like to know where the door is. Please."

Ellen looked tense. She went over and showed Fiona an electrical outlet behind some hanging clothes. "It's this. Press it."

Fiona did, and the whole front of the jewelry cabinet popped open. "Whoa."

"Don't ever use it. Don't ever go in there. Mr. Edwards will kill me or one of the others if he finds out."

"I understand."

They went back into the bedroom.

She sat at the table where her meal had been set out, and took a bite of the egg soufflé. Fiona wondered what the guy had meant when he said that he couldn't save Fiona, that only Kelan could. Save her from what? What if she could save herself? Would these girls help her? Either way, she had to make a plan.

"Ellen, when is this wedding supposed to take place?"

"Tomorrow."

Oh, God. That gave her very little time to get out. "No." She shook her head. "That's not happening tomorrow."

Ellen shared a swift look with Bryn. "You don't have a choice."

"Of course I have a choice."

Ellen took the seat next to her. "None of us has a choice in our lives anymore. Not here."

Fiona studied Ellen. "They can't think this marriage would stick."

"In this world it will." Ellen shook her head.

How could this world even exist today? How could it be so unknown that she—or anyone—could disappear into it? "I don't live in this world. I'm going back to mine."

"Can she do it?" Bryn asked, looking at Ellen. "Can she get out?"

Fiona sent them a curious glance. "Do you know the way out?"

Ellen reluctantly nodded.

"Then why don't you leave?"

"Only one of us is allowed to go to the surface at a time, when some errand takes us there. If that person doesn't return, one of us is killed." Ellen took Bryn's hand as she came to stand next to her. "Two of our friends have died that way. We don't challenge that rule anymore."

Fiona frowned. "How long have you been here?"

"I've been here four years. Bryn's been here two."

"Do your families know you're here?"

The girls shook their heads. "We haven't been able to communicate with them."

"You couldn't even sneak in a phone call?"

Ellen shook her head. "Our families don't have phones. They expected us to be gone only a few months. Our community does tithes in the form of a service."

Fiona frowned. "Ellen, are you guys from the Friendship Community?"

"You've heard of our village?"

She'd heard some of Greer and Remi's long work there while Remi was quarantined. More terror unleashed by her father and his cohorts. "My father did a terrible thing to your people. He sent one of his associates to infect them with a disease called smallpox. Many died before it was contained." She showed Ellen her inoculation site. "I got the vaccine, but those who didn't in your village, or those where the disease was too far progressed for it to help, had terrible sores like this one was but all over their bodies."

"Ellen," Bryn said, "we have to get home to them."

Ellen nodded. She got up and walked around.

"Have you not been out of King's Warren in all the time you were here?"

"No," Bryn said. "None of us have left."

Ellen stopped pacing and looked at her. "You will be the first to leave. If we write letters to our families, you could take them with you and see they got delivered."

"I'm not getting married."

"The ceremony is going to happen."

"Perhaps that's your custom, but it isn't mine."

"Even to save your life?" Ellen asked.

"This is crazy. This is not reality. I can't be forced to get married. None of this is real." She looked at the other girls. "But I will get out. And I will take your letters and get them to your families. And I will come back for you."

Fiona turned away from their disbelieving eyes. She was going to get out. If not by herself, then when Kelan came back for her. This wasn't going to be her life. She yanked the drawers in the sideboard open, searching for some paper and pens. She found some in the third drawer.

The girls sat at the table and began scribbling madly. Fiona silently ate her breakfast as she watched them. Not only was she going to get out, she was going to keep her promise to come back for them.

* * *

The bunker conference room was empty when

Max and Ryker brought the boxes in from Catherine's storage unit. There were ten of them. Owen helped them unload.

"Let's not dig into these until Blade's here," Owen said. "I think it's going to mean a lot to him to be part of it."

"Fine," Ryker said. "But I want to be here too."

Owen looked at him. "I don't have a problem with that." He looked at his watch. "I need to ask a favor, Cord."

"What's that?"

"Most of our team is down in Colorado today. I could use another pair of eyes here at the house until they get back."

Ryker looked from him to Max. "Sure. I'm off today."

"Max, get him a handgun. I want him armed."

"I'm a convicted felon, Owen."

"An exonerated one."

"The exoneration hasn't come through yet. And I haven't shot a gun in almost three decades."

"Noted. When things calm down, I'll have Blade spend some time with you at the shooting range so you're ready if we find ourselves short-handed again."

CHAPTER THIRTEEN

Fiona was in her closet after the girls left. She waited anxiously for enough time to pass that she could follow them into the tunnel without their knowing. She heard someone enter her room. She came out of the bathroom to see whom it was.

Mr. Edwards. Whether he was King or not, the man gave her the willies. With his wiry build, his strange, short nose, and his predatory grin, he seemed more of an enforcer of sorts, not the man capable of masterminding tunnel systems like those in King's Warren, and all the other wicked things he'd put into motion.

But wasn't that the powerful thing about King? No one really knew who he was or if they'd seen him.

She caught her hands together so that he wouldn't see them shaking. "Are you King?"

The man laughed. "I told you who I am."

"I'd like you to leave my room, Mr. Edwards."

The fake affability left his face. "I don't care what you'd like. Your wants, your needs, your hopes, your dreams matter nothing against those of your father.

Your entire life you have been spoiled and coddled. Now, he's calling upon you to do your duty. You will stand up and do as he wishes."

"My father can go to hell."

Mr. Edwards' hand shot out, but stopped before connecting with her face. She cringed as if the strike had happened. "We all do what is asked of us."

"Maybe you do, but I don't blindly follow madmen. If you're going to kill me, do it."

Again, the thin smile of his carved space across his teeth. "You aren't required to live very long. Just how long that is will be entirely dependent on you."

Fiona thought of all the deaths her father had caused. What if she couldn't find a way out and Kelan couldn't find a way back to her before the wedding tomorrow? She had to go along with the crazy they all lived by here; she had to live long enough to return to reality.

Her expression must have changed, for Mr. Edwards visibly relaxed. "Very good. Yes, very good." He walked away, but paused by the door to her suite. "I have a special treat planned for you—lunch with your fiancé."

"The War Bringer."

"The *true* War Bringer. The man hand-selected by King for a very important role. Be ready in fifteen minutes. You will be escorted to him."

* * *

The guards came for her precisely fifteen minutes after Mr. Edwards left. She followed them meekly, and hated that weakness about herself. She couldn't battle her way out. Maybe she could think her way out. If she truly was King's daughter, then she had his smarts. She'd chosen to be like her mother—always letting kindness rather than cunning be her guide.

Not for the first time, she wondered about her mom...how had she crossed paths with King? Were they in love? Was she just a useful female? And why, why had her mom never mentioned this dark world?

She glanced around her at the elegance of the hall she was escorted through. It looked like a European art museum. Interspersed with the sculptures and paintings were huge floor-to-ceiling red and purple banners with words in languages she didn't know. Occasionally, they were in English, and those talked about a new world order.

It was a grand show. A theater of dominance. The scale and arrogance reminded her of the Nazis she'd learned about in history class, how rapidly their claimed superiority became true superiority, letting them perpetrate crimes on their own people and the whole world.

Was this another attempt to grab power? A Fourth Reich crawling up from the grave of the Third Reich? She had no doubt Kelan and his team would stop it. In time. But they weren't here and she was. She had to play her role and harvest what information she could for them.

She was going to step up, step in, become...what she hated.

And it would be the most convincing performance she'd ever done, because her life depended on it. Maybe Kelan's too...and that of everyone else living at Blade's.

They turned down a few hallways. All of the doors they'd passed were closed. They didn't encounter anyone along their way. They came to two massive carved oak doors, which her guards pushed open for her. Crossing the threshold, she lifted her head and straightened her shoulders then stepped into the room and into her role.

Mr. Edwards was there, with another man, one tall and muscular like Kelan, but opposite him in every other way. This one was blond with blue, soulless eyes. He looked her over as if she were a luxury car that pleased him. This wasn't the first time she'd seen him. He was the fourth contender at the arena fight.

"Fiona, this is Erick Ansbach. Erick, your fiancée—and King's daughter—Fiona Addison."

Fiona gave him the look of an ice queen. "You were at the fight," she said.

He grinned. "So were you."

She looked at Mr. Edwards. "This is your War Bringer? A man who waited to confront his opponent until three others had worn him down? He stabbed the fight's announcer in the back."

Anger quickly replaced Erick's previous humor. "He was stopping the fight. It was interrupted by the police anyway, but I look forward to finishing it."

Fiona lifted a brow, dismissing his comment, dismissing him. "Mr. Edwards, surely my father has better stock available than him. Or does he want a brood of biddable minions?"

"Fiona!" Mr. Edwards shouted, so affronted by her arrogance that he responded emotionally.

Fiona sighed and gave Erick a slight shake of her head. Her bravery came at a steep cost; her heart was beating so hard, it was about to pop out of her chest and take up residence elsewhere. She started for the door. "Bring me the rest of the choices."

"Fiona Addison, your father chose Erick after long and careful deliberation."

"My father, Mr. Edwards, didn't ask my opinion. And he's not the one who has to live with the guy I marry." She opened the door. "I'm going back to my room." She sent a last disgusted look at both men.

The guards outside the room did not try to stop her. They did escort her all the way to her room, however. Fiona stepped into her room and they closed the door behind her. Maybe she'd scrambled everything enough that the wedding planned for the weekend would be delayed, buying her and Kelan more time to get her out.

* * *

Both men looked at the open door Fiona had just exited through, feeling a mixture of awe and worry.

Erick broke the tense silence.

"You said she was innocent. Malleable."

Mr. Edwards smiled. "She's King's daughter. Did you, by chance, underestimate her?"

"I will remind you that there are no other choices for her. Our union was contracted long ago."

Mr. Edwards smiled and set a hand on Erick's shoulder. "You've been living in our world. She hasn't. You can understand it's a bit of a shock to step into it out of the blue."

"She is overly attached to the mutt from the warehouse. The imposter War Bringer."

"She is overly attached to her entire world, but don't worry about the mutt. I have a plan to deal with him...and his entire team."

"They've been hunting King. And you let them continue to exist. Are you weaker than I thought?"

"They are well connected. I cannot eliminate them without bringing greater scrutiny down on us. Or I couldn't, until now."

"What changed things?"

Mr. Edwards smiled. "Your wedding."

* * *

Fiona walked into the garden room next to her bedroom. How had her mom gotten involved with these people? And why hadn't she warned Fiona about them—prepared her at least for what might come? She'd always wondered why her mom had married Alan. When he turned out to be one of King's pawns, Fiona tried to think whether there was any indication that her mom had known. King probably funded the education she thought Alan had been paying for. Her mom, up until her death, was neck deep in this world.

Fiona decided she had to stow those endless questions. Right now, she had to get out of here. She walked back into her bedroom, making a beeline for her closet and secret tunnel door.

"Hello, daughter."

Fiona stopped dead. The voice—or rather voices—had come from the sitting area in her room. Slowly, she pivoted to face whoever was in her room. It was just one person. A man, dressed from head to foot in black. He wore some sort of facemask that covered his head and neck, everything except his eyes, but black sunglasses covered those. He wore a plain baseball cap over his hooded mask. A turtleneck, sports coat, jeans, gloves, and boots completed his terrible ensemble.

"You aren't my father. You don't have the privilege of addressing me that way." Where her bravado came from, she didn't know. Anger; maybe fear. Perhaps he was just going to kill her anyway, so what did it matter?

He chuckled, and his voice modulator fractured the sound into a thousand pieces, all laughing at once. "Mr. Edwards was right. You have gumption."

"Get out of my room."

"Whose room?" He stood. He was tall. Not as tall as Kelan, but close. He was fit and moved with ease, but she was unable to discern his age—or anything about him that she could tell Kelan.

"You know what? It's your room. You have it— I'll leave."

"I've watched you grow."

She stopped and turned back to him. "Did you? Well, thank you for keeping your distance."

"Who said I kept my distance?"

Repulsion sent a shiver across her skin. He came closer. "The breeding program we started so long ago is beginning to bear fruit. Tonight, we will carry on the good work. One thing your mother did right was ensure you stayed a virgin, until that boy almost ruined our plans for you, your sophomore year at college. Remember Danny? Your escapades with him caused your mother's death. She would have let you be impure."

The man seemed to smile behind his mask, as if any of that was amusing. At least it was confirmation that her mom had been murdered. Danny had died the same week as her mother—also while driving under the influence. Was King responsible for that as well?

Fiona did force a smile of her own. "What an honor it is to know my father is a murderer."

He laughed at that. "You please me. Greatly."

Fiona wondered if he knew that she and Kelan had been intimate here, in this room, in this monster's hidden complex.

He faced her. Fiona felt the hair rise on her neck. "Ironic, isn't it, that I let your lover take your virginity last night."

Was he a mind reader, too? Fiona froze, worried anything she might say would make things worse for Kelan. Did they have him? Was he here somewhere or did he get out?

"I do nothing without a purpose. Your feelings for him seem genuine. When he dies, his pointless death, caused by your inability to control your impulses"—his voice rose to an angry pitch—"and your utter disloyalty to me will break you. His death will earn you a second chance to be the daughter I wish you to be. You see, it's useful to lose something you love. Makes you grow up. Makes you appreciate the life you have—and the lover I will give to you tonight."

Fiona wrapped her arms around herself. This man, father or not, King or not, was missing all of his oars.

He went to the door, then paused and looked back her. "Your former lover had no right to take the title War Bringer. I engineered my War Bringer. He is the culmination of generations of careful breeding to be the perfect warrior. He will unify our people and take us into the new era we've been working toward for so long. Kelan will pay for his hubris—and yours in choosing him."

The man left her room, slamming the door behind him. She heard the lock engage.

Now was the time; she had to leave.

* * *

Mandy was waiting in the living room with Zavi when Selena came down with her overnight bag. She was wearing a white silk shirt loosely tucked into her waistband in the front but untucked in the back. Her shirt showed a bit of her white lacy bra through the thin material. Her skinny jeans made her legs look longer than they were, and a pair of wicked-looking stilettos completed her outfit.

She didn't in the least look afraid for what was coming. Mandy went over to her and took her hands. "The bad guys are going to lose their heads over you."

Selena smiled and leaned close to whisper, "That's because I'm going to separate them from their necks."

Mandy laughed. "Please keep my man safe."

"You know I will."

"And come back safely yourself."

"We'll be fine. And hopefully we'll bring Fiona and Kelan home with us."

"Goodbye, Miss Selena. Fight a good fight," Zavi said.

Selena exchanged a look with Mandy, then laughed and ruffled Zavi's hair. "I'll fight a winning fight."

Rocco came into the front hall. He nodded to Sel. "I'll meet you out front in a minute. And you've got shotgun."

"Fine, but I'm driving on the way home."

Rocco stepped into the living room. He lifted Zavi and smiled at Mandy. Her eyes began interrogating his. He reached out to touch her hair. "I'm fine. I got this."

"I need you to come home safely."

"That's my plan, Em."

"I love you."

His gaze held hers a moment before he answered. "I love you, too." He brought her close and kissed her mouth. "I'll be back tomorrow at the latest. Take care of Zavi."

"Always."

He hugged his son then set him down. "Be good for Mandy."

Zavi put his hand in Mandy's. "Always, Papa."

* * *

Once he and Selena were out of Wolf Creek Bend, the highway took them down to Laramie, and then to Cheyenne. Selena put a rock station on the radio. It was noisy and irritating, but it let his mind wander.

He looked at the rolling, empty hills and thought about the convo he had with Mandy last night after sex. She'd snuggled close to him, just the way he liked it, then tore at his soul a little.

"How are you doing?" she asked.

"Fine."

"Rocco, it's me, remember? I'm the one person you let

inside."

So he did, and they'd barely talked since. "It's hard, you know, living. It hurts," he told her. Mandy looked up at him. He gave in to the pull of her eyes.

"It's a choice," she said.

"Living?" He sighed a relieved breath. It was like she finally understood.

"No. Your reaction to life. It's a choice."

"For you, maybe. For me, there's only pain."

Mandy was silent for a moment. "Do you love me?"

"Yes."

"Do you love Zavi?"

"Yes."

"Does that love hurt?"

"Yes."

"Why?"

"'Cause I'm losing my grip. I'm losing you."

"No, you aren't. You will never lose me." She leaned over him and touched her hands to his face, smoothing his hair back. "Decide to feel differently, Rocco. Decide to feel the warmth of our love. Just that. Nothing more. Nothing complicated. Just warmth. We can build on that."

"I killed my wife, Em."

"No, you didn't. War and hate and anger killed her. She let it own her. She rode a dark horse, Rocco."

"I put her on that horse."

"It was a choice—her choice."

"That horse has come for me."

Mandy stared at him. "Maybe so. But you don't have to get on it. You can choose a different horse. You could choose

Kitano. He's fighting back. He's rejecting the darkness. He's living in the light. You can, too."

Rocco sighed. He wished it were that easy. Just decide to feel differently.

As if he had a say in the madness suffocating him.

* * *

A limousine was parked out front of Yusef's motel. Rocco got out then held the door for Selena. They collected their bags from the trunk and walked over to the entryway, where Yusef was talking to Jafaar while two of his men looked on.

Rocco exchanged greetings with the men, then introduced Selena to Jafaar.

"She is beautiful, my friend, but she cannot come with us," Jafaar said.

"It is considered ill-mannered in this country to attend a wedding unescorted."

"The invitation was only for you."

"If she doesn't come, I won't be joining you." Rocco looked at Selena. "You see, she's my bodyguard."

Jafaar's brows shot up. He called a warning to his men. They both drew their weapons. Selena tossed her bag at one, then used that distraction to hit the other guy's wrist, bending it back toward him and freeing the gun. She used a pressure point to twist his hand and turn him around so that it was halfway up his back before he even registered he'd lost his gun.

She pocketed his weapon then slammed him down on the hood of the car. "Don't point a weapon at my boss, got it?" she said, her elbow digging into the guy's back.

Jafaar laughed. Selena eased her hold on his man and let him straighten up. "I can see her value. I'm sure King will make an exception."

"Very good," Rocco said. He nodded at her to give Jafaar's man his gun back.

The other guy tossed Selena's bag back to her. She stowed it with Rocco's in the trunk.

CHAPTER FOURTEEN

Kelan slowly came to his senses. The air was still; not even a scant breeze cooled the sun burning his back. He could hear ants moving through the sandy dirt as they hurried to get their piece of him. His eyes slowly focused on the busy black column, watching until they climbed up his face and into his mouth and nose.

He pushed himself to a seated position and wiped the dirt and bugs off, spitting them out of his mouth. The blue, blue sky spun around him. He had to shut his eyes until the world settled down. When he realized he was no longer in the tunnels, he leapt to his feet, ready for a threat. How long had he been unconscious?

He was alone. In a sea of prairie. It seemed the land rose and fell like the swells of an ocean.

Where was he? There wasn't a house or vehicle or road in sight. The sun was well into the western sky. If the fake light in the garden room had been accurate, it was early morning when he'd been taken from Fiona; he'd been out for hours.

He climbed the nearest hill and tried to see if he could spot the mountains, as he would be able to if he were anywhere within fifty miles of the front range. All he saw was a whole lot of nothing. Sparse buffalo grass. Dirt. Sage and rabbitbrush. No mountains.

When he turned around again, he noticed there were tracks where he had been lying. Truck tracks. He studied them from his vantage point. They dead-ended where he'd been dumped, then backtracked the way they'd come. He jogged in a direction parallel with them. He lost sight of them in a couple of areas that were particularly rocky, but they always picked up again when the gravel gave way to dirt.

He looked where the tracks were headed. There were no buildings and no clues to where he was. He could be anywhere on the plains—in or out of Colorado. Best thing to do would be to find a phone and check in with the guys. But that was also the last thing he wanted to do. He needed their help to find the tunnels, but if he went to them, they'd insist on following him back in—possibly to their deaths; didn't take a fool to see the only reason he had been left alive was as bait to trap the whole team.

I can't save her. Only you can. He remembered that guy's warning. Who was he? Not King—he was too young.

He continued to jog. He didn't know where the entrance to the tunnels was, but the truck he'd been on from the warehouse last night hadn't driven more than an hour east of Denver to the arena. From there to the tunnel had been less than another hour. It gave him a specific search area for when he reconnected with civilization.

The thing was, he had no idea how far he was from the arena or the tunnels.

He looked for signs of human habitation—a dirt road, a telephone pole. Anything. The tracks were still clear, which was good, because if he wasted time going in the wrong direction, he could wander for days without seeing anyone.

* * *

Fiona returned to her closet, hoping at last to be able to sneak out. Ellen and her friends had spent the afternoon with her, talking, adjusting the wedding gown, writing more letters. Mr. Edwards had not returned with more husband choices for her or to press his case. Obviously, her acceptance of the situation was irrelevant.

Well, they could just find another princess, because this one was out of there. She was about to open the secret door, then remembered the letters the girls had written. She rushed back into her room for them—she couldn't leave without them. Not only was it important that their loved ones hear from them, but the letters were the only proof she'd been in this nightmarish place.

Before she could get to the secret door, it swung open and Ellen came through. She was carrying a long garment box.

"Hi." Fiona tried to smile, but she was frustrated that her exit was foiled again. Ellen didn't smile back. Fiona caught the edge of emotion she was barely holding back. "What's in the box? The wedding dress you've been working on?"

"No. It's for tonight."

"What's happening tonight?"

"Another ceremony."

"Oh."

"I'm here to help you bathe and dress."

Fiona tilted her head. "I think I can dress myself." She needed to get Ellen out of her room so that she could make a run for it.

Ellen nodded. "As you wish. I'll just leave it here, then." She set the big box on the oblong ottoman in the middle of the room. When she straightened, she asked, "Are you sure I can't assist you?"

"Quite. Quite sure."

"I will return in an hour for you. Please be ready."

"Okay. An hour. I'll be ready."

Fiona set the letters down and opened the box. Inside was an exquisite red velvet robe trimmed in white fur. It wasn't fake fur. She touched the soft skin, saddened that an animal had been sacrificed for that use. She lifted the robe out, but didn't see an accompanying dress.

Not that it mattered, because she wasn't going to be there to attend the ceremony.

She looked at the secret door, hoping Ellen wasn't

waiting on the other side of it. She pushed the electrical outlet as Ellen had shown her to do. She heard a click. The whole front face of the cabinet released, revealing a black, empty corridor.

Fiona stared at it in shock. She grabbed the candle she'd brought into the closet and used a box of matches to light it. She stepped just inside the tunnel, looking around to find out how to open the door from the other side. It was easier than from the closet side; the tunnel side had a latch to pull.

She closed the door and went down the sloping tunnel, away from her room. She had no watch, but she estimated that she had about forty minutes before the alarm would go up that she had escaped. She had to get as far away as possible in that time. Her access tunnel stopped at another, larger one. She went right. The tunnel had a slight curve, as if it made a wide circle around some central core of the warren.

There were other people here. Not enough that she could get lost in the crowd. They looked harried and didn't make eye contact. She did as they did. At one point, there was a map on a wall. She tried to think where she was in relation to where she'd come into the tunnels. It was set up like spokes and concentric rings. The farther out, the smaller the shafts.

She couldn't see where any of the tunnels had true exits, but then she wasn't thinking super clearly. Any minute, Ellen would notice she wasn't in the room. Then Mr. Edwards and the guards would come for her. She picked a spot on the map that looked as if it might lead into another wheel and spoke system.

Ten minutes later, she entered a new tunnel system. She followed one of the channels to its end at an access tunnel like hers. She'd just turned into it when she heard some commotion from the area where she'd been. She blew out her candle and stood in complete darkness, then began feeling her way along the steep ascent up the tunnel. Her heart was beating so loudly, she feared it was a beacon for those who hunted her.

She paused for a minute to calm her breathing. Up ahead, she noticed there was a slight shimmer of light coming from the end of the shaft. She went in that direction, praying the room or space she stepped into would be empty. She had no idea what she was getting in to. Hopefully, at the very worst, there would be someplace she could hide. Her best plan at that moment was to go from hiding place to hiding place until she could find her way out.

When she got to the door at the end, there was a latch like the one in her access tunnel. She listened to the door for a while, but could hear nothing other than her own breathing. No, that wasn't true. She could hear the uproar that had been trailing her grow louder. She had no choice. She had to go forward.

She pushed the lever. The door popped open. She peeked around the edge of it, seeing what looked like an ordinary basement space, finished and nicely decorated.

Stepping into the room, she realized the access chute was behind a large bookshelf...near a power plug that doubled as a button release for the lever. She pushed the bookshelf almost all the way closed, keeping it open enough in case she needed to make a quick exit, but closed enough that if someone flashed a light up toward it from the tunnel side, it would appear to be closed.

Fiona stood still and silent, getting her bearings. What a surprise it would be to have some stranger walk up out of one's basement. Best idea would be to slip out unnoticed.

She crossed the room to crack the door to the main level. She heard voices...two men talking. She closed the door again and looked around for a place to hide. She hoped whoever lived here didn't have a dog.

Her gaze landed on a phone. She took it out of its docking station and dialed Kelan. It rang once.

"Shiozski here," a man answered, but it wasn't Kelan. It was Max. Still, his familiar voice filled her with savage relief. She could barely speak.

"Hello?"

"Max."

"Fiona! Baby, where are you?"

"I don't know."

"Never mind. I'm tracing your call. Stay on the line as long as you can."

"I got out through the jewelry cabinet in my closet," she whispered. "I went through tunnels and tunnels. It looks like I'm in the basement of a house, but I can't be sure."

"Aw, Fee, it's so good to hear your voice. Are you hurt?"

"No. Where's Kelan?"

Silence. *"We—we've lost contact with him."*

"He was with me last night, then they took him out this morning. I think they drugged him. Oh, God, Max. I don't know what's happening here. They say I'm King's daughter. This place is insane and huge."

"Yeah, Val told us about Daddy dearest. Some of the guys are in Colorado, probably not far from you. Stay put. They'll come to you. Got your location. I'm sending it to Val."

"Max—something's happening tonight. I don't know what. Some part of the wedding ceremony. I'm supposed to marry this guy. They call him the War Bringer."

"Fee, hang tight. The team's almost there. You aren't going back. Just stay with me."

Laughter came over the line. Someone else was on the phone with them. *"Oh, yes, she is."*

"Fiona, get out of there," Max ordered.

Fiona tossed the phone to the sofa. She heard people moving upstairs. The room she was in had small windows mounted high in the walls. She wondered if she could get out in time, then decided she had to try. Before she could move a chair under the window, the bookshelf hiding the entrance to the tunnels opened. Men spilled into the room.

She fought them off as best she could, but she was severely outnumbered. At the same time she was struggling in the basement, she heard a scuffle upstairs. The men who had been up there came running down the stairs. Her captors forced her back into the tunnel.

She heard one of them say to the ones who'd come downstairs, "Get back up there. Kill anyone who comes for her." The man grinned at her. "You just got your boyfriend killed."

Two men held her arms folded behind her. She leveraged their weight to kick him in the face. His head shot back on his neck, and he stumbled backward. When he righted himself, he charged toward her, his fist raised.

She braced herself for the blow, but it never came. One of the other guards caught his hand. "Don't forget who she is and what's about to happen," he warned the guy.

He straightened then rubbed his jaw where she kicked him. "Of course. Mr. Edwards will deal with her."

CHAPTER FIFTEEN

Kelan followed the tire tracks to an empty steel-frame building. No cars were around. No homes, either. There were no trees or shrubs for cover, but there also weren't any windows on the side of the building he was approaching.

A few feet from the building were several abandoned cars parked in a neat line of wrecked metal. Tall brown grass grew up wherever daylight hit—in the wheel wells, the busted floorboards, the narrow spaces between bumpers.

He ran forward, as quickly and silently as he could, then crouched behind the cars and listened. He could hear the whine of a power drill and a radio. Some men laughing about a chick they'd had the night before.

Shit was about to get real. He had no idea where he was, and no idea how to get back into the tunnels. He needed a phone to call in a pickup from the team. And he needed to get hydrated. He checked the shadows, trying to judge what time it was. Depending on where he was, the guys could be hours coming for him.

He didn't have hours. Fiona was in dire trouble *now*. The guys would need time to research and make a plan, maybe check in with Lobo. The tire tracks in the dirt by where he'd been left led here—he couldn't waste this lead.

Someone came out of the building to take a piss in the weeds. Kelan waited for him to come around the row of trashed cars, then stood up. The guy grabbed for his gun. Kelan stood, holding his hands up. "Hey, man, I could use some water."

The guy walked toward him, his pistol held at shoulder height, his arm fully extended. "You're the guy they dumped. How'd you find us?"

Kelan nodded as he moved forward. "It's a long story, and I really could use some water first."

The guy motioned with his gun for Kelan to come with him. "Let's go."

Kelan moved cautiously forward. When he was within reach of the gun, he grabbed the guy's wrist, slapped the gun in toward his chest, and disarmed him. Two other guys heard the commotion and came running out.

Kelan grabbed the first guy by the throat and spun him around for cover as he used the guy's gun to shoot the two men firing at him. Seconds later, the man he held was dead weight and the other two were lying flat on their backs.

These guys knew he'd been dumped. They had to be involved in King's world. Why else would they shoot first and ask questions later?

He took their weapons and stuffed them into his waistband. Leaning up against the steel siding, he listened for sounds of more people inside. The tools were silent. The radio music spun on, covering the sound of anyone else who might still be in the building.

He checked the mag in the pistol he'd taken, then cautiously turned the corner. He could see across the opened overhead door, but not into the building. He did a quick look then stepped inside. The big garage was empty. An MP5 was disassembled on a table, in the process of being cleaned. Perfect. He was going back in the tunnels and needed all the firepower he could gather.

He scavenged what he could from the dead guys. One of them had an employee badge, which he took. Another had a KA-BAR in an ankle sheath.

He went back into the garage, where he finished the cleaning then reassembled the MP5. He found more rounds and magazines in a metal locker. He loaded all the magazines then stashed them in his thigh cargo pockets.

Weapons in place, he checked the fridge and found half a case of bottled water. He downed three bottles then stuffed one in another cargo pocket. Next, he had to decide whether to phone in to ops to check in with the guys.

He looked around the garage, trying to tell if there were any clues about where the tunnels were or how to get back to King's Warren. There was a sweet Range Rover on a lift platform. Its door panels were in the process of being altered for drug transportation.

Kelan stared at that platform it was on. He remembered coming into a garage after the fight at the arena. They'd pulled inside, stopped, then they'd been lowered to an underground parking garage. Could this have been that same elevator?

He looked around for the button to operate the lift. It was there on the wall. A big green button. Kelan hit it and watched the Range Rover slip below the floor. He hit it again, calling it back. Time to call in to ops—but he sure as hell wasn't waiting for them before going after Fiona.

He'd collected phones from each of the guys. One of them wasn't screen-locked. He dialed Max. Because the number he was calling from was unknown to the team, the call was routed around to the usual message centers. Kelan pressed his code, and Max picked up immediately.

"Go, Kelan," Max answered tersely. *"Where the hell are you?"*

"Wherever the hell this phone appears to be calling from. Somewhere out on the plains. No idea if I'm still CO anymore, either."

"Never mind. I got it. You're out east of Bennett. What the fuck are you doing there, bro?"

"I'm goin' after Fiona. And once I have her secured, I'm gonna fillet King."

Silence, then, *"We just got a call from Fiona."*

"Where was she? She okay?"

"She was about five miles south of your current location. No. She said something about tunnels. She got out long enough to call us—well, call you. Kit's on his way out there with a few of the guys."

"Have them come to these coordinates. The other site that Fiona called from has to be a trap; why would they have left me alive and let Fiona slip out long enough to summon the team otherwise? They're waiting to ambush."

"Copy that. Rocco and Selena are somewhere on site as guests of Jafaar's. We think he's wherever King is. We lost contact with them once they hit the prairie. Their signals were jammed when they got to the tunnels. They're attending a celebration honoring King's daughter's nuptials."

"Oh, hell no. I'm going in. I don't want Fiona in there another night. She is not getting engaged or married or whatever tonight."

"Negative. You're going to wait for the team."

"I am not waiting. There's a vehicle elevator in the garage that I'm in. It goes down to a parking garage, and from there, into the tunnels. I'm starting two floors down. Come find me."

"Fiona said the complex down there was huge. How are we going to know where you went?"

"Follow the bodies."

"Shit, K—"

Kelan cut Max off by hanging up. He slipped the MP5 over his shoulder, hit the down button, then raced back to the Range Rover and jumped inside through the open sky roof. He scanned the area as the platform descended. He could only see one guard patrolling the area. The guard came over to see who was on the elevator. Kelan rolled out of the Range Rover before it settled on the ground. He slipped behind a couple other parked cars. When the guard saw that the vehicle was empty, he called up to the guys Kelan had laid out above. Their silence made him reach for his radio. Kelan rushed him, knife in hand, and sliced his throat.

He took the guy's AK-47 and jogged across the parking garage to the stairwell. Inside, another guard stood on alert. He tossed the AK to him, then shot him while he reached for the weapon. This guy's pistol had a silencer. King must want to keep things quiet should Kelan and the team infiltrate the wedding proceedings. Kelan took his pistol and mags then hurried down the steps.

He came out of the stairwell into some sort of landing or utility area. The flooring wasn't as richly appointed as that down the main hallways. He walked out of the stairwell with such authority that it took the single guard a second to become alarmed, and by then, he had a hole in his forehead.

A woman came out of the ladies' room as he turned down the hallway toward what appeared to be a main event ballroom. She glanced up at him, not in the least afraid. She wore an evening gown that looked as if it belonged on the red carpet.

She sucked in her breath and puffed up her chest. Tucking in her chin, she smiled at him. "Oh, but aren't you delicious," she purred in an accent that sounded British. "King has the most fearsome guard corps I've yet seen at one of these functions."

She was flushed and something wasn't right with her eyes. They were dilated, as if she were stoned or horny as all hell, like this whole event was some big orgy. Maybe it was, and Fiona was the night's centerpiece.

The woman rubbed her hand on his arm. "Oh. Gives me shivers."

He had to stink from sweating during his long run that afternoon, but that didn't seem to put her off. "Where were you headed, ma'am?"

"Just back to the ballroom. Will you walk with me?"

Kelan nodded. Wearing the clothes from the closet in Fiona's room meant he was dressed as any of the other guards, so he didn't stand out. They passed one of the real ones. The woman he was with smiled at that guy, too. Her flirting gave Kelan the cover he needed to get her safely back with the others. When they reached the doors to the ballroom, he pulled her hand from his arm and urged her inside, then closed the doors behind her. He was just slipping the AK-47 through the handles when the guard they'd passed noticed the dead one.

"Hey!" he shouted, starting for Kelan at a run. He didn't make it very far before a bullet in the head dropped him in place.

The blocked door wouldn't hold the guests very long. And there had to be other ways in and out of that big ballroom. He just needed the hallway clear a little while he retrieved Fiona from their room.

* * *

Rocco and Selena circulated about the ballroom. It was densely populated with celebrities, wealthy businessmen and women, and high-ranking politicians, the who's who of international powerhouses. No phones, cameras, or technical equipment of any sort was allowed in the ballroom. All guests had been searched, and any electronics they carried were confiscated until they left the premises.

Fortunately, the tour Rocco and Selena had taken a couple of hours earlier, before anyone arrived, let them stash the two phones they now used with the hidden cameras Greer had set up for them. They were recording everything that Rocco and Selena looked at.

Their tour had let them see all of the rooms that would be in use that night, along with the security offices that monitored the public rooms.

It was a massive underground event center in a renovated silo, like the one under the White Kingdom Brotherhood's compound, except quite a bit bigger. Most of the rooms were standard fare for an event center—kitchen, restrooms, storerooms, lobby, quiet room with wall-mounted phones. Even the multistoried parking garage was all very normal.

The room that shocked Rocco was the rotunda several floors below. It looked like something from an ancient castle. It had to be fifty feet in diameter, with two courses of thick arches encircling an altar. The arches had a Moorish flair, with alternating dark and light stones. There were ten arches in all that led to an outer ring, which had only five arches, five exits to other hallways, which he and Selena were not allowed to inspect.

The floor of the rotunda was paved with heavy stones, the lines of which made a star. The points of that star aligned with the five exits. The ceiling of the rotunda was painted in a midnight-blue background with the moon and stars in the foreground. Rocco wasn't familiar enough with the constellations to know which were being highlighted.

It was a beautiful room that might have been relocated from a world heritage site and reconstructed here in King's bizarre underground world.

"What do you make of the rotunda?" Rocco asked Selena.

She sipped a glass of wine as she looked around the room. "It was stunning, and oddly overwhelming. I didn't dig the pentagram on the floor. What do you suppose they do there?"

"Don't know. That was the one room that had no surveillance cameras in it. Jafaar and a few of the other witnesses were heading there when they left here."

"And what the fuck is a 'witness'?" she asked. "If this has anything to do with Fiona, then we need to get down there ASAP."

Rocco nodded. "Let's make our way to the exit."

They were just feet from the door when a woman came inside. She laughed and looked at a man who stayed on the far side of the doors...with an AK-47 in his hand. The hairs rose on Rocco's neck until he realized that man was Kelan. He heard the rifle being shoved through the handles.

He turned and smiled at Selena. "Time for shit to hit the fan." They crossed the room to the kitchen exit, making a plan as they went. "Get out of this ballroom and see if you can find something to block the other doors," Rocco said. "The fewer people out wandering around, the less collateral damage that'll happen once bullets start flying."

"Some of the suits of armor in the hallway have swords or battle axes I might be able to liberate for that purpose."

"Then keep your eyes on the stairs. Kit's bound to be on his way in. Let him know where Kelan and I are."

"Roger that."

"Selena"—Rocco paused and looked at her— "remember you're not bulletproof, okay?"

She smiled. "You sure about that?"

He shook his head, then took off for the hallway that had the stairs down to the rotunda.

* * *

Kelan jogged down the hallway to the stairs at the far end. Coming out in their corridor, he saw the door to Fiona's room was open. He stepped inside cautiously, weapon in hand. He heard weeping. A quick sweep of the suite showed no one lying in wait for him. The crying was coming from the closet. He stepped into the bathroom and pushed the closet door open.

A girl sat on the padded bench, holding her face in her hands. As soon as she became aware of him, she gasped and jumped to her feet. He held a finger to his mouth.

"Where's Fiona?" he asked.

"They have her."

"Do you know where?"

She nodded.

Kelan regarded her silently. She had a bruise on her cheek and her lip was split. Would her help lead him into trouble, or was it his only option? "Can you take me there?"

Again, she nodded. "They are going to take her to the rotunda."

"Is that where the wedding is being held?"

"No." She started weeping again. "The wedding is tomorrow. Tonight is the initiation."

"Why are you crying?"

"Because it's horrible, and I could not help her escape." She looked beyond him. "And I cannot help you, either."

A commotion sounded in the other room. "Get down and stay down!" Kelan ordered the girl. He stepped out of the closet into the bathroom as the suite filled with armed guards. He slammed the bathroom door shut and locked it, then ducked behind the half wall of the shower.

When the guards kicked in the door, he shot the first two to come through. The next two were right on their heels and got into the closet before the second one hit the ground. He hurried to block them, but they came out a second later dragging the girl between them, a pistol to her head. Another man paused at the shot-up entrance to the bathroom.

"You've made quite the disturbance out of my party," he said. He was a middle-aged blond man who was clearly the leader of this little group.

"Your party. So you're King."

"I'm many things to many people. Drop your weapon."

"I came for Fiona. No one else has to get hurt." Kelan looked at the guards as he said that.

The blond man chuckled. "You don't get it, do you? No one else but Fiona matters. Not you. Not me. Not any of us here. Only Fiona is instrumental in King's plans."

"Why?"

"Because he's made her so. If you come with me peacefully, I will allow you to have one final farewell."

Kelan instantly calculated the outcomes of several

different strategies. Most would cost the life of the girl he had found crying. He couldn't let her be killed in cold blood. Holding up one hand, he slowly set his MP5 on the ground. Two of the remaining guards yanked his hands behind him and zip-tied them, then finished disarming him.

How much time had passed between when he hung up with Max and now? Was the team close? Where were Rocco and Selena?

"You cost me the lives of many men," the man said through clenched teeth. "And on a night like this night, so critical to King's success. Your death will be slow and painful and certain, but I haven't the time to see to it properly at the moment." He looked at the guards holding Kelan. "Take him to Pen 9 and secure him."

CHAPTER SIXTEEN

Fiona's fear deepened as her captors dragged her back up the dark tunnel to the secret door in her closet. Kelan was gone without a trace, and now she knew even his team hadn't heard from him. Had they killed him?

The only thing sustaining her was that she'd made contact with Max. He'd said some of the guys were nearby. Would they be able to find their way into these tunnels?

When they stepped into her closet, a smiling Mr. Edwards was there, with Ellen, whose face was red and swollen.

"So nice of you to join us, Princess Fiona." The fake cheer left his face. "You're late. It will not make your father happy." He pushed Ellen forward. "Get her ready and downstairs in a half-hour, or there will be further consequences."

He went out of the closet, and a minute later, she heard the door to her room shut.

Ellen came forward and took Fiona's arm. "Please, you must do as he says," she whispered urgently. "If you don't, he'll beat me again. We have to get you ready for the initiation, and we don't have much time to do it. Please." Ellen walked as if a herd of horses had trampled her, and Fiona had no doubt it was all because she had tried to escape.

She nodded. Ellen took her into the bathroom. It was a shambles. Blood was spattered over the walls, floor, and ceiling. The acrid scent of recent gunfire stung her nose. The bathroom door was shattered.

Bryn went into the bedroom, then came back with a beautiful white silk slip draped over one arm. "They're gone."

"Your man was here," Ellen said in an urgent whisper.

"Kelan was here?"

Ellen nodded. Her face was tight. "They made me lie to him about where you were, then they took him to one of the holding pens."

Fiona turned and looked at her. "Where? Where is he? I have to go to him."

Ellen looked at the other girl. "Mr. Edwards said he would bring you to him when we were finished."

"Then let's hurry."

"We have to bathe you."

"There isn't time. I showered yesterday. Please, we have to hurry."

Ellen nodded. "Please, put this chemise on, then we'll start."

Fiona hurriedly stripped to her bra and panties. Ellen looked at her. "Everything must go."

Fiona didn't argue. She dropped her underclothes, then the girls helped her put on the tissue-thin slip. It went to just below her knees. They had her sit on a stool, then draped towels over her shoulders to keep any makeup from discoloring her slip. She felt naked. Why wouldn't they let her put something more on?

She couldn't help but think of last night, when she was here with Kelan, in this bathroom, getting the terrible stage makeup off. Were they going to put all of that on her again?

But why was it so critically important that she be perfectly groomed for this evening's event? Why wouldn't anyone tell her what was happening?

"Fiona, I think we will get to help you dress again tomorrow, but if we don't see you before you leave, there's something you must know." Ellen was kneeling in front of her. "And I need you to make a promise to me."

Fiona frowned then nodded slightly.

"I've sewn our letters into the cape you'll be wearing tonight."

The letters! She'd gathered them before trying to escape, then still hadn't brought them with her. She was glad Ellen had found them.

"If you leave tonight, promise me that you will get them to our families in the Friendship Community. If you don't leave tonight, pack the cape and the letters to bring with you."

"I will. I promise."

Ellen's nostrils flared. The breath she took was

187

jagged as she looked with relief to Bryn. Fiona almost started crying.

Max had said Kit and the guys were on their way. There was an end in sight. This wasn't what the rest of her life would be like. She would get to see Kelan in just a few minutes. Maybe she could stall for time there with him until the guys found them.

It was going to be all right soon. Very soon.

"Don't press your lips together like that," Bryn said. "Stay still so I can put the liner on."

At last, the makeover torture was finished. Fiona looked at herself. The woman looking back at her from the mirror was someone she didn't recognize—someone beautiful, regal, poised, older than her mere twenty-one years. Twenty-one.

It was her birthday today.

She closed her eyes. This was the day she and Kelan had looked forward to sharing. He'd planned a special day for her, for them.

She stood up and moved away from the mirror, trying to keep hope alive. The team was coming for them. They would be found. Soon. Very soon. Tonight, even.

"What now?" she asked the girls. They passed a worried look among themselves.

"We have to do your nails."

Fiona watched as they fixed long, ruby red false nails on her. Then Ellen led her into the dressing room. She selected a diamond and pearl necklace that hung low beneath the collar of her slip. She retrieved a pair of matching earrings and put them on Fiona.

"Where's my dress?"

"Fetch her cape," Ellen instructed Bryn.

Fiona pushed them away. "No. I'm not going out like this."

"Your dress is kept in a special location. We'll take you to it. But first, shoes."

The girls helped her into a pair of red evening pumps that added three inches to her height.

"I have never been to an initiation ceremony, but I understand you'll be given to your husband during it."

"I'm not getting married."

Ellen looked at her and blinked her bruised eyes. "I am not able to change your destiny."

Fiona nodded. "I will change it."

"Remember your promise about the letters."

"I will."

* * *

Kelan was led back to the stairs and through a door on the landing. This led to another staircase and to tunnels painted a utilitarian gray. A couple long corridors later, they were at their destination—a series of holding pens. Ten in all.

He tried to see if the other cells were occupied, but couldn't make anything out through the narrow slit in the door. He heard at least two other inmates banging in their cells, so he knew he wasn't alone down there.

Pen 9 had an interesting design. There was a four-foot-wide ledge rimming a sunken floor in the middle of the room. A steel cabinet stood to one side of the room near the door on the upper deck. The gray cinderblock walls were austere. There were a couple sets of chains with cuffs on one side of the wall.

One of the guards grabbed a chair from the ledge and set it in the sunken area of the room. The light overhead was housed in a metal cage. There were no windows. The only egress was the door he'd come through. So far, he hadn't seen anything he couldn't get out of.

They zip-tied his ankles to the legs of the chair and his wrists to the arms. The blond man consulted with one of the guards, who then removed a tray of metal implements from a tall steel cabinet and placed it on a folding TV table next to Kelan's chair.

Kelan was biding his time, waiting for the right moment to break free. He hoped he would get to see Fiona first.

"Make him bleed," the blond guy from Fiona's room ordered. "There's no reason he should be sitting in comfort here."

One of the guards came over and planted a fist in Kelan's jaw, slicing his lip on his teeth. A few more punches made Kelan rethink his plan to wait it out for Fiona.

"Where's the rest of your team?" the blond man asked.

"How would I know? I've been out of contact since before I got here."

"You telling me you didn't call when you took out my men at the garage?"

"I called. Got voice mail."

The man nodded at the guard, who landed a few more punches. Blood pooled in Kelan's mouth. He spat it out on the floor. He kept one thought in his mind: *Fiona.*

"Try again."

"Try what again?" Kelan asked.

The man chuckled. "Not very smart, are you?"

He shrugged. "I parted ways with my team. It's why they wouldn't take my call. They don't approve of me and Fiona."

That gave the blond guy pause. "Nor do I. Nor does King. But after tonight, it'll all be over."

Dread for what Fiona was going through started a hum in his head. He was going to have to make a move. But just as he decided that, a knock sounded on the door. There was some rustling of clothes, then a vision came into his line of sight, one so stunning Kelan had to blink a few times to be sure he was seeing what he was seeing.

Fiona stood at the steps to the ledge, covered toe to neck in a red velvet cape trimmed in white fur. Only her forearms and head showed, both so pale against the red as to be striking. They'd done her makeup again, but this time softer, more regal and less stagy. Her hair was arranged in a tangle of braids above her head, threaded with pearls. Her nails were long and red. Her lips as red as her cape.

Even in pain, his body quickened at the sight of her. She pulled free of the guard holding her and raced down the steps and over to him, spilling her cape on the floor as she knelt before him. So anxious was she to hold him that her cape accidentally toppled the stand with the tools on it.

Kelan bowed his head, helpless to do more to comfort her.

"Kelan!" She sobbed against his thighs.

"Fiona," he choked out. "Fiona. I love you." He became aware that she wasn't holding him beneath the cover of her cape. Instead her hands were busy at his ankles with a knife she'd swiped from the spilled tray. She was clipping the zip ties holding him. *God. Damn.* The girl could think on her feet.

"Give us a minute," Kelan ordered the blond man.

He nodded toward one of the guards, who came forward and yanked Fiona to her feet. The motion opened her heavy cape, exposing her sheer slip, the only thing she wore.

"You've had your minute," the blond man said, stopping Fiona before she could be taken from the room. "Look at your lover. What happens to him next depends on you. Surrender yourself to your future, and we'll let him go—after your wedding. Continue to fight, he dies tonight."

Fiona met Kelan's eyes. Hers were full of fear and sorrow and anger. And something else. Determination. To live, to fight, he didn't know.

"Fiona, do what they ask you to do. I will find

you."

The guard nearest him backhanded him in the face. "Shut up."

Tears sparkled on her face, but didn't disturb the makeup she wore. Maybe it was stage makeup after all. They took her from the room.

The blond man exchanged words with the guard nearest him, then left the room. Water had begun to spill across the sunken floor, slowly pooling around Kelan's feet.

It was now or never. Kelan pushed up from the floor and swung the chair legs against the man standing next to him. He went down. Kelan grabbed one of the knives from the table and stabbed him in the throat. One of the other men jumped down into the sunken area with him. Kelan held the chair he was still bound to, jumped down on it, and landed hard in the seat, shattering the chair just as the man reached him.

Kelan rolled over backward and came up with a sharp spike that had been a chair leg. He drove it into his eye. The guard's Kevlar vest made any other target in a fast-moving fight too difficult to hit successfully.

There was now only one man left, and he had his hand on a lever to send electricity through the water. Without thought, Kelan flipped to a handstand using the remnants of the arms of his wooden chair as stilts just as the lever dropped. He walked on the wooden spikes across the electric field and flipped over to stand on the ledge surrounding the sunken, deadly pool.

The man rushed toward the door. Kelan helped him get there, smashing him against the steel panel. "Where's the rotunda?" The guy only gurgled. Kelan banged him against the door again. "Where is it?"

"I will die before I tell you."

Kelan tilted his head. "So be it." He pushed the guard into the electric pool and watched him convulse then go still. He shut the electricity off, then took up his weapons, which had been deposited on a shelf. He reloaded his half-empty clip, then took the pistol he'd claimed from one of the guys above ground and holstered it. He holstered the KA-BARs and slung the MP5 over his shoulder.

In the steel cabinet of torture implements, there was a stack of zip ties. He grabbed a bunch and stuffed them into one of his cargo pockets.

As much as he hoped to end the blond man if he ran into him, Kit and Lobo would probably rather he didn't. Didn't mean the bastard wouldn't need a stay in the hospital before being turned over to them, however.

Kelan went out of the narrow hall that fronted the various pens and into the larger room outside them. A guard who had been sitting at the desk jumped to his feet. Kelan pointed his MP5 at him. "Do you want to die?" The guy was young. He shook his head vigorously. "Then disarm yourself."

The kid did as asked. Kelan took him over to the stairwell and zip-tied him to the railing.

Someone was hurrying down the stairs. Kelan pointed his MP5 at the tuxedoed guy, recognizing him a split second before shooting.

"Need help?" Rocco asked.

Kelan grinned. "Not gonna say no." He looked at the guard he'd disarmed. "Where do they have Fiona?" he asked, doubting what the girl in Fiona's suite had told him.

"Who?" the guard asked.

"She's in the rotunda," Rocco said. "I know where it is."

They went down some corridors, then into another stairwell. Kelan's boot crunched on something small. A bead. No, a pearl. Fiona had been wearing pearls in her hair. He looked around, wondering if she'd been manhandled out here before being taken to the rotunda. His eyes caught another pearl on the stairs going down. He nodded at Rocco, then they hurried down the stairs. Every few steps was another bead or clip or something from Fiona's costume.

"Where were you?" Kelan asked Rocco.

"Jafaar left me and Selena with the guests while he and the other witnesses went to participate in some private ceremony. When you blocked the door to the restrooms, I knew shit was going down."

They stopped at the bottom of the stairs...at a complete dead end.

CHAPTER SEVENTEEN

Fiona's two guards dragged her down the stairs. She considered resisting, but where was she going to go? Mr. Edwards was in complete control of this entire place. A vision of Kelan, battered and tied to a chair, flashed through her mind. *"Do what they tell you,"* he'd said. *"I will find you."*

But who was going to find him? Who was going to save him? She'd only been able to cut his feet free, but hopefully that would give him the mobility he needed to fight back.

A little seed pearl fell from the set woven into her hair. It was the second one she'd lost. Maybe the string was coming undone. She reached up to feel for the rest. She pulled a string of them free and let one fall every few steps.

Down and down they went. Where were they going? Ellen had said they were taking her to her dress, but why hadn't she been allowed to come with Fiona?

One of the guards pulled his badge and pressed it against the corner of the wall. A small panel lit up inside the doorway. It beeped when his badge was successfully read, then the whole wall moved to the right. Her guards pushed her into the dark room beyond and let the big wall slide closed behind her, leaving her alone.

She looked around the space, confused at the extreme shift in decor. Small, flickering flames danced from sconces in the stone walls. The floor she stood on was highly polished stone, inlaid with what looked like ancient patterns of scrolls and plants and...monsters? Hydras, dragons, centaurs—classical beasts that were both beautifully rendered and terrifying in their presentation.

She looked behind her. The sleek steel wall she'd just come through was faced on this side with heavy stone like that of an ancient castle. It was as if she were at a theme park, standing on the dividing line between two worlds.

A couple of women came toward her. They were wearing gray velvet capes similar to her red one. Their dark hair was also arranged into complex updos, but without the adornment that hers had.

One carried a small tray with a glass of red wine on it. "Welcome, Princess Fiona. We've been waiting for you. Would you care for a sip of wine? It will ease your nerves and help you relax."

Fiona hesitated. "Where's Ellen? She was going to help me dress."

"She's on her way." The other woman smiled at her. "You're twenty-one today. You can drink wine."

Yes, she was, wasn't she? Though it wasn't at all the birthday celebration she and Kelan had planned. Fiona picked up the glass and took a long sip. The wine was dry, not sweet. It warmed her mouth and throat. She hadn't realized how chilled she was. She took another long sip. Why had they brought her here? Why was her being here worth torturing Kelan to achieve?

"What happens to him next depends on you." What did that mean? What was it that she could do or not do that would impact Kelan?

She started to lift the glass for another sip, but it fell to the ground instead of coming to her lips. The figures on the floor moved. *Moved.* The dragon lapped up the translucent red liquid while the centaur laughed. She drew back in horror, then looked at the women who observed her. One nodded to the other. They took hold of her arms and guided her away from the broken glass.

She was glad they had a hold on her, because she was feeling a little strange. "Ymshs," she said in an effort to thank them, but her tongue hadn't moved. It was paralyzed, stuck to the bottom of her mouth. She asked what was happening, but those words made even less sense.

They walked into another room…or rather, one of her legs moved; the other just dragged behind her. The two women bore her entire weight. Was she having a stroke? What was happening?

Thinking was getting harder to do. Everything

seemed distorted. They walked at least a mile into a huge, round room, stopping at a raised stone altar. There were little beings holding it up. Baby human monsters. With teeth. They twisted around to look at her. She tried to scream, but her mouth didn't open. One of the women drew her cape from her. She expected a rush of chilly air, but couldn't feel anything. Someone lifted her onto the platform, setting her down on her robe. The red velvet was the only color in the whole room. Maybe it was just brighter looking than anything else because of the stream of moonlight spilling over her.

The women who'd helped her come in here disappeared into the shadows. It was sick how they left. They didn't walk out backward; they just got smaller and smaller then were gone. She couldn't move well enough to look around the whole room, but she realized she wasn't alone. There were alcoves spread about the space with statues in them. Some of the statues wore black robes, some white. As she watched, they stepped out of their cubbies and came closer. No, that wasn't right. They didn't move—they got *bigger*.

A man came to the side of the altar. She recognized him but couldn't quite place who he was. Where did she know him from? As she studied his face, it morphed from handsome, Nordic features to those of a leering, horned satyr. He leaned over her and ripped her slip apart, baring her before all the statues. He ran his hand down her body, over a breast, her ribs, her pubic mound, then down one leg, which he lifted and resettled in the channel at the corner of the dais.

Moving to the other side of her, he repeated the process with the strokes and lifted her other leg into its place, leaving her open and helpless. She couldn't fight, couldn't scream, couldn't do any of the things Angel had trained her to do.

Her only defense was to close her eyes. She couldn't even feel the tears she knew she wept.

* * *

"She came this way," Kelan growled as he paced the length of the wall. "She dropped those pearls for us so we could track her. She didn't disappear into thin air." He and Rocco began to pat the steel wall where the stairs dead-ended, trying to see where it opened. Kelan's hand touched something that lit up. An access panel. "Rocco! I've got it!"

Kelan lifted the badge he'd taken from one of the mechanics above ground, and tapped it against the panel. The door slid to the side. The room inside was dark, lit only by a few candles. Two women stood guard. They each carried a tray with a single glass of red wine on it.

"Welcome," they said in unison.

Kelan could hear a hum coming from the area behind the women, a circular area with Moorish arches in two rings. He couldn't see into the room from where he stood, but these women were definitely meant to keep them out.

"Would you care to refresh yourselves before joining the others?" one of the women asked as they pushed their trays toward him and Rocco. Both he and Rocco swiped the trays off their hands, an action that opened them to the daggers the women thrust up toward their chins. Kelan caught the woman's upward-thrusting hand in both of his, using her forward momentum against her as he turned the blade to her throat and sliced the side of her neck. Rocco stabbed the other woman, shoving her blade into her chest. They both dropped to the ground at about the same moment.

Kelan and Rocco stepped into the outer ring of the rotunda. What he saw chilled his insides. Fiona was laid out on a stone table, nude. Her eyes moved, but her body didn't. A man was touching her...a man he knew. He was the fourth contender in the arena fight.

Kelan looked around the room, where caped men and women hummed and swayed. Their hoods were down, but in the dim light, Kelan couldn't quite make out their faces. All of them stood except for one man, almost directly opposite him, who sat in a huge, golden, throne-like chair.

"Is that King?" Rocco asked in a whisper.

"Probably."

"Jafaar's here."

Kelan looked at Rocco. Before he could speak, an

alarm went off. The people in the room started to buzz around, uncertain where to go to get out. Kelan looked back at the women they'd dropped; one of them had crawled over to a rope pull and was still clinging to it even slumped back against the wall as she was.

"I'm going for Fiona," Kelan told Rocco. "Wait a minute, then go in for Jafaar. Perhaps he'll think the alarm sounded above the stairs, too. See if you can find another exit and get him out." He met Rocco's eyes briefly, knowing it went without saying that if his cover was blown, Rocco was going to have to take out Jafaar. His death could be absorbed into the mayhem that was shortly about to break loose, while Khalid's cover could remain in place.

Kelan walked into the rapidly emptying rotunda. The blond guy was climbing up onto Fiona's table. He was naked. His erection hung low between his legs. Kelan thought about a dozen different ways of ending him, but knew he had to get the guy away from Fiona first. He walked up to the guy and punched him in the ear, toppling him off the other side of the tall marble altar. Kelan grabbed the edge of the red fabric under Fiona and pulled it up over her. When he looked up, he could see King in the distance getting up off his throne.

Kelan slipped his knife from the sheath at his waist and sent it flying across the room. It caught in King's cape, but Kelan couldn't do more than that because Fiona's assailant had regained his footing and was coming at him.

Kelan blocked a right hook, then a left hook. He twisted his arms around the guy's arms and yanked him in for a headbutt. He stumbled back, dazed. Part of Kelan wanted to draw out the fight, break every bone in his body. Twice. But he noticed other guards coming into the rotunda, and knew he couldn't risk the danger to Fiona. When he came forward again, Kelan kicked his knee out, then swung his MP5 forward and put a bullet in his heart.

He turned to face the guards, but realized he wasn't the only one fighting anymore. Kit, Angel, and Selena had taken care of the six that had rushed into the room after the alarm. Kelan looked through the arches to the entranceway to make sure no more were coming.

There weren't any at the moment.

The noise ringing in his head settled down to silence. He looked at Kit, then wiped the sweat from his face as he glanced around the room. Angel and Selena were clearing the space. Kelan turned his attention to Fiona. Her eyes were open and staring at the ceiling. He forced himself to smile at her as he checked her pulse, even though she probably couldn't see him. He could feel the faint beat of her heart against the tips of his fingers.

"I got you, Mahasani. You're safe now. We're all safe. The team's here. I don't know what they did to you, but we'll get it sorted out at the hospital." He eased his hands over her face, lowered her eyelids, then wrapped her up in the thick velvet robe and lifted her off the altar.

"Kit," Kelan said, thrusting his chin toward the big throne that King or someone representing him had sat in. "See if my knife nicked whoever was sitting there. It might have been King."

Kit nodded, then looked at Fiona. Kelan knew what he was thinking; that King had been in the room as a witness to his own daughter's rape. What a sick bunch of bastards these were. Even after what happened to Blade and to Hope, Kelan was shocked by their depravity.

Kelan carried Fiona out of the rotunda to the entrance he and Rocco had come through. Selena and Angel came back. "It's clear. Everyone's gone," Selena said as Angel went to move the dead woman away from the wall panel.

"Where's Rocco?" Kit asked.

"He went with Jafaar out of here," Kelan told him.

"Jafaar was in here while this was happening?"

"Yeah," Selena said. "He was a 'witness,' whatever that is. Rocco and I were left upstairs with the other guests." She brushed a bit of Fiona's hair from her face. "She gonna be okay?"

Kelan nodded. "They drugged her, but she's breathing. I don't know if she's been raped. I only saw one guy with her, and I think I terminated him in time."

Angel pulled the lever that opened the wall panel from this side. They went up the stairs, Angel taking point, Kit and Selena covering the rear. At the main level with the ballroom, it was a madhouse. Armed FBI agents were directing people out of the event center via stairs that went up to the ground level.

When they got outside, the field was swarming with people. Tents were being set up to process everyone and to collect evidence. Floodlights had already been deployed, brightening the field like daylight. Order was swiftly banishing chaos.

Several police vans, cars, and canine units were spread around the garage, with cops setting up a perimeter. People were shouting, crying, claiming diplomatic immunity.

Kit led Kelan over to an ambulance. The medics brought a gurney over. He gently settled Fiona on it. The medic opened Fiona's red cape, revealing her naked body. He sent Kelan a narrow-eyed look. The other medic quickly pulled a blanket over her. They lifted her into the back of the ambulance and began working on her.

Kelan felt tears on his face as he looked at his woman being tended to by the EMTs. It shouldn't have come to this. He should have been able to take better care of her. His negligence had let this happen.

Kit put a hand on his shoulder. It was good he didn't start peppering him with questions. He was out of words.

"Angel—go find a store that's still open and buy a pair of sweats for Fiona to wear home. Then clear out our motel room and meet us at the hospital. I'll text you which one we're going to."

"On it." Angel jogged off toward their SUVs.

"I want you to go back and see if you can find any trace of King or Rocco," Kit ordered Val, Blade, and Selena. They took off for the garage and the stairs down to King's opulent hideaway.

One of the medics jumped out and came over to them. "You know what she's on? Did she OD?"

Kelan shook his head. "She was drugged, but with what, I don't know. Is she going to be okay?"

"Yeah. We'll get her to the hospital, get her detoxed." He started to close the doors to the ambulance.

"Whoa, whoa, whoa." Kelan pulled him away from the door. "What are you doing?"

"Taking her to the hospital."

"I'm going with her."

"Follow in your own vehicle." He told Kelan which hospital they were going to.

"No. I'm not leaving her side."

"Kelan—" Kit tried to pull him back.

He faced his team lead, and said between clenched teeth, "I don't know these guys. They could be working for King. I'm not fucking leaving her side. If I have to drive her to the hospital myself, I will."

Kit sighed. He said something to the EMT. The other EMT got out of the back, vacating his spot so Kelan could go with Fiona.

The first medic faced Kelan. "You need to disarm yourself before you get in my ambulance."

Kelan didn't fight that order. He handed Kit the weapons he'd collected during the night. He felt a bit like Val handing over his MP5, three pistols, several knives, and all his mags and zip ties.

"I'll meet you at the hospital," Kit told him.

"We're good. Stay here and help Lobo sort this out."

Kit shook his head. "I'm gonna make sure you get settled, then I'll come back. I want them to check you out, too. And I need to talk to you anyway. See you at the hospital." He nodded to the EMT, who shut the door, leaving Kelan alone with Fiona.

CHAPTER EIGHTEEN

Kelan sat on the hard bench in the sterile cavern of the ambulance. He leaned close to Fiona and held her hand the whole way to the hospital. Their ordeal was close to being over, but until he and Fiona were back at Blade's, he couldn't let his guard down.

The ambulance sirens were loud, and the cab swayed perilously. Kelan held her hand, rubbing it between his. Five minutes into the ride, her fingers tightened on his. His eyes shot to her face. She was trying to look up at him. He moved so that he was crouched over her, making it easier for her to see him. He touched her face, smiling with relief.

"Fiona, can you see me? Can you hear me?"

Mangled sound came from her mouth. She didn't yet have use of all her faculties. He touched her face. "Just blink if you can hear me." Kelan nodded as he made that suggestion. She did blink, very slightly. Again he laughed. His relief was enormous.

"We're on the way to the hospital. They're going to check you out. I won't leave your side. Do you understand?"

She blinked.

"You're safe now. You're out of the tunnels. The team's on site. Including Lobo and half the Denver police force. Kit's following us to the hospital. As soon as we get you checked out, I'll take you home. Everything's going to be all right now."

Fiona closed her eyes at that. A tear slipped down the side of her face.

The ambulance pulled into the hospital and the sirens went silent. The back doors of the ambulance opened, and Kelan stepped out to help the EMTs pull Fiona's gurney out of the ambulance. He hurried with them into the hospital. They rushed her to the emergency ward. As they transferred her from the ambulance gurney to a hospital bed, the EMTs debriefed the medical technicians. They drew the curtains over the medical cubicle that she was in, separating her from Kelan. He stayed outside the curtain listening to the medical jargon being thrown about.

When the EMT guys came out from behind the curtain, one of them nodded at him. "You should get yourself checked out, man." Kelan looked down at himself, recognizing the pain his own body was in.

When Kit arrived, he said the same thing as the EMT. "Look, I'll stay with her," he said.

"I'm not leaving until I see her."

A nurse pulled back the curtain. Fiona was sitting up in bed. She was wearing a hospital johnny, and actually smiled at them a little bit.

The nurse told him they'd drawn blood to see what was in her system, and that in the meantime they had her on an IV to help flush it through.

"Why don't I put you in the bed next to hers so that we can check you out too?" the nurse asked.

"Not until I've had a chance to talk to her. Give me a minute, please."

The nurse went to prepare the next station over. Kelan moved next to Fiona's bed and took her hand. The blanket that they put on her was nicely warm. "Are you feeling all right?"

Fiona nodded. "Can't talk much," she said, her words still slurred.

"That's okay. The effects of whatever they gave you are wearing off." He looked over at Kit, who stepped up to the bed and took her other hand. "They want to check me out. I'll be just in the next bed over. Kit's going to stay here with you."

Fiona nodded. She moved her head slightly and smiled at Kit. Kelan gave Kit a hard look, making it clear he expected his team lead to stay with his woman until he could resume his post.

Behind the curtain in the next cubby, Kelan shucked his boots, cargo pants, and tee, then sat on the hospital bed. The nurse brought over a warm blanket to cover his legs, then wheeled him off to have some x-rays done. A half-hour later, they confirmed he had a couple of broken ribs. Some of the cuts on his face and chest were stitched up. And his bleeding knuckles were disinfected and bandaged.

When he was brought back to his cubby, he dressed. Kit came in. Fiona was being processed with a rape kit. "She's going to be a few minutes. How about you bring me up to speed on everything that happened after you left the biker bar?"

Kelan sat on the edge of his bed. Kit stood next to him so that his words wouldn't carry. "What day is it?"

"Saturday," Kit said.

"Val told you what happened at the bar?"

"Yep."

"I was taken to a warehouse. Fiona was laid out on a table—a gurney, I guess. They'd changed her into some kind of a revealing dress. Put makeup on her. She wasn't conscious. Two guys came into the warehouse. We fought. I killed them. While we were fighting, another guy wheeled Fiona into what I thought was another room, but it was actually the back of an eighteen-wheeler."

"Yeah, we found the truck."

"I was held in the loading dock area while they got her situated in the truck. Some guy said through a speaker that I was the War Bringer they'd been told was coming." He frowned as he looked at Kit.

"What does that mean?"

Kelan shook his head. "I don't know. They hadn't seen my ink at that point; they couldn't have known I have it tattooed on my arm. The guy who was on the speaker was a shot caller. He took us to an arena. It was some kind of fight club setup in there. That same guy later took us to King's Warren."

"We found the arena. Is King's Warren where they had Fiona?"

"Yeah. I don't know who that guy was, but he was the one who pulled me out in the morning. No idea whose side he's on, but it feels as if he was helping me. They had Fiona sit on a throne and watch the fight. Whoever won was to become her champion and get sucked into King's world. The audience was chanting 'War Bringer,' like it meant something to them, too. The last guy who came up to fight me was the same one I killed in the rotunda."

"So this shot caller pulled you out in the morning? What happened to you then?"

"I was tranqed and left out on the prairie. But they made it easy for me to find my way back to the garage with the lift, which is where I was when I called Max." He looked at Kit. "I left some bodies there, too."

"Yeah, we found them. Kind of a bloody breadcrumb trail you left for us. And the next time Max says to wait, you better fucking wait."

"I couldn't. The guy from the arena said that he couldn't save Fiona, that only I could. I had to get back in there. There was another guy in the warren who took me to a cell and tried to kill me." Kelan grinned at Kit. "Didn't work."

"I see that." Kit looked at Kelan's bruises. "They came pretty damned close, though."

"When I got out of the pen, Rocco was there. He

knew where the rotunda was from his tour of the site earlier with Jafaar. We found Fiona, then you guys caught up to us."

"You think you can describe the two shot callers well enough for a sketch?"

"Oh yeah."

The nurse came in and said that Fiona was ready for him to return. Kit went to sit in the waiting room so he could watch for Angel. Kelan held Fiona's hand as the doctor told them she had no injuries or bruises that would indicate she'd been sexually assaulted, but they had collected some samples and were sending them in for tests to confirm.

"She'd been drugged with a date-rape cocktail of ketamine and Rohypnol. Give her lots of fluids to get it out of her system. If you notice any odd aftereffects, contact us or your primary care physician. We're going to keep her here until she recovers her mobility, just to make sure she doesn't have any seizures, then we'll release her."

Fiona nodded, then began to weep, the relief too overwhelming. Kelan climbed onto her bed, resting on his good side. He pulled her close. "I'm so sorry. I should have done something different, tried harder to keep you safe, Fiona."

"Nothing you could have done, Kelan. Can't outthink my father."

Her voice was getting back to normal. What a relief. "Your father isn't going to win."

"Not the war, perhaps, but a lot of the battles."

"Not for long." He kissed her forehead. "Let's shut our eyes for a bit until they release you."

Kelan closed his eyes. He must have dozed off for a bit, because he startled awake when she started to stroke his arm. She turned her head toward him, and he heard her whisper his name. His arms tightened around her. He spread his fingers into the hair at her temple, tilting her toward him for a kiss.

"I saw him. King."

"When?"

"He came to my room."

"What did he look like?"

She shook her head. "He was covered head to toe. I can only tell you he was almost your height."

"What did he say?"

"A lot of things. That he'd watched me grow up. That he'd killed a boy I dated for a little while last year. And my mom, too. And that you were on his hit list."

"That's fine. He's on mine." Kelan kissed her forehead again. "I'm sorry about your mom and your friend. You said you thought she'd been killed that first night you were with us."

"He said you had no right to call yourself the War Bringer, that he had selected the true bearer of that title." She looked at Kelan. "He'd picked the satyr to be his War Bringer."

Kelan shook his head. "I have no idea why a term I picked for my own use has any meaning to them." He frowned as her words sank in. "A satyr?"

"The guy who almost raped me. He was a satyr. He was the fourth guy in fight, the one I tried to stop."

"That's just the drugs distorting what you saw, honey. And he's not going to be hurting anyone ever again. He died in the rotunda."

* * *

Angel arrived about the time they were ready to release Fiona. He brought with him a shopping bag of clothes for her and another with some blankets. "I didn't know what size she wore, so I just guessed. It should be good enough to get her home at least."

"It will be. Thanks, Angel," Kelan said.

Kit came over to say goodbye. He took Fiona's hand and gently squeezed it. "You're going to be okay, Fiona. We gotcha now." He looked at Kelan. "I'm going to talk to Angel, then head out. He'll drive you home. Get some rest. We'll have a full debriefing tomorrow when you get up."

Angel set their bags down in the chair. "Let me know if you need help. I'll just be out front with Kit." He paused and looked back at Kelan. "Oh—your stuff's in the bag, too."

"Thanks, Angel," Kelan said. He got off the bed and pulled the curtain for privacy. He couldn't wait to get back to the house and take a long, hot shower. He looked at Fiona, imagining she felt the same way. He lifted out her clothes from the bag and set them on the bed, then removed the tags.

"We'll get you dressed, and then we'll get out of here." He helped her sit up in the bed. She let her bare legs dangle over the edge so that he could pull her panties on. She was so petite and frail that his hands shook. He helped her to her feet, then finished pulling them all the way up. There was no bra in the bag, but there were a couple of tees along with a pink workout set of pants and a zip jacket.

"Kelan!" She grabbed his arms. "What happened to my cape?"

He nodded to where it was folded on the floor. "I was going to have them throw it away."

Fiona's eyes widened as she shook her head. "Please, hand it to me. There's something I need to get out of it."

"Let's finish getting you dressed first," he said. He helped her into the tee, then into the stretchy pants and jacket. He had her sit on the bed again as he put her new socks and slippers on.

Kelan grabbed the red cape and set it on the bed next to her.

"I need scissors. Can you find me some?"

Kelan opened one of the drawers in a bank of cabinets. He handed her a pair. She cut into the velvet fabric and pulled out some white envelopes. Setting the scissors aside, she handed him the envelopes.

"There were two girls there from the Friendship Community. They weren't allowed to leave. Did you see them?"

"I may have seen one of them."

"We have to go back and get them."

"You're not going anywhere near there ever again. I'll call Kit on our way home and ask him to keep an eye out for them."

Kelan helped Fiona off the bed, then wrapped an arm around her waist, trying to support most of her weight himself. They made their way out of the emergency room hall and into the waiting room. Angel was there. He took one look at Fiona, who was walking on legs as unstable as a newborn foal, and made as if he was going to swing her up into his arms. Kelan held a hand out and stopped him—he wasn't certain how comfortable Fiona was being touched by other men just then, and he didn't want to find out. He gave Angel a warning look. "She's okay; walking is good for her—helps get that shit out of her system."

Angel glared at Kelan in helpless frustration. He turned and walked next to them as they went outside. Angel opened the rear passenger door of the team SUV. Kelan helped Fiona inside and tossed their bags in the front seat.

Fiona leaned forward and touched Angel's shoulder. "I really am okay, Angel. Just a little queasy."

He rolled down all of the windows then turned up the heat. He handed her a bottle of water, which Kelan opened for her. "Best just keep washing it through," Angel said.

Kelan opened the blankets and wrapped them around her. "Let's go home, Angel."

CHAPTER NINETEEN

All the girls were awake and waiting in the living room when the three of them arrived at the house. Kelan felt Fiona pull back against him. He thought about making their excuses and getting her out of there as fast as possible, but it occurred to him she might feel more comfortable in the long run if she got her reunion with them over with now. And, truthfully, everyone in the household had been worried sick since she was taken, so they needed to see her just as much.

Mandy came over and wrapped her arms around Fiona. She started to cry all over again. It fucking wrecked him.

"Oh, Kelan. God," Eden said as she waited for her turn to hug Fiona.

"What happened?" Ivy asked. Her eyes were wide with horror as she looked him over.

Kelan glanced at all of the women who'd been confined to the house while they tracked down Fiona. "It's a long story. But we're here and we're fine. Kit and the others are at the site down in Colorado where

King was holding Fiona. They may be there a while. Lobo's got his guys there, and there's a huge police presence, too."

The good news, which he didn't yet tell them, was that he didn't think they would be targeted next. Fiona had been taken because she was King's daughter. They could probably resume their lives— Ivy at the diner, Remi at the university. Mandy and Eden had their work here. Hope was still in hiding from the WKB, so she wasn't out and about anyway.

"Will you take care of her for a second?" he asked Mandy. "I have to go get something from my room."

Upstairs, he grabbed his smudging stick, then hurried back down. Fiona looked ready to drop. If it weren't such an important step in cleansing her spirit, he would have postponed the task. In the living room, he held out his hand to her. "Fiona, will you come outside with me?"

She put her hand in his and let him draw her to her feet. On the patio, he lit a sage and white cedar smudge stick, and let it smoke in an abalone shell. "Spread your arms."

She didn't question him, didn't argue, just docilely did as requested. He floated the smoke over her body, feet to head, front to back, all while speaking words he knew she didn't understand.

"Why are we doing this? Am I impure?" Her voice broke on the last question.

"No, you are not impure. Each of us is surrounded by an energy field. It's a little sticky, and it keeps some of the energy that passes near it. Smudging helps clear that away, releasing what clings to you but doesn't belong to you. It will help you regain your own balance." When he was finished smudging her he smudged himself and then extinguished the stick. "Now we shower."

When they came back into the living room, it was empty. He was glad they wouldn't have to field more questions just then. He wrapped his arm around her waist as he helped her up the stairs.

"Will you let me help you shower?" he asked as they reached her room.

"I can manage. I think I need to be alone." She folded her arms in front of her and hunched her shoulders.

Kelan kissed her forehead and nodded. "That works. I'll take your letters down to Max to hold for Greer. Then I think I'll have a shower myself." He didn't immediately leave. "Are you hungry? Do you want a sandwich? A cup of tea?"

"A cup of tea would be heaven. But Kelan, you don't have to wait on me. Look at yourself. You are in worse shape than I am."

"I'll bring tea when I come back." He hugged her and was so damned reluctant to let go.

* * *

Fiona stood in the middle of the big bathroom in her room at Blade's house. It was hard to get her head

220

around the fact that she was home. Safe. Out of her father's clutches.

Steam from the shower was making her hot in the knit top she wore. She really ought to strip and get in the shower before Kelan came back, but she couldn't seem to make her arms unfold or feet move. She felt numb. Empty. Like a void. She couldn't even summon tears.

She didn't want to shut her eyes for fear the images that she had seen, which now made no sense, would haunt her dreams. The water in the shower ran and ran, creating white noise that droned like the chants that had filled the rotunda.

It hadn't been statues standing around her and their white and black robes—they'd been people. People had been watching her almost get raped. She blinked, trying to clear her mind, a futile action because the fog was so dense, but she couldn't let it go.

She kept seeing the satyr who had climbed on top of her, with his horned head and grinning face. It was a memory. Memories were real. They should make sense, but these didn't. And monsters don't exist...unless they had the name "King."

What had happened to her? Had the drugs they'd given her distorted everything she'd seen, made her hallucinate? And there were bits that she couldn't remember. How long had she been on the table? What had happened before Kelan came in and everyone started running?

She was glad the hospital had run a rape kit. At least she could put that out of her mind. Still, that thing had touched her. Kit was there at the end. And Angel and Selena. Had they seen her laid out in her shame on that table?

She was still standing in the center of the bathroom when Kelan returned. He stood at the bathroom door for a moment, then walked over to the shower and shut it off. His hair was wet, and his face newly shaven. His T-shirt hid most of his bruises, which was good, because they were hard to look at; he had them because of her.

* * *

When Kelan returned to Fiona's bathroom, she was still standing in the middle of the room, fully clothed, arms folded about her. He shouldn't have left her. This was the bubbly, vibrant, ballsy woman who had waited for him in her closet, waving an ancient Colt pistol at him. She was shattered because of his inability to protect her.

He shut off the shower, then wrapped an arm around her shoulders and led her out of the bathroom. He rearranged the pillows on her bed, stacking them so that she could sit up, then flipped back the covers and waited for her to get in. She took off her knit jacket and left it at the foot of the bed. He covered her up, then didn't know what to do with himself. Should he climb in bed with her? Should he try to get her to talk? Should he just sit quietly with her, guarding her while she slept?

He handed her the cup of tea and a ham and cheese sandwich he'd made for her. She took a bite of the sandwich and a sip of the tea, then set the plate back on her nightstand. He was sitting in her armchair with his feet braced on the bed.

"He looked like a satyr. The guy who tried to rape me—he looked like a satyr."

"The ketamine cocktail they gave you distorted what you saw. Remember what he looked like in the arena? He wasn't a satyr. Why don't you have another sip of tea?"

She didn't take more tea. Her hands were tightly clasped in her lap. "Those weren't statues set around the room where they had me on that block, were they?"

"No."

"Why would they do that? What were they doing to me?"

"It was a ritual of some sort. Why they did it? Who gained from it? I don't yet know."

"Did Kit find Ellen and Bryn?"

"No. They searched the entire silo and did not find the girls."

"There are more tunnels than the ones they could see. I got out by going through the jewelry cabinet in my closet. Maybe they're hiding in the other tunnels?"

Kelan nodded. "It's possible. After I meet with Kit and the team in the morning, I'll go back and look for them."

Fiona pulled the covers up to her chest. "I'm going to try and sleep now."

Kelan got up to shut off the lights for her. "No— leave them on."

"It's easier to sleep with them off," Kelan said.

"Yes, but if it's dark, I might close my eyes. And if I do, I'll see it all."

Okay. That was it. That was all he could take. He went around on the other side of the bed and stretched out next to her. He pulled her against his side. "Most of that's coming down from the ketamine and roofie high. Let your mind go—it'll begin sorting it out. I'm holding you. I won't leave you. If nightmares do come, then the moment you open your eyes, you'll see I'm still with you."

Fiona nestled into him. "This happened because of me. Because I insisted on staying at CSU. Because I'm the spawn of King."

Kelan's face was pressed to the crown of her head. He shook his head and sighed. "This happened because of me. Because I failed to keep you safe like I said I would." He adjusted his hold on her. "I've got you. Close your eyes and sleep."

* * *

It was close to two a.m. when the team returned from Colorado. The light was still on in the den. Val poked his head in and saw Owen sitting at his desk.

He was writing something by hand. He covered the paper and stood up as they came in.

Val knew that Kit had updated him on the news that Fiona was King's kid. What Val wasn't prepared for was the intensity in Owen's cold eyes.

"Tell me. Everything."

"Can it wait until the morning?" Kit asked. "We're beat. It's been a hellishly long few days. We'll do a full briefing with the team in the morning when Kelan joins us. For now, let's just leave it that he and Fiona are safe. Lobo's team is processing the site. And Rocco's cover with Jafaar is still intact."

Owen's face tightened. He nodded. "I'll wait until the morning."

Val started to follow the guys out of the den, but then he remembered seeing Fiona as Kelan held her. She was going to want her hair back to normal ASAP, otherwise every time she looked in the mirror, she'd be reminded of her abuse. He hadn't told her or anyone yet, but he was going to make damn sure she got the extensions removed tomorrow. It was a small thing he could do for her. Maybe the only thing. But it was something, anyway.

"Hey," he said, turning back to Owen. "I'm gonna see if Fiona will let me take her to the salon tomorrow to remove the hair extensions they made her wear. Don't make a big deal about it and freak her out. She's already been through enough."

Owen met his eyes. His nostrils flared. "What did they do to her?"

"Rocco didn't give you the down-low?"

"He did. I want to hear it from you."

Val sighed. "They drugged her, then made a spectacle out of what would have been a ritualistic rape—had Kelan and Rocco not gotten there in time."

Owen didn't blink. He made a fist and pressed his knuckles against the top of Blade's desk.

"They held the ritual in a special rotunda. There was a pentagram in the tiling on the floor. Someone, maybe King, sat on a throne, watching the proceedings. There was blood on the knife that Kelan threw at him, so we might have a DNA sample. If it matches Fiona's and Lion's DNA then it might be King's."

The muscles in Owen's cheeks bunched. "Was she bound?"

"Not physically, but the drugs they gave her paralyzed her."

"Is she all right?"

Val shook his head. "Honestly, I don't know. We won't know for a while." He drew a long breath and slowly released it. "I'm not sure how an innocent like Fiona can recover from such abuse." He gestured between them. "You and I, the team, we have armor we've built around ourselves. If something gets under it, we know how to deal with it. She had no defenses, O. Nothing. And Kelan is damn near wrecked over it."

"I'll talk to Kit. Kelan needs to take the time he needs to deal with this."

CHAPTER TWENTY

Wynn brought a bouquet of daisies to her grandmother's room at the palliative care center in Cheyenne Sunday morning. The room smelled of industrial disinfectant, but it was clean and not a horrible place to convalesce. The staff was nice, but they were often spread thin. Wynn frequently helped bathe her grandmother and change her bedding on her twice-weekly visits.

She would have had no choice but to continue assisting with her grandmother's care here, if not for her new job teaching and babysitting Zavi. Now, she could afford to move her to a more expensive facility that had better options for her care and rehabilitation. And she could do it without having to surrender the deed to her grandmother's house. Just the thought of that made Wynn's heart ache. That house was the one her grandfather had built for Grams when he came home from the Korean War. It was the house where her mother had been raised, and where Wynn herself had lived after her parents died.

She pushed those thoughts out of her mind. The

center was doing a fair job caring for her grandmother, but things were going to change for the better very soon. She brushed her grandmother's white bangs from her forehead and kissed her, wondering how aware of her surroundings she was.

"How about some light, Grams?" Wynn asked as she lifted the blinds, letting sunlight pour into the room—it was the only natural thing in the entire hospital.

"I brought you some new flowers. The daisies were gorgeous, so I selected two bouquets of them." She threw out last week's flowers, replacing them with the fresh daisies.

Thanks to Rocco Silas, Wynn now had the income to afford a better situation for her grandmother. She'd just signed the papers to have her released. They'd be moving her Wednesday. Wynn wanted to be there for the move, but the only available time the new home could do it was during the week while she worked. They assured her they'd take great care of her. Wynn was excited for the change. Hopefully, the new environment would help her grandmother recover more of her faculties.

She pulled a chair over to her grandmother's bedside and took her slim hand. It was so hard seeing her indomitable matriarch in this bed, just a shell of her former self. Grams closed her eyes at the contact. Wynn knew her grandmother was still in there, somewhere, wanting out.

"I found a new job, Grams. Right here in

Wyoming. It's outside of Laramie, not far at all. I'll be able to visit you every weekend." She told her grandmother about her new situation, the boy she was hired to teach, his special capabilities.

Near the end of the visit, after brushing her grandmother's hair, she told her about the upcoming move to a new home.

"I love you, Grams. We'll get through this, just like everything else. Good things are just around the corner for us. You'll see."

* * *

Kelan woke to the feel of Fiona in his arms. The whole night through, her body had touched his. He smiled. This was the most sleep he'd had in all the days since she'd been taken. To know that she was here, with him, both of them safe…it was a feeling he'd feared he'd never know again.

He watched while sleep slowly released its hold on her. It was late in the morning. Almost ten. They'd missed breakfast and their workouts. He was grateful the team had let them sleep. She opened her eyes, blinked, then squinted from the light flooding the room.

She reached over and touched him. "Kelan."

"That's me." He smiled.

She pushed herself up and frowned as she looked around her room. "I feel as if we've slept for a week."

"Maybe we did—but I think it was only one

night."

She settled back down, into the space between his arm and body. "What happens now?"

He wished that nothing was happening, that he and Fiona could stay in bed an entire day and night and day again. He wanted to love her in every way he'd ever imagined…and invent a few new ways, too.

"I suppose you shower, and I'll go meet up with the guys, see what happened after we left the tunnels. I know they will want to talk to you, if you're up to it. You're the only one of us who has actually seen King."

She nodded. "But you have to know that he was covered head to foot. I didn't actually see any of him."

"That's okay. There might be something in that interaction that has more meaning than you think. Let's talk it over with the team and see what happens."

Her eyes widened as she looked up at him. "Kelan—the girls!"

"I haven't forgotten. I'll see if they were found."

She pushed herself up to look into his eyes. "And if they weren't, will you go back for them?"

"Yes." Her eyes filled with tears. He frowned, then stroked her cheek with his thumb. How could her skin be so incredibly soft? "Talk to me, Fiona."

"I love you. I love you so much, and I don't even yet know everything that means to me. I love you on a visceral level, as if our hearts have connected in a way that isn't rational. And yet here I am, sending you back into danger."

Kelan grinned. "You love me viscerally?"

"Don't go back, Kelan."

"Don't be afraid for me. I will find your girls and bring them back. I'll do this errand, and a thousand more for you. I will do anything that gives your mind peace."

A short sigh broke from her. She leaned forward, dragging her body up and across his so that she could put her face in his neck. She drew a deep breath against his skin. The air tickled his skin and lifted gooseflesh across his arms and back.

Kelan turned to her. Digging his hand in her hair, he held her face to his and looked into her eyes as his lips met hers. Her arm slipped about his shoulder, avoiding his broken ribs. He tensed; he was hungry to peel off their layers and explore her body with his. It was good he'd gone to bed fully clothed; she wasn't ready for them to be intimate again yet—not after everything that had happened. It took a force of will to make him roll over her and climb off the bed.

He took Fiona's hand and pulled. "Up." When she stood in front of him, he said, "Take a shower. Get something to eat. Rest. I'll come find you when the team's ready to talk. I'll be there with you the whole time." He kissed her forehead. "I love you. Viscerally." He grinned at her, but couldn't raise a smile in her somber eyes.

* * *

Kelan grabbed a cup of coffee from the sideboard in the dining room, where Kathy always kept a pot going, then went down to the bunker via the hidden stairs in the den.

The team was slowly coming in. Everyone had started late today. No one had assigned seats, so he just sat wherever. Kit hit his shoulder as he went by. Greer fist-bumped Kelan, then sat next to him. Rocco nodded at him from across the table.

When everyone was assembled, Kit flipped a folder open, ready to start the meeting, until Val stopped him.

"Wait, Kit. Just hold up." Val held up a hand. "Can we all take a moment to give Kelan a hug?"

Kelan frowned. "No."

Max barked out a laugh.

Val smiled. "I'm glad you're back. And Fee, too."

"Thanks," Kelan said.

"We all are," Owen said from his place by the wall. "After this meeting, I expect you to take some time with Fiona."

Kelan met Owen's cold eyes. That was an unusually generous suggestion, especially at such a critical time. "I will. And I appreciate that, but I'm not finished with this. I need to see it through."

"Right." Kit stood up. "So here's what we know. King's Warren is a complex covering several miles of underground tunnels from two separate missile silos.

Lobo and his team are still working the site. It's been the holy grail of stolen antiquities, art, and jewelry. It's going to take the FBI months to catalog everything they found."

Kit nodded at Greer, who popped some images up on the huge smart screen. The long red and purple banners that lined the main hall filled the screen. Kelan read their slogans about world domination, moral cleansing, and population control—he'd been too focused on other things the times he was in the hall to notice them in detail.

"And in case you're wondering, this wasn't a casual clubhouse," Kit commented. "Looks like they have grand plans, which they may already have begun implementing."

An alert sounded in the ops room. Max checked his phone. He looked at Kit, then Kelan. The room became silent.

"Got the results back from the test we ran on Fiona's DNA. She and Lion do share the same biological father. They're half-siblings." He took a breath. "And the blood from your knife, Kelan—it matches their father's."

"So it was King in that rotunda," Rocco said.

Kit's mouth became a thin line. "Or if not King, then at least their dad. We just don't know who or what this King is." He was silent a moment. "Let's start at the beginning. I want to make sure everyone's on the same page. Rocco, you and Selena got into King's Warren first. Tell us what you saw."

They told the team about the security system, the guard corps, the floor plan for the areas they toured. Greer played the video they'd collected. Some of Rocco's footage included what happened in the rotunda. Greer had blurred the image of Fiona on the altar.

Kelan wanted to be sick.

The lights were dim and the video switched to low light, making the images green and grainy. It did capture a figure sitting on a throne and the others in the ten alcoves. And it showed the bastard who looked like a satyr to Fiona climbing on top of her.

Then the feed shifted. Kelan ran into the rotunda and all hell broke loose. Rocco followed a minute later, running around the outside ring toward Jafaar.

"Jafaar was at the ceremony?" Kit looked at Rocco

"Yeah. Said he was a witness," Rocco told them. "All the witnesses brought guests, but only the witnesses were permitted in the rotunda."

"Those guests, the ones left in the ballroom, were the one percenters of the one percenters," Selena added. "We were rubbing shoulders with aristocrats, sheiks, celebrities, you name it. It was like a rave for the world's glitterati."

Kit looked at Owen. "Lobo said there were some power players coming in to town, but no one knew what their agendas were."

"Well, Jafaar was no stranger to King's Warren," Rocco said. "He knew another way out, as did the other witnesses. His limo was waiting there for him.

Theirs were, too. You can't really see it on this feed. I bet there are a dozen more entrances we don't know about." The video showed some dark footage of them running through tunnels. They came to a staircase, which they went up for a few flights before finally reaching an exit hatch. The video ended there.

"I shut it off in case Jafaar's driver scanned me again. When we left, we went up to Yusef's. Jafaar kept saying how pissed King was going to be that his carefully planned initiation of his prime warrior had been ruined."

Kelan frowned. "So the whole initiation event had more to do with King's warrior than with Fiona? They destroyed a girl's life for a fighter?"

Rocco looked at him. "Not just any fighter. When I asked Jafaar why that mattered, he said King's War Bringer was long foretold to be a uniter of the regions in the new world order. The fact that it didn't happen and that King's daughter had been taken would have devastating implications for his power bid." Rocco glanced around the table. "I should note that Jafaar did not seem heartbroken over that turn of events."

Kit's brows lowered. He nodded toward Kelan. "Your ink says 'War Bringer.'"

Kelan lifted his sleeve. His ink was no secret. He'd had it since before he entered the Army.

"It's an odd label," Blade said. "Odder still to have it used by King and Kelan. I understood it's tribal meaning when you used it. But what does it mean to King?"

"Maybe there's something in your mom's papers that will help us understand," Kit said. "Your turn, Kelan. Tell the guys what happened after Val left you at the biker bar."

"Wait. What papers?" Kelan asked Blade.

Blade pointed to a pile of boxes set in the corner. "I found a note she left in her jewelry box." Greer put that note up on the smart screen. "She'd taken these from Bladen. He was a librarian for a secret org. We haven't had a chance to dig into them yet."

"Go on, Kelan," Kit ordered.

Kelan shrugged. "I was taken to a warehouse where I had to fight two guys for Fiona. After that, we were both transported to a steel building that was being used as a fight club. The announcer there told them I was the War Bringer. That phrase has meaning to King and the people around him."

"This event seemed highly organized, with odd roles and labels for different people," Selena said. "It wasn't a simple party—it had a purpose, but what that was, I don't know. People knew their roles—they were familiar with what was happening. This isn't the first time it happened."

Owen moved his stance. Kelan could feel his tension. "Were the guys who took Fiona part of this org?"

"Like everything else," Kit said, "it's unclear. Lobo thinks King put a bounty out for her capture. Lobo tracked down the owner of the house she was stashed in that first night. He's one of the big sex traffickers in Denver. The bounty King offered and the opportunity to become one of King's sex suppliers sent a powerful ripple through that trade."

"What happened to the girls we recovered?" Kelan asked.

"They were checked out at a hospital, then were handed over to a women's shelter."

"The arena fight was supposedly to select who would be Fiona's champion." Kelan frowned. "It was run by the same shot caller who brought Fiona and me to King's Warren—the one who got me out the next morning. He said he couldn't save Fiona, that only I could."

"So was he helping you?" Blade asked.

Kelan got up and started pacing the length of the conference room. "Maybe. I'm not convinced the arena fight was part of King's scene. That guy could have taken Fiona and me straight to the tunnels. Why divert for a bit of entertainment first?"

"Describe him," Owen said.

Kelan glanced at the boss. "My height, light brown hair, gray-blue eyes, muscular, in his thirties."

Kit frowned as he looked Owen. "You know him."

Owen's lips thinned. "Wendell Jacobs. Our rogue Red Teamer."

"Sonofabitch," Blade cursed. "Is he King?"

"He's not old enough to be Fiona and Lion's dad," Kelan said. "And yes, I think he is helping. He could have killed me when he took me out of the warren.

Instead, he tranqed me and made it easy for me to find my way back to the tunnels. He was definitely the one who ended the competition before Fiona's attacker could join the fun." Kelan looked at Greer. "I heard a police siren. Everyone scattered."

Greer nodded. "I'll see if a trouble call hit the police blotter."

"Wendell's more involved than you thought," Val said, watching Owen.

"What's he doing hanging out with King?" Max asked.

Owen looked at them. "Good question. Find out the answer."

"Well, there's more. Fiona actually spoke to King. She said he visited her in her room Saturday."

"We need to talk to her," Kit said.

"I know. Take the video off the screen. I'll go get her." He paused on his way out the door. "This is not going to be easy for her, so keep it chill."

Kelan returned a few minutes later, leading Fiona by the hand. He pulled out a seat for her at the table opposite Kit, then sat next to her.

Kit leaned forward. "Fee—Kelan said you had some info for us. I know this is a difficult thing to do, talking about what happened, but we need to know what you know." He looked at Greer, who set a digital voice recorder in front of her. "We're going to record it so that we don't miss any of your story."

Fiona nodded.

"Can you tell us about meeting King?"

She looked at Kelan. He tried to give her a reassuring look. "I had just come back from meeting the guy I was supposed to marry this weekend. Erick Ansbach—the one who…who…"

"He's the guy King wanted her to marry," Kelan finished for her.

She nodded. "He tried to cheat at the arena fight. Kelan had just fought three men, and more outside the arena before he ever went in, and probably more even than that. It was too much."

Kelan smiled and shot a look at Kit. "She stopped the fight. Then the sirens made us all clear out."

"Kelan said to play along with whatever was happening, but none of it made sense. When they took me to meet Erick, I told Mr. Edwards that I was disappointed they had selected a substandard fighter, that I refused to marry him."

"Mr. Edwards is the one you told me about?" Kit asked Kelan.

"Right. The other shot caller," he said.

"After that, King came into my room."

Kelan noticed the tension deepen in the room as the team focused on what she was saying.

"There's not much I can tell you about him other than his height and size. He wasn't as tall as Kelan, but he was trim. He was covered from the top of his head to his feet. He wore gloves, some kind of mask that covered his face, neck, and hair. He wore eyeglasses and a baseball cap. And he used something that changed his voice. I don't even know if he really was my father."

"Okay." Kit nodded. "What did he say to you?"

Fiona drew a long breath, sending another glance toward Kelan. She closed her eyes. Kelan was glad they were doing this debriefing now rather than waiting; he knew Fiona was going to block the memories as she began healing.

"He said a lot of things. I don't know what it all meant. He watched me grow up. He talked about a breeding program they started long ago. He said he killed my mother and a boy I sometimes dated because he threatened my"—she paused and looked at her hands in her lap—"virginity. He said he killed my mother because she was supposed to keep me pure. He made it clear that they died because of me."

Kelan reached over and held her shoulder. "Fiona, you didn't kill them. He did."

"But if I had made other choices—"

"He would still have killed them. He was done with your mother and your friend was in the way."

Her eyes looked tortured when her gaze met his. "He let us have our night together because that way, when he kills you, your death will break me, and then I'll have a second chance to become the daughter he wanted."

"Yeah, that shit's fucked up," Max said. Kit gave him a quelling look.

"He said he'd engineered his War Bringer, after generations of careful breeding"—she looked at Kelan—"and that you had no right to the same title

240

because you're a mixed breed. He said his War Bringer was a pure Arian son." She paused. "He left then."

"Thank you, Fiona," Owen said, breaking the silence that followed her words. Greer shut off the recorder.

"Were the girls in the tunnels found?" she asked, looking around the table.

"No," Kit said.

"You told Kelan they were from the Friendship Community?" Greer asked.

She nodded. "They wrote letters to their families."

"I gave you the letters yesterday," he said, looking at Max. "These girls are being held against their will. If Lobo hasn't seen them, I have to go get them out."

Max leaned forward. "I'm going, too. I want to look for Lion and his boys. It would be easy to hide a large group of kids in a place like that." He looked at Kelan, then Fiona. "While you were in the tunnels, did you see or hear about the watchers?"

"No," she said.

"Were they using Lion and his boys as guards?" Max asked.

"The guards I saw were adults, not boys," Kelan said. "Doesn't mean they aren't there. I just didn't see them. I want to make a stop on our way down and talk to a friend of Fiona's. Stacey Atkins. She was integral in getting info about Fiona to King's people. I want to see what she knows."

"Who is that?" Kit asked.

241

"My friend from CSU."

"The girl got close to Fiona and found out everything about her—her taste in clothes, in jewelry," Kelan said. "Helped King prepare for taking her."

"Shit. All right. Kelan, take her upstairs. We have a little more to do here before you head out."

The team stood when Fiona got up. She nodded at Kit. Kelan took her hand and led her back to the elevator. "You did great. Really great."

"I don't know how that helped."

"We now know more of the things that King's interested in. It's good." He pulled her into a hug as they rode the elevator up. "Don't let him do a mind freak on you. You can't control his crazy."

She nodded, but he could tell from the tension in her body that warning was way the hell too late. He was still worrying about that when he rejoined the group.

Angel stood up, putting a few images on the smart screen. "So about those silos. I did some digging. Colorado has its share of active silos, but it also has a large number of decommissioned ones, those were mostly built in the late sixties, like the one under the WKB compound. They stretch for miles in an almost straight line from north of the airport to south of Colorado Springs. Really, along the whole front range, like every ten miles. Some of them have been sold to private owners. Some are abandoned but are still on the government's books. Some have dropped off the record completely." He clicked a button and red dots showed up where the old silo sites were. "These were the ones I could find record of."

A frisson scraped Kelan's spine. "Can you overlay the arena where I fought?"

Angel did. "Here's the farmhouse Fee called us from, and here's that garage with the auto lift in it. I don't have the coordinates for the exit Rocco and Jafaar used, but I bet it's somewhere in this line." His map showed a silo beneath the garage.

"Who owns the farmhouse?" Kelan asked.

"Same company who owns the arena and the garage."

Kelan realized now that all the trees and the shrubs surrounding the arena weren't to keep it cool in the summer or provide windbreaks; they were for privacy from the ground and air. "Who owns that silo?"

"That's one of the ones that have dropped off the books. It's not on DoD's list, and it's not on the EPA's list of superfund sites."

"Good work, Angel," Kit said. "Do some more digging to find out where and when that silo and any others dropped out of the system. See if there was any remediation work done. Find the original plans for the site. Selena, give him a hand. Greer—dig into the company. I want to know everything there is to know about them—who they are, what they do, who works for them. And I want to know about this Erick Ansbach that King wanted Fiona to marry. If they engineered him, anyone who's connected with him may be of interest to us. Rocco, Blade, Val, and I will crack open Bladen's library."

"Blade, let your dad know we're getting into the boxes. He wanted to be here for that," Owen said.

CHAPTER TWENTY-ONE

Mandy stepped quietly to the doorway of the third bedroom in the suite she shared with Rocco and Zavi. Zavi's smallpox vaccination still had a beige Band-Aid on it, but it no longer seemed to trouble him. The doctor was coming up to the house later to give Wynn her vaccination.

The two of them were sitting at a small table discussing the alphabet. The bedroom had been transformed into a cute classroom, with a couple of tables in different heights, a big whiteboard, and bookshelves filled with fun stories. Zavi even had a cubby where he could keep his schoolwork organized.

It all looked so ordinary, as if the room had never housed Rocco's dark retreat. The closet was empty now. She wondered where he had moved his secret nest. He seemed to need ever more alone time since she'd told him about the baby.

Zavi saw her and his face lit up. "Hi, Mandy!"

"Hi, baby. How are things going?" she asked Wynn.

"Wonderfully. We're learning about each other.

Zavi's showing me all the things he knows."

"I know a lot," Rocco's boy assured her.

Mandy smiled. "You are the brightest boy I know. Are you hungry? Kathy has lunch served up."

"Yes! Miss Wynn said we can go for a swim after lunch." Zavi hurried over to take her hand.

"I think it's time we introduced Miss Wynn to the rest of the team." She looked down at Zavi. "Would you like to do that?"

He nodded. "It's important. We're a very big family now."

"We are indeed."

* * *

Wynn followed Zavi and his stepmom downstairs. The closer they came to the dining room, the louder things got. Men's voices, deep and rich, laughing. Softer women's voices. She was curious about the group and what they did. The house was big and rambling, lavishly decorated. Rocco and Mandy had been able to put together a perfectly equipped classroom for her work with Zavi. And the furnished apartment they'd provided her over the garage was even nicer than the one she rented in Cheyenne.

What did the people here do that made such an environment possible? She'd done a comprehensive internet search for Zavi's parents. Other than some obituaries regarding Mandy's parents and grandparents, she'd found an article about Mandy's plans for her hippotherapy center...and its subsequent explosion from a faulty gas line. So sad. She found nothing on Zavi's dad, but that didn't surprise her, since he'd been serving overseas for a while.

She researched Tremaine Industries, too, but didn't find anything other than their company website. She looked up the company's founder and CEO, Owen Tremaine, but only learned that he had no social media presence, which for a man who headed a company like his wasn't surprising.

Perhaps the most important element of her research into her new employer and living situation was the fact that they clearly weren't wanted by the FBI or anyone. That gave her some small comfort. Hopefully, they weren't associated with any crime families who knew just how to keep a low profile in a technology-driven world.

She felt her nerves tighten as they stepped into the huge dining room. Zavi took her hand, then stepped up onto the chair at the head of the table. She thought about correcting him about standing on the furniture, but his parents were there, and no one else in the room seemed to mind.

The chair gave him the height he needed to get everyone's attention. The introductions took some time, because it was never a simple matter of his listing names for each person. Everyone's association with each other was detailed, too, which she found surprisingly helpful. Casey was there, the other potential student she might need to help tutor or babysit.

A man with pale blue eyes and blond hair came into the room. He stared down at Zavi in a way that would have terrified Wynn had she been the recipient. Instead, the boy just met his look, stare for stare.

The man lifted his brow. "I believe you're in my chair."

Zavi grinned. He reached up and touched the man's chest. Wynn held her breath. It was like watching a cub bite the paw of a huge male lion.

The boy looked at her. "Uncle Owen, this is my teacher, Miss Wynn. Miss Wynn, this is our chief, Uncle Owen."

Wynn had the strangest thought that she should curtsy or something. She held her hand out. "Uncle Owen."

"It's just Owen." He shook her hand, then lifted Zavi off his chair.

She looked around the room, uncertain as to what to do next. Mandy smiled at her. She explained the buffet system to her, offering the choice of eating at the table, outside, or in her suite. Really, there were no rules. If she didn't like what was offered, she could help herself to something else in the kitchen. Kathy often had leftovers available to munch on.

Wynn was surprised by the group's generosity. She started toward the far end of the buffet line, but was stopped by a late arrival to the room. A tall man with swarthy skin came up the stairs from the living room.

His hair was short. His dark eyes were clear and sharp. She noticed him give her a quick, almost instinctive once-over, from head to toe and back again. Heat warmed her face as his dark eyes settled on hers.

She was a tall woman. It was unusual to find a man who made her feel short. He held his hand out without breaking eye contact. "I'm Angel."

She slipped her hand in his. It was larger than hers just like all the rest of him. "I'm Wynn. Zavi's teacher."

He smiled. The skin of his face wrinkled by his eyes and made lean folds beside his mouth. His teeth were big and white. God. He stole her breath. "Welcome, Wynn." His words rolled from his chest in a baritone rumble.

"Thank you, Angel." He still held her hand. His grin widened.

"Down, boy," Blade called from across the table. "It's the teach's first day. Give her a break."

He nodded and released her hand but not her eyes. "Right." Again the grin.

Wynn smiled and lowered her eyes. How was she going to survive this job? She looked around the room of hot, capable, probably deadly men, and thought she'd best spend most of her time away with Zavi or in her own quarters.

* * *

Kit, Val, Rocco, Ryker, and Ty moved Bladen's boxes to the long conference table.

"This is what your mom hid before she died?" Val asked.

"Yeah," Ty said. "Something about the jewelry box had been nagging at me since Allie brought it to my dad. I thought maybe my mom wanted to keep something of value from Bladen, just save one thing for me. But maybe there was more to it than that. I wondered if there might be a hidden compartment in it like Bladen had in the desk. It didn't make sense that my mom would have risked her life or that of her friend to hide jewelry from the bastard—he'd already taken everything that belonged to my family. So I started poking around."

He displayed the scanned image of his mom's letter on the smart screen. "I found this, along with the instructions to get into her storage unit. We were lucky that the facility still existed and her unit hadn't been touched. Max and my dad retrieved them while you were in Denver."

Ty looked at the boxes. "I don't know if she was killed because she took these boxes, or if Bladen had already decided to dispose of her once he offed her dad. Who knows."

"Maybe this is what Amir's guys were looking for when they tossed the house," Rocco said.

"Could be."

Kit took a pair of nitrile gloves from a box and then passed the box around. "I want this stuff processed for fingerprints, so let's be careful with it. Shit has a way of disappearing, so let's get every piece logged and scanned for backup."

They pulled the items out of the boxes and set them on the table. Some were loose sheets of paper and some were ancient manuscripts. There were scrolls, leather-bound binders, ledgers, and journals. The newest documents in the batch were from a quarter century ago...the oldest were more than six centuries old. They were in French, German, English, Spanish, and Latin. Others were in a cryptic script that seemed a cross between simple symbols and some arcane text they couldn't quickly identify.

That mound of data may hold the clues to King's empire. It was a windfall that Ty knew could get their headquarters blown up if King ever discovered they'd retrieved it.

* * *

Kelan stepped through Fiona's opened door. "Hey."

She turned from the window and smiled. It was a warm September day, but she had a big sweater on. Her hair was wet. Maybe she'd caught a chill after her shower.

"You didn't come down for lunch."

"I didn't feel much like being around anyone yet."

Kelan nodded. "I understand. I brought our lunch up here. Will you have a bite?"

She looked at the tray he held—sandwiches, salad, melon—and nodded. They sat at the table. He handed her a glass of iced tea. "I could get you some hot tea if you'd prefer."

"This is fine."

When Kelan had finished the first of two sandwiches, he broke their silence. "Val would like to take you to the salon in town to have your hair extensions removed. Would you like to do that?"

She nodded. "Yes. When can we go?"

"As soon as you finish eating. I'll let him know. Max and I are going to head back down to the tunnels. And I'm going to stop and see your friend Stacey. I want to see what she has to say for herself."

"I don't want to ever talk to her again."

"I don't blame you. I'm sure the FBI is going to be interested in the role she played in your abduction."

Fiona toyed with the salad in her bowl. "I don't think I can go back to school."

Kelan nodded. "Why not sit out a few days and make up your mind then?"

She nodded, still pushing her food around.

"You know, everyone here was worried to death about you. They'd love it if you came out of your room and visited with them. Maybe go sit in the sun, or talk to the girls."

"I will." She looked up at him and smiled, but the gesture was so fleeting that it left him feeling hollow.

Kelan stood up. "I don't know how long we'll be. Don't wait supper for us if we're not back."

Fiona's eyes widened. "You're sure it's safe for you to go back?"

"Perfectly. The FBI is all over that place."

She stood and faced him. He pulled her into his arms. "When you're ready, we'll do something fun. We missed your birthday. I still have your gift to give you."

She rubbed her cheek against his chest. "I don't feel much like having fun. Maybe we should just skip this birthday and wait for next year."

Kelan rubbed her back. "We could do that."

* * *

Walking with Val toward the salon that afternoon, Fiona enjoyed the sun's heat on her face. The girls in the tunnels had lived with very little natural light for months and years. She thought of the other girls in the brothel. They could see the sun but not go out into it.

Val wrapped his arm around her. "Wanna talk? I'm a good listener."

Fiona shook her head. "Not yet. I'm still trying to process all of it. What I saw, what happened." She looked up at him. "My father's like a cancer, isn't he?"

Val considered that then shook his head. "No. He's more like a tropical virus that until now had existed in a closed, controlled environment. But that environment has been ripped open, exposing him and spreading his disease rapidly. We'll get him, Fiona.

We're closer than we've ever been, thanks to you."

Someone moving toward them on the sidewalk caught his attention. Fiona felt him tense. It was a young woman. She looked Goth. No, that wasn't quite right. She looked like a Goth fairy. She wore two camisoles, the outer one a pale aqua, the other peach. A wide, studded black leather belt hung low over her hips. Skinny jeans ended with black Army boots. A long finger held a black leather jacket over her shoulder. A coffee cup was in her other hand. Her makeup was impeccably applied—no, it was more like she'd sculpted her face with tones and colors that perfectly complemented her outfit. The smoky shadowing around her eyes made their pale green color pop.

Val had stopped walking and was grinning at her.

Fiona stopped too, but kept close to him. The girl didn't miss the fact that Val didn't step away.

"Ace," Val said.

She nodded at him, then her gaze sliced toward Fiona.

"This is my friend, Fiona." Val touched her long hair. "We're going to get her extensions removed."

A small smile touched Ace's mouth. Fiona watched as her brows lifted. "Oh. Ohhh. Uh-huh." She grinned as she met Fiona's gaze. Her entire demeanor changed. Fiona looked up at Val to see if he caught the shift. After the mind game Stacey had played on her, she was much more observant. Maybe that was fallout from all that had happened, a scar that would always color her world. She hoped not, but once you saw things you didn't pick up before, you could never go back to not seeing them.

Val was still fingering her hair as he looked at Ace, who chuckled and went around them.

Ace turned around, walking backward. "Hey, Val. I'm going for a hike up on Bobcat Trail Tuesday. Want to come?"

"What time?"

"One?"

He nodded. "I'll meet you in the parking lot."

Ace looked happy. "Nice meeting you, Fiona. Good luck with your hair!"

Fiona waved. "Thanks, Ace. Have fun on the hike."

Val gripped Fiona's arm and started forward, but Fiona didn't move. "What?" he asked.

Fiona lifted a brow. "You like her."

Val tilted his head and frowned. "Fee, have I ever met a female I didn't like?"

"Don't play it down. You *like* her."

"So?"

Fiona frowned. "She thinks you're gay."

His brows lowered and the humor left his face as he glanced back at Ace. "No. And I'm not."

"I know you're not." Fiona gave him an exasperated look. "But you're missing the point."

"Which is?"

"She went from standoffish to friendly as soon as she decided you were. Why would she do that?"

"I don't know. Maybe I'll find out on our hike."

Fiona started down the sidewalk. "I hope you'll let me know how it goes." Val's mood had darkened. She smiled, trying to cheer him up. "How is it that you know about removing hair extensions, anyway?"

"It's a long story." He looked at her disappointed face. "But the short version is that I worked at a salon the last two years of high school."

They'd reached the shop. He opened the door, putting an end to their conversation, which was a shame, because now she really was curious.

CHAPTER TWENTY-TWO

Kit and Ty went upstairs for a break. They took glasses of iced tea outside to the patio. "What do you make of Bladen's library?" Kit asked.

Ty looked into the distance, burying his gaze in the hills beyond the lawns of his yard. "I think whatever it is, it's older, bigger, and better organized than we ever thought. And given all the languages represented in the library, it's not confined to the U.S."

"True that. It's going to take a while to get through all the documentation and start putting the pieces together."

"I'd like to see Rocco given the lead on this."

Kit dipped his head as if thinking about, then tossing, that idea. "Not sure about that."

"He's sick to death of monitoring social media accounts for whispers of insurgency."

"We still need that done. And he has the most fluency of all of us in the languages of our enemies."

"I speak those languages well enough to monitor chatter while he delves into the papers. If we just keep his mind busy, keep it active and engaged and held together, like a broken bone in a cast, he may heal."

"Don't think that works for a broken soul the way it does for a broken bone. He's more like a cracked mirror where the pieces are still in place but refracting in different directions. He has to choose to pull it together. We can't do that for him."

"No, but if we can keep him focused on important work long enough, it may become his new normal. Might help him heal," Ty said. "It's not an impossible task. In fact, it's perfectly suited to a linguistic savant like him. He has access to every documented language the government has; he can review all the keys established in translating all of the ancient languages. Maybe he'll discover something new, an incorrect translation of something in the papers, or even just an alternate translation that we can use to halt the Omni World Order's spread of power. He still needs handling, Kit. For the sake of the team and your sister and his kids."

Kit nodded. "Make it happen."

* * *

Kelan and Max got to the apartment complex of Fiona's friend early Sunday afternoon. Four police cars were already there. Kelan and Max weren't allowed near her apartment. Yellow crime scene tape had been stretched across the open hall, cordoning off access to her place.

They asked a couple of the cops what was going on, but couldn't get a useful answer. None of the bystanders seemed to know what was happening either.

When they turned to go back to the car, Kelan saw another of Fiona's friends standing in the crowd that had gathered to watch the cops. He recognized her from that night at the Swinging Monkey Tiki Bar. She looked terrified, but when she saw Kelan, her face brightened. She hurried over to talk to him.

"Kelan! How's Fiona? I've been trying to call her, but her voice mailbox is full. What are you doing here? I thought you two were getting married this weekend."

Kelan frowned. "What made you think that?"

"Stacey said you two were getting married this weekend."

"She did?"

"Yeah. She was working hard to make sure Fiona's wedding planner had everything Fiona might need." Her face darkened. "Oh God. Stacey's dead. Does Fee know that?"

"No. What happened?"

"I don't know. I came over to get her for lunch." The girl covered her mouth as tears flooded her eyes. "She was dead on the floor of her living room. I don't know when she died."

Kelan shared a look with Max.

"The cops said Stacey OD'd on heroin." She shook her head. "That's not possible. She never did drugs." The girl gave him a sheepish look. "Well, okay, maybe some pot, but never anything involving needles. Ever."

"Have you met anyone unusual lately?" Kelan asked. "Anybody asked you to do them a favor, run an errand, do anything that pertains to Fiona?"

"No. What's happening, Kelan? Am I next?"

"Did you see Stacey with anyone you didn't know?"

"No."

He looked at Fiona's friend. "We weren't getting married this weekend. We were just going to celebrate her birthday. But we couldn't do that because she was kidnapped on her way home Thursday night."

The girl gasped. "What's going on? Are women being targeted here at school?"

Kelan shook his head. "Not women in general. Just Fiona and anyone who helped her kidnappers get her away."

"Did Stacey help them?"

"I think so, but she may not have known she was helping them. Is there anything that you can tell me that might help me find who did this?"

The girl thought for a second. "She said that you—or Fiona's fiancé anyway—wanted to surprise Fee with the perfect wedding weekend, so she helped gather all the info on her sizes and likes and color preferences, everything the wedding coordinator wanted. We all thought it was so romantic."

"Who was the wedding coordinator?"

The girl shook her head. "I don't remember. I'm not sure Stacey ever told me."

"You've been very helpful. If I could give you a bit of advice?" Her big eyes looked up at him. "Don't get involved in this. Don't ask questions. Don't show any interest at all. Don't raise your head and get yourself noticed."

Her brows lifted. "One of my friends was kidnapped. Another has been killed. And you want me to pretend it didn't happen?"

"Yes. For your own safety. I'm working on finding the culprits. I will make sure Stacey receives justice. Please, don't get involved. Stay alert and aware." He handed her one of Lobo's cards. "If there's something you think of, something you happen to see, give Christian Villalobo a call, then stay out of it."

"FBI?" she asked, after reading the card. "You're with the FBI?"

"We're only advisors to the FBI. Christian will be able to help you." Another friend came over to hug the girl, so Kelan and Max left without further conversation.

At the SUV, Max drove and Kelan took shotgun. "Heroin OD. You buy that?"

Kelan shook his head. "No." Despite what had happened, Fiona would be devastated to learn Stacey had died the way she did. He wished that was news he didn't have to tell her.

"Your girl's not taking phone calls from her friends?"

Kelan sighed. "It's only been a day. She needs some time to work through everything."

Max nodded. "If there's something Hope or I can do, you'll ask, right?"

"I will. Thank you."

* * *

The drive south and east to the garage took a little more than an hour. A large perimeter had been set around the property and was heavily guarded. One of Lobo's team members let them onto the site. He said Lobo was down in the ballroom, where a temporary command post had been set up.

The guys took the stairs to the ballroom floor. FBI agents were documenting the paintings, antiques, and sculptures in the central hall.

"Fuck. Me. This looks like a museum," Max said.

Kelan nodded. "It's an underground palace."

Loco Lobo was talking to a couple of his agents. When he saw them, he came over and shook hands. "Owen send you guys down to help?"

"Sort of," Kelan said.

"No," Max snapped.

Kelan gave him a frown. "My girlfriend—" he started, but Lobo interrupted him.

"She deserves a medal."

"She does. She said there were a couple of young women held here against their will. They were from the Friendship Community."

"Shit. The Friends are involved in this too?"

"Seems King doesn't let go of any resource he might put to use later," Kelan said. "I need to know if you've found those girls. And if you haven't, we have to."

"Let's see." Lobo opened a file on his phone and flipped to a manifest listing the civilian workers who were removed from the site. "Have a look. It's a short list."

Kelan scanned the list. He didn't see the names Fiona had given him. "They're not there." He frowned. "This is a huge place, possibly encompassing miles of tunnels. To service guests, cook, clean, and maintain it, they'd need a helluva lot more staff than this."

"Mind if we go looking for them?" Max asked.

"Help yourself."

They started to leave, but stopped. "Lobo—have your people documented the secret tunnels?" Kelan asked.

His brows lifted. "Secret tunnels?"

"Yeah. My girlfriend accessed a tunnel from inside her closet. She followed it to the farmhouse. I was removed from the site via that same tunnel, but they tranqed me before I could see much."

"Shit. How big is this place? I'm coming with you."

Kelan led the way down to the room where Fiona had been held. Max looked around at the opulence and decadence of the suite. He started to grin, but one look at Kelan made him swallow whatever he was going to say.

They went into the closet. Kelan found the electrical outlet that Fiona had told him about. He pressed it into the wall. The whole front of the jewelry cabinet opened.

"Whoa." Max was shocked. He shined his light down the long tunnel. "Where does this go?"

"No idea. Fiona said she took mostly right turns when she ended up at the entrance to the farmhouse."

Lobo radioed in for some additional agents to follow them.

Kelan found a light switch, which he flipped on. Compared to the opulence of the main hall, this looked like a complete afterthought. Exposed wiring was anchored to the top of the tunnel, powering a dim light every ten feet or so.

Two hours later, they returned to the same place they had started. Agents were moving about the space, documenting its layout, which looked to be a wheel and spoke arrangement. How much of the architecture was left over from the original footprint of the silo, and how much had been constructed over the last forty-some years, was as yet unknown.

They found evidence of human occupation—bits of clothing here and there. A shoe. A basket. Some dishes. But they had not found anyone.

"Maybe whoever was kept here against their will took advantage of our being here and got out," Lobo suggested.

"Maybe. It's possible. But if they knew the way out and had a support system outside to help them get away, why not take advantage of it before this, when they wanted to leave? Why stay here if they didn't have to?" Kelan shook his head. "I think they're still here. Maybe there's another level."

"Look, let's separate and see if we can find any access entry points to other floors," Max said. "They had them all over at the WKB's silo complex."

Kelan took the search quadrant assigned to him. So many of the hallways and tunnels intersected each other. He went down one of the spokes that they hadn't passed through yet. There was a steel sewer cap in the floor.

Maybe that was one of the chutes Max had mentioned. He knelt and lifted the heavy disc aside. Shining his flashlight down into the dark depths, he couldn't see much beyond the ladder fused to the wall and that the ground at the bottom looked dry. He put his flashlight in his pocket and slipped into the chute.

Twenty steps down, Kelan dropped that last few feet to the bottom of the shaft. Light shone down from the floor above, but everything in there was absolute darkness. He stayed kneeling on the ground, listening to the sounds around him. There was a dull, rhythmic roar. The engine of a distant ventilation system. He couldn't hear people, but that didn't surprise him.

He closed his eyes and spent a moment absorbing

the darkness and the silence. Off in the distance, he could hear…the muted sound of dogs barking, a sound that grew, as they seemed to be moving nearer. He held still. His eyes were getting acclimated to the dark and the shadows it hid. He could see the arched opening that led out of the shaft.

The dogs were close. Kelan shut his eyes and calmed his energy, aligning it with theirs. They grew quiet as they approached, moving more slowly. He drew a long breath, then another, staying in a place of silence, using his stillness as a vehicle to reach his ancestors. He called upon them to guide him, to help him harm only his enemies and protect all others.

When he opened his eyes, the dogs were sitting in a half-circle ten feet from him…and people were gathering outside the archway. A lot of them. He rose to his feet and moved toward them. He was taller than most of them, but that was true in normal populations as well.

Lanterns had been lit, dispersing some of the darkness. The people wore simple clothes made from organic fibers, dyed in dozens of colors—not unlike those from the Friendship Community. Some were decorated with intricate needlework. Several children were in the front of the group, having been the first to follow the dogs. Women came forward and snatched them up, dragging them away to the back of the group, leaving the men in the front to face him.

None of them had weapons. They were soft and vulnerable. What if it hadn't been him to enter their world, but one of King's men?

"You're the War Bringer," one of the men said. "The true one."

"I'm Kelan." He preferred to keep things real, but nothing in this strange situation fit that term. Whether the moniker he'd chosen as a protective symbol before he went into the Army was meant for him alone or was the icon of a greater purpose was yet to be determined. "Who are you?" he asked as he moved forward.

The crowd parted, clearing a path to an old man whose white beard reached his heart. This man stood unmoving in front of Kelan. "We're workers here."

"Are you here against your will?"

The man looked around. There had to be almost two dozen people. "Not at first. But once here, we weren't allowed to leave."

"There have to be a dozen exits out of here."

"And all of them were guarded by King's men."

"I don't know where King is, but the FBI is all over this place. If you want to leave, I can take you out."

"Can we take our dogs?"

"Of course."

"Will you wait while we gather our things?"

"I'll wait. I'm looking for two girls—Ellen and Bryn. Do you know them?"

One girl moved to the front of the group—the girl from Fiona's closet. "They didn't kill you."

Kelan grinned. "No. Nor you, I see."

Ellen gestured to the other girl to come forward. "We've been hiding down here ever since the initiation was interrupted."

"Fiona sent me for you. I'll take you home once the FBI has finished interviewing you."

"Will they keep us from going home?" Ellen asked.

"No. Is everyone here from the Friends?"

Ellen shook her head. "Not everyone, but we've been talking about bringing them all back with us."

Kelan nodded. "Get your things and let's get out of here."

A few minutes later, he was helping people bring their animals up the ladder. Once everyone was out, he did a quick walk-through of the tidy but ramshackle place where they lived to confirm that everyone was out.

When he climbed out of the shaft, Max and Lobo were there leading another group of about the same number. Lobo looked stunned. Kelan grinned.

"I can't believe this was here and we didn't know," Lobo said as they started back for the command post.

Kelan looked at the crowd following them. "And you haven't checked the other silos yet. Who knows what they hide."

"I'm going to set up temporary shelter for them in the ballroom. We'll start taking their statements tonight."

"They want to return to the Friendship Community."

"They'll need smallpox inoculations first."

Kelan nodded. "I'll send Doctor Beck Williams down with Greer and Remi to take care of that tomorrow."

"Kelan—I'm staying here tonight," Max said. "I want to ask them if they've seen Lion and his boys here. I think I better do that individually or else they won't want to talk about him."

Kelan nodded. "I can stay and help."

"No. Get home to your woman. She needs you more than I do right now. I'll head back with Greer tomorrow."

CHAPTER TWENTY-THREE

Fiona became restless in her room. She wandered out to the stables to see if Mandy was still there, and found her working with one of her newly donated horses. There were bags of sand on the saddle. Mandy led the horse around the corral where she worked with her clients.

"Hey there!" Mandy called, bringing the horse around to the mounting ramp. "You're just in time. Feel like helping me for a bit?"

"Sure. What do you need?"

"We're doing great with the sandbag weights, but I think he's ready to be tested at the next level. I need you to ride him while I lead him. Make sure you move around in some ways he might not expect. Not all of my clients have full motor control; we need to simulate that experience so that he doesn't spook when it happens."

"I'm in. Tell me what to do."

Mandy removed the sandbags, then Fiona got in the saddle.

"So as I walk him around, how about you sway

side to side?"

Fiona did that, careful of the horse's reaction. She wanted to get him used to the motion, not scare him.

"What brought you out here?" Mandy asked.

Fee lifted her shoulders. "I wanted to talk." She looked at Mandy. "I need some advice." There wasn't much about what had happened that she was ready to say aloud—except for what Kelan had told her about his claiming ceremony.

"Shoot."

"Kelan asked me to come up with vows that I will make to him as part of the claiming ritual. He commits to four, and I do the same—we exchange them during the ceremony."

"I like that."

"I don't know what ones to make."

"I suppose they would be different for each couple."

"What vows would you make to Rocco?"

They moved a couple times around the corral before Mandy answered. "I can think of two off the top of my head. One is that I would be endlessly patient as he works through his illness. He had PTSD long before he had me."

"I like that."

"The other also has to do with his illness. He still battles paranoia. It causes him to not trust. My vow would be that I would always be truthful with him. Sometimes he doesn't believe me when I say I love him. But if he knows I will never lie to him, then he knows I'm telling the truth."

That broke Fiona's heart. What a battle Mandy was fighting. She never complained, at least not that Fiona ever noticed.

"What are the things that you can promise from your heart to Kelan? Things that only have to do with the two of you? He's an good man, Fee. What are the things you can do to honor him? How will you make his days wonderful? Because I'm sure he will do those same things for you."

Fiona felt a wave of sorrow. "What if…what if the best thing I can do for him is to let him go?"

Mandy frowned. "You don't love him?"

"Oh, I do. So much so that I'm terrified to think of life without him." She wiped a tear that slipped down her cheek. "But I'm King's daughter. What kind of life will that be for him? He will always be on guard for an attack from the thing that is my dad."

"Fiona—Kelan's a warrior. I think he's up to what you're both facing."

"But why should that be his life?"

"Have you had this talk with him?"

Fiona shook her head and blinked more tears away. "I can't."

Mandy's eyes watered, too. She looked away from Fee, then stopped the horse they were training. The wind tangled about them. "Why is everything always so hard?"

Fee lifted her shoulders and drew a long breath to calm herself—she couldn't go back to the house all red-faced. "I guess because it all matters so much to us." Fiona dismounted. They walked shoulder to shoulder into the stables.

* * *

Fiona skipped dinner. Kelan and Max were still down in Colorado. She couldn't quite deal with the worried looks she knew the other girls would still send her way.

After talking to Mandy, she'd spent the afternoon trying to figure out what she was going to do: stay for the claiming ceremony or leave before things got worse. There was only one answer coming to her. She was going to have to go.

Kelan was like an Arabian horse—all heart, all loyalty, running until it died because its master was too uncaring to see it wouldn't quit.

Kelan would never give up on her. And King would never stop coming after them, after their kids, after the people they loved. Joining their lives together meant she imperiled his entire family.

That was not okay.

Somehow, she was going to have to find a way to say goodbye.

She was just finishing getting into a pair of baggy pajama bottoms and a tank top to sleep in, when a knock sounded on her door. Hope was standing there, a tray in hand.

"Hey. You weren't at supper. I thought I'd come

check on you."

Fiona smiled and stepped back so that Hope could come in. She set the tray down at the small table in the corner of the room. "Ivy made a sandwich for you. They wanted to come up, but I thought a bunch of us might overwhelm you."

Fiona plopped down in one of the chairs at the table. Hope pushed the tray toward her. A bowl of broccoli cheese soup and a crusty roll. It looked delicious. "Thanks, Hope."

Hope tilted her head to the side and gave a little grin. "Couldn't let my sister starve, could I?"

Fiona frowned at her. Sister?

"We share a brother. That makes us sisters, no?"

"I suppose it does."

"Your hair looks cute."

Fiona touched her curly bob. It had taken a while to get the extensions removed. Val had stayed with her the whole time. And every time the girls in the salon had shifted their attention from her to him, he returned their focus to her. She'd left there feeling almost like herself again.

"I always wanted a sister," Fiona said, looking at Hope as she took a bite of the sandwich.

"Me too."

Hope made small talk while she ate, telling Fiona about everything that had happened while she was away. It was so perfect, all of them, living here. She'd been terrified of the guys when she first came to Mandy's. And now, they really were family. She had more sisters than just Hope, too.

How was she ever going to be able to leave all of them?

Hope folded her legs in front of her on the chair and braced her heels against the edge of the seat. She set her chin on her knees and focused on Fiona. She reached for Fee's hand and squeezed it.

"I want to tell you something, something I haven't told the others." She told Fiona about the day she and Max met, how the club was cutting her clothes from her body with the intent of raping her. "My dad was among them. I didn't know he was my dad, and I don't think he knew I was his daughter. I was just some chick to abuse for the amusement of the club. King had sent me to the club to be killed. I'm sure of it."

Fiona thought back to her twisted memories of what happened in the rotunda. She couldn't bring herself to talk about it yet. She was pretty sure, though, that King had been at the ceremony.

He was never, ever, ever going to leave her alone, was he? She looked at Hope. "Can I ask a favor?"

"Anything."

"I need to burn something."

"What?"

"Something they made me wear the night Kelan got me out of there."

Hope smiled. "Let's do it. Grab whatever it is and meet me outside. I'll get the firepit ready." She took Fiona's empty tray and left.

Fiona pulled a hoodie on over her tank top, then stepped into a pair of flip-flops and grabbed the bag with her cape in it.

Hope had a roaring fire in the big pit. Ivy was there. She gave Fiona a hug, but didn't talk, didn't ask questions. Her quiet acceptance of Fiona's pain chipped away at Fiona's frozen spirit. The three of them watched the fire burn for a little while, letting the kindling burn down and firewood catch the flames. Mandy and Eden came out. Remi followed them.

"I think it's ready now, if you are," Hope said.

Fiona took the cape and the shredded slip from the hospital bag. She tossed the silk slip on the fire first. It hissed and flared up, then burned the silk like a bit of dried paper. When it was just black ashes, Fiona dropped the red cape on the pyre. It was slower to catch, just from its sheer mass. Ivy handed her the poker. She pushed at the garment until it began to smoke, then watched as flames broke through and began to eat the thing.

She wasn't sure how long they stood there silently watching the fire, but she was so mesmerized by it that she didn't hear anyone come up behind her. Warm, big arms circled around her, pulling her back against a rock-hard chest.

She set the poker aside and turned to wrap her arms around Kelan. He bent and kissed her temple. Fiona realized the other guys had come to stand with their women, too.

"Burning that cape?" Kelan asked.

Fiona nodded.

"Good."

They watched the fire for a few minutes. Fiona looked up at him. "Were you able to find the girls?"

"Yes. We found quite a few people living in areas even deeper than where they had you. It's a labyrinth there."

Hope crossed her arms over her chest. "Any hint of Lion and the watchers?"

"No. Max stayed on site to talk to the people we found. He was going to do some more exploring to see if there were other hidey-holes they might be in."

"Maybe he could use my Malinois. I've been training her to find lost people—dementia patients who've wandered off. Kids who've gotten lost in woods. I've started working with her to find humans under rubble."

"That's a great idea," Kelan said. "Maybe you could go down tomorrow with Greer and Remi. They're picking up Doc Beck, too."

Eden looked over at Greer, who was standing with his arms around Remi. "We'll be ready when you are in the morning."

Fiona remembered the diamond and pearl earrings that were in the bottom of the bag from the hospital. She fished them out and handed them to Greer. "Give these to Lobo tomorrow. They made me wear them during the ceremony. Maybe they were stollen from someone."

The group got quiet after that. Fiona stared into the fire for a long while. It wasn't until Kelan poked the logs that she realized the others had all gone inside, giving the two of them privacy.

He took a blanket from the plush loveseat, then coaxed her over to sit with him. The altitude they were at made the temperatures of these late summer nights changeable—sometimes warm, sometimes cool like tonight. He covered her then pulled her close. "I'm glad to see you out of your room."

"Hope came and talked to me."

"There's something I need to tell you."

Fiona braced herself for whatever his news might be—a new revelation about King or some other negative news.

"I stopped in to see Stacey in Fort Collins."

Fiona looked at him.

"She died of a heroin overdose."

"Oh my God."

"I don't think she knew she was helping King. I think she truly thought she was helping us."

"She didn't do drugs, Kelan. She wasn't a user."

"I told Lobo about her."

Fiona leaned forward and folded her knees in front of her. "I can't go back to CSU. I'm the reason she was killed."

"She was killed because King's a sick sonofabitch."

"But he was after me. He could try again."

"He could."

"And if he does, who knows who else will get in

the way or be steamrolled by him."

"Can you switch your classes to online ones?"

"Not this semester. I can drop my classes, though."

"That might not be a bad idea."

"Kelan." Her voice was barely a whisper. "I have to leave. I can't stay here."

"Why?"

"Because King has left me no choice."

"He will kill you."

Fiona nodded. "Maybe. But if he does, then at least he'll leave you alone."

"Fiona, sacrificing yourself will not end our troubles with him. While you were gone, Blade found some papers that his mother took from his stepdad. They describe in great detail this Omni World Order movement that King's heading up at the moment. It's much bigger than one man, or one small group of anarchists. It's an international movement that began decades, if not centuries, ago. We haven't gone through all of the papers, but some of them are very old."

Fiona looked up at him as she tried to absorb all of that information. "I don't know how I fit in to all of that, but I do know King is using his power to come after all of us because he wants me. He's already taken Lion. I don't want something bad to happen to everyone here. To you. If I let him take me, then the rest of you won't hold any interest to him anymore."

"Do you think that every one of us on the team

didn't already have targets on our backs simply because we're coming after him? We're safer together than separated. If you leave, King will kill you and still hunt us. And he isn't only interested in you. It's much bigger than you. If you stay, you can help us figure it out."

"If anything happened to you because of me, I would not be able to live with that pain."

"If you leave out of fear, I would not be able to live with that pain." He pulled her closer. "We're at war, Fiona. We're getting very close to King. I can feel it. Will you wait this out a little longer before deciding?"

She looked at the fire, wishing she had that luxury.

After a while, when the fire burned to embers, Kelan put the screen over it. "Let's quit for the night." He held a hand out to her. They went inside by the living room. Fiona waited while he locked the doors. They went upstairs. He paused at her door.

Her heart started beating fast. Would he come in?

He lifted her chin, looking into her eyes for a long moment before he bent and kissed her cheek. "I'm just next door if you need me."

She needed him. Desperately. But sooner or later she was going to have to break that bond. Maybe sooner was better than later.

She nodded and went into her room. Standing on just the other side of the closed door, she waited for the sound of his door shutting.

He wasn't wrong in the things he'd said at the fire

tonight. In fact, he was spot on. It just meant she was going to have to do some serious planning before she left.

CHAPTER TWENTY-FOUR

In all the craziness of her abduction, Fiona didn't even realize that Zavi's tutor had started until she ran into her in the hallway the second day she was home. She liked her right away. And she could tell Zavi was enthralled with his new teacher.

"Have you seen my classroom, Fee?" he asked.

"I haven't."

He took her hand and led her back to the classroom. He walked her around the whole room, pointing out what everything was.

Fiona smiled at Wynn. "I'm sorry I didn't know you were here."

"Oh, please, don't worry about it. You've had enough on your mind! Besides, I haven't been at breakfast and you haven't been at the other meals."

Fiona gave a small smile. "I've been hiding."

"Why were you hiding?" Zavi looked up at her.

She ruffled his hair. "I've just been in a mood, that's all."

Wynn smiled. "And that's understandable."

"Zavi seems pretty happy you're here."

"That makes two of us!" Wynn said.

"Well, I don't mean to keep you. Have a wonderful day studying, Zavi."

"We will!"

Fiona wandered outside after that. She sat on the stone wall of the steps that led down to the lower lawn. There had been a frost overnight, but that had burned off a while ago. It would be hot later, but the morning was wonderfully crisp and fresh, the sky brilliantly blue. Fiona pulled the quilt she'd brought out with her tighter about herself.

Everyone seemed to have something to do. Mandy had her horses. Eden her dogs. Hope was working on the team's vehicles. Remi was back at the university. Ivy was no doubt at the diner, catching up with work that had been put on hold during Fiona's ordeal. Even the kids were occupied: Casey at school, Zavi with Wynn. The guys and Selena were down in the bunker. Kathy was busy in the kitchen cooking up a big meal—something she hadn't been able to do while the team was spread out, searching for Fiona. And Dennis, her husband, was prepping Ty's property for the change in seasons.

Everyone had something they needed to do. Everyone but her. It was Monday. She could have gone back to class. She hadn't decided yet what to do about that.

King was such a madman that there was no telling what he would do next. She couldn't continue to endanger her fellow students at the university. She couldn't take a job for the same reason.

Would this nightmare ever end? She bent her head, blocking the happy blue sky from her eyes. After a while, she heard someone approaching. Not Kelan— she recognized Angel's cheery whistling. He could whistle entire tunes the way some people hummed them.

He sat on the opposite side of the stairs from her, his back straight, his hands folded in his lap, his attention entirely on her. She tried to ignore him but should have known better than to think that was possible.

"Missed you at practice today." He cut into the silence she'd been enjoying.

She shrugged, still facing away from him. "It's not like it did me much good when it came time to use it."

"Yeah. Sometimes shit's just stacked against us. Did you know that there were thirty-five men arrested from the silo who were on King's guard corps? Even Kelan was overwhelmed by them."

Fiona didn't answer him.

"I heard you fought back at the shack you were kept in." He grinned at her. "From what Kelan says, you were fucking epic."

Fiona tilted her head and looked at him. "They weren't expecting that. Took four guys to get me." She rubbed her nose. "But it didn't change my fate. They still took me. And my resistance didn't do anything for the girls whose only way out of the house was into the jaws of dogs trained to kill them."

"We've talked about fighting. You know that leaving the situation is always your first best option. You run from an assailant when possible, fight when it's not. Self-defense is a tool, like anything else available to us. You used it in the ways you were taught."

"But it did no good."

Angel shrugged. "Maybe. You don't know that. The girls you were locked in there with, I bet they'd never had another person—much less a female—fight for them before. What courage did your bravery inspire in them?"

Fiona's eyes watered. She squeezed them shut. "I can't see an end to it, Angel. I can only see the dark."

They sat in silence for a while. It was uncomfortable and long, and Fiona really just wished Angel would go away. As if he heard her thoughts, he stood. "I want to see you at practice tomorrow. It's good for the body and mind, even if it's useless in real life."

He started up the steps. She felt bad hurting his feelings. All she'd done was pass her hurt on to him. Really, he should have left her alone.

He paused at the top step. "Fee, maybe you should talk to Rocco. He's lived in the dark a lot longer than you. He might know some things he can share."

Fiona thought about that. Yeah, maybe it would help. "Where is he?"

Angel's lips folded against his teeth as he looked

off into the distance beyond the house. "He's working on something in the bunker for now. Later you might find him over at Mandy's. Sometimes he likes to hang out in her old barn." He lowered his head, then looked back at her. "If you go there, make some noise so he knows you're there."

Like the whistling Angel had done as he approached. Fiona's eyes watered again. She nodded. "Thanks, Angel."

* * *

Fiona walked back into the house a little while after Angel left. Ivy was in the living room, putting some papers in her briefcase.

She looked up and smiled. "Hey. I wasn't sure if you were still here or if you'd gone back to school."

Fiona didn't smile. "I'm not sure I'm going back to school."

Ivy nodded. "I understand. Look, if you wanted to get out of here for a little while, you could come with me. I have a bit of work to do at the diner, then we could go for coffee or grab Selena and head down to Cheyenne. Maybe we'll throw caution to the wind and spend the day in Denver."

Fiona nodded. "Yeah. I'd like that."

"Good. How soon can you be ready?"

"Fifteen minutes?"

"Sounds perfect. Come down when you're ready. Bring a book to read so you have something to do while I knock out a few things in the office."

Fiona met Ivy in the foyer a few minutes later. "Should we tell someone we're headed out?"

"Selena knows."

They went through the garage and down to the small parking lot that was off to the side. Fiona slipped her arm through Ivy's. "I feel like an escapee."

Ivy laughed. "Feels good, doesn't it?"

"To get out, yes." The thought of leaving instantly brought Kelan to mind; leaving him did not feel good. "I don't think I'd feel so cornered if"—she caught herself before complaining. There was nothing she could do about the man who'd fathered her— "things were different. I just don't know where I fit. How I belong."

They split apart as they went to their sides of her car. "Then I'm glad I got you out of the house for a bit." They got in and buckled up. Ivy looked over at her. "Things will be easier for you once you get back to school."

"I'm not sure I'm going back." Fee shook her head.

"Are you afraid that there'll be repeat of what just happened?"

"Maybe." She looked at Ivy. "I'm King's daughter. I'm a liability to anyone near me. People die when they get close."

"Oh, Fee. I'm so sorry this is happening. Have you thought about switching to online classes?"

Fiona sighed and shifted her gaze to look out the

window, watching the soft hills slip past as they headed toward town. "The thing is, I'm not even sure that I want the degree I've declared anymore. Why does the world need another business admin anyway?"

"Ah." Ivy flashed a look at her. "The whole existential conundrum. I just went through some of that myself. It sucks." She smiled as she gave Fiona a sympathetic look.

"What did you do about it?"

"Spent a lot of time thinking about what's really important to me. To Casey. To Kit." They pulled into town. "If you don't want to go into a business field, what else interests you?"

"I don't know. Seems there are other things that matter more than getting a business degree. Like helping the girls I met over the past few days—the ones stuck in the sex-trafficking ring or ones from the Friendship Community. Seems like there ought to be a way I could help people rather than harvesting money from them."

"I'm in business here with the diner. I don't think of what I'm doing as harvesting money from my customers. If I'm successful, I'll earn an income, true, but I provide a valuable service to my community in the process. Employment—with benefits—for a dozen people in an environment that cares about work and home life balance. The diner's a hub for our neighbors. And we provide reduced-cost meals for seniors. I think we're a positive addition to the town, and I like being a part of that."

"I didn't mean—"

Ivy smiled. "I know. Sounds like you want to go in a different direction than you did when you started down your degree path. That's okay, Fee. That's part of what college is about." She pulled up outside of her diner. "You know who would be a good person to talk to about this? Remi. She's found a way to work with niche, at-risk populations. Maybe she can help you identify your next steps."

They got out of the car. "I'll talk to her," Fiona said as Ivy came around to her side.

"You know, there are many ways of helping people, even with a business degree. Maybe a little time off to figure things out isn't a bad thing."

Fiona nodded. "I hate being lost."

Ivy laughed. "Welcome to the human race."

They parted ways inside. Fiona settled into a booth. One of the waitresses brought her a slice of apple pie with a big scoop of vanilla ice cream and a cup of coffee. She opened her e-reader and flipped through a list of books she'd wanted to read. She sampled several different ones, but couldn't seem to get into any of them.

Kelan had asked some good questions last night at the firepit. If she did decide to go, how was she going to survive? How could she keep King from finding her? She'd need a job. A place to live.

The thought of leaving cut to the quick. Maybe there was a way of doing it in steps. Maybe Ivy had an opening for a waitress. And didn't she have an empty apartment on the third floor of this building? It was sort of safe here, given all the surveillance that the team had put in to protect Ivy. And Ty's dad worked here.

If she could work here, then at least she would be making her own way, not living off the charity of the team...and Kelan.

But would he let her go?

Fiona brought her dishes to the kitchen, then went to see Ivy, who was in her office doing some paperwork. She looked up from her desk and smiled. "Getting bored?"

"No."

"I'm almost finished. Five minutes, max."

"I was wondering...do you have any openings for a waitress? If I'm going to sit out a semester, I need to earn my keep."

Ivy took a long time answering. "Have you talked this over with Kelan?"

Fiona fought tears. She didn't want to go, even in these small steps. She just couldn't see any alternative. "Some. I kind of want to have things organized before I tell him more. And I was also wondering if you would rent one of your apartments to me. That way, I can get my feet under me before deciding what's next."

Ivy gestured toward the side chair next to her desk. "Fee, do you love Kelan?"

Fiona blinked her tears away and swallowed hard.

"Yes."

"You know I told you about my crisis a little while back? I learned something going through that, something unexpected. Our guys love us in a deep and abiding way. We aren't just adornments to them; we're essential to their lives. I can't, in good conscience, agree to something that would hurt Kelan and negatively impact the team. I've been there. I did that. I know what that cost is."

The tears did fall then. "King will never stop, Ivy. I'm a danger to them if I stay."

Ivy teared up, too. She took a set of keys out of her desk drawer. "Ace has the apartment on the second floor. Go take a look at the one on the top floor. I'm not saying I agree to this. I need to hear that this is okay with Kelan—not because he's the boss of you, but because you're a couple now. You need to do things as a couple. Really, really, think this through, Fee."

Fiona took the keys and stared at them in her hand. Every instinct she had screamed it was a bad decision. She looked at Ivy. "I will. Thank you."

CHAPTER TWENTY-FIVE

Fiona walked up the two flights of stairs. There was only one apartment on each of the floors above Ivy's diner. She unlocked the door. A wave of stale air swirled around her. The windows were closed, trapping in the heat of the September day. Flies buzzed at the front window. There wasn't any furniture, but there wasn't any debris from the last occupant, either. It had the standard complement of rooms: living room, kitchen, dining room, bathroom, and two bedrooms. It was a big space for just one person.

Fiona heard the stairs creak. She'd left the front door open. Someone knocked on her door then popped a head inside.

Ace.

Her purple hair was shaggy. She wore big hoop earrings with half a dozen littler rings in the cartilage farther up her ears. Her makeup was perfect, like she had a crew of makeup artists at her full disposal.

"Hi," Ace said. "I heard someone up here and was curious."

Fiona smiled. "I was thinking of renting this place."

"I thought you lived up at the big house with Ivy."

"I do."

Ace folded her arms and stepped deeper into the apartment. Her perfectly sculpted brows lifted. "That's kind of an odd arrangement."

"I guess so. It's like a sorority house on campus…except it's different."

"What are they doing up there? The guys?"

Fiona looked at Ace, measuring her interest in the team. "I don't know. It started out as a team retreat. I guess they liked the area and decided to stay longer."

"But what do they do? I've heard the gossip, and I've seen the pictures of them and their guns the time the deputy pulled them over."

Fiona shook her head, feeling uncomfortable with the direction of Ace's questions. "I don't really know. I've been preoccupied with school."

Ace nodded toward the bruise on her face. "Do they keep you there against your will?"

Fiona touched her bruise. "No. Not really. It's complicated." She looked out the window to the town's main street, avoiding Ace's intense and pale green eyes. "You ever wanted to just disappear, Ace?"

"Yes."

"How would you do it?"

"Why do you want to disappear?"

Fiona felt ill. "I've recently learned I'm the daughter of a crime lord. He wants me under his control. I'm a danger to anyone I'm around."

Ace seemed preternaturally still. "Who's your father?"

"A bastard named King."

"Shit." Ace tore her eyes from Fiona and glared at the wall.

"Do you know him?"

"I can help you disappear."

"Do you know King?"

"He sounds like a power-mongering sonofabitch. I know his type."

"He's everywhere. He knows everything. I don't know how I could slide under his radar."

"I do."

Fiona met her eyes, held them in silence for a long moment. "Will you help me?"

"Yes."

"How do you know about disappearing?"

"I've had some experience doing it. Do the guys know you're King's kid?"

Fiona nodded. "In fact, they helped me get away from him recently." She pointed to her chin. "Hence the bruise."

"It isn't easy disappearing. Everyone you meet or talk to or accept help from becomes a target of those after you. If you're in a controlled situation now, might be best to hang tight there a while."

"What were you running from when you disappeared?"

"Some bad people."

"Are you safe now?"

"For a little while."

"You should come to the house and talk to the guys. They would help you."

"That's what Val said."

"Maybe you should listen to him." Fiona couldn't help but grin at the irony that she was giving this tough girl survival advice.

Ace returned her smile as she followed Fee to the door. "Maybe I will. I tell you what. I'll come talk to the guys about my issue, if you'll rethink leaving the big house. For a while, anyway."

Fiona busied herself locking the door. Before she could answer, Ivy called up to them. "Fee! Come down here. I have something to show you."

Fiona looked at Ace, then both of them hurried down the stairs. Ivy met them at the main level. Her face was tense, her eyes bright. Fiona frowned. "What is it?"

Ivy turned and walked into the back door of her diner. The girls followed her. She stopped at her office and pointed to a box sitting on her desk. It was a shiny red decorative gift box about six square inches.

"This just showed up. The label says it's for you."

Fiona stared at the box. How did anyone know she was here? "Where did it come from?"

"I don't know. I went to the restroom, and it was here when I got back. I asked the crew out front, but no one saw anyone bring it in."

Fiona started forward, but Ace stopped her.

"Don't open it," Ace said. "Call your husband, Ivy. Do it now."

Ivy took her phone out of her pocket and dialed Kit.

"Ivy-mine, s'up?" he said. She had the call on speaker.

Ivy drew a deep breath. "Kit, there's a problem. Well, it may be a problem. It's probably nothing, just odd."

"What is it?"

"A box was delivered here for Fee."

"Is she there?"

"Yes. It's just—no one saw anyone bring it."

"Max, check the videos at the diner," Kit said, slightly away from the phone. *"Don't touch the box, Iv. I'm on my way."*

Ivy hung up. "Let's wait for them out back."

A few minutes later, they saw one of the team's SUVs drive up the alleyway. Kit and Kelan got out of the front, then Kelan held the back door for Eden and Tank.

Kit went over and hugged Ivy. Kelan looked at Fiona. She hadn't told him she would be there with Ivy. He slipped an arm around her back and kissed her hair. "You all right?"

"Yeah." She was great. Better than ever. Absolutely coming apart at the seams.

Kit and Kelan went into Ivy's office first, clearing it for Eden and Tank. The girls stayed in the hall, watching them. Eden let Tank sniff around. He didn't catch any scents that interested him. After a minute he sat and looked up at Eden, who shook her head. "No drugs or explosives. The box is clear."

Kelan pulled a pair of nitrile gloves on and opened the lid. He held still a minute, then pulled out a card that was tucked inside the pink tissue paper lining. "Shit."

Fiona covered her mouth.

Kelan handed the card to Kit, then showed him what was in the box.

"What is it?" Fiona asked.

"Nothing," Kelan said.

"Kelan, what is it?"

He shook his head. "More bullshit from King. You don't need to see this."

Kit handed the card to her. It read, *Everything must die sometime. Remember our talk. A flower for your twenty-first birthday, daughter.* Inside the box was a black rose, withered and brittle.

Fiona handed the box to Ivy and hurried out the back of the diner. She leaned against the brick wall in the alleyway, sucking in big gulps of air.

King had known she was there.

And he probably also knew who was with her. Working here, living here wasn't a safe option—for her or Ivy or anyone.

Oh, God.

She would never be able to outrun him.

Kelan came outside. He came right to her,

catching her face in his hands. "Fiona, Mahasani, look at me."

She didn't. She couldn't. She was frozen. Her lungs had quit pulling air.

He rubbed the knuckles of one hand over her sternum. "Baby, breathe." He blew warm air in her face. Her breath caught. She lifted her eyes to him. He gave her a small smile, then stroked her cheeks with his thumbs. "That's it. Don't let King's stupid Halloween gag spook you. He's an ass. Of course everyone, everything dies. In due time. In the proper order of things. Except him. He will die soon and violently, and far younger than he ever expected. Got it?"

Fiona reached for his wrists. "I wanted to leave."

"No, you didn't. You wanted to make us safer, which will only happen if we're together." He pulled her into his arms. "Come home with me."

The others came out of the diner. "Max said a guy dressed like a farmer in a plaid shirt and jeans, wearing a baseball cap, came into the diner with a gift bag," Kit said. "He went straight to the back, left the box on Ivy's desk, then left. The cameras didn't get a good shot of his face. I checked for bugs, but didn't find any." He looked at Ivy. "I think you should come back to the house."

She nodded. "Just let me get my things."

Fiona handed her the keys to the apartment. Kelan noticed that exchange and frowned. She avoided his eyes, looking at Ace instead.

"What about Ace?" she asked Kelan.

The guys looked at her. She shrugged. "Don't worry about me. I can take care of myself." She came over and gave Fiona a hug. "Think about what I said."

"I will. And likewise."

Ace smiled, then waved and went back into the building.

"What did she say?" Kelan asked.

"She said not to run."

The hard look he gave her didn't need words. That she would heed advice from a stranger but not him cut deep.

"I'm driving Ivy home," Kit said. "I've got the box. Let's see if there's any info Greer can get off it."

* * *

Kelan sat on the edge of his bed later that night. He'd brought Fiona down for supper that night, then stayed with her in the billiards room afterward, when everyone gathered for some downtime.

Fear had such a grip on her mind that he didn't know how to reach her. She'd been withdrawn the whole evening. He wanted to hold her, be with her while she worked through everything, but he'd told her he wasn't going to put his needs before hers. So until she came to him, he was going to give her room.

The trunk sitting in the corner caught his attention. His mom had sent it out a couple of weeks ago. It was a big thing, full of the tools he'd need for their claiming ceremony. He'd been so excited to show it to Fiona, but now it was going to have to wait.

Kelan knelt beside the trunk and opened it. His mom had sent a ceremonial gown made of white deerskin for Fiona. He had no idea how old it was, but the beadwork had been restored a couple of decades ago.

The wrist cuffs he'd wear after their ceremony were in there, too—wide leather embossed with Celtic eagles. He pulled those items out and lifted the petite irons, four with straight, masculine lines and patterns, four with feminine ones of curving lines and knots—both sets done with Celtic styles.

There was the sage he'd use to purify their ceremonial space, and the paint he would use to mark the four directions, the four seasons.

Kelan put everything back in the box. He'd waited his entire life for his claiming ceremony with Fiona—he could wait until she healed, too.

* * *

Fiona began to doze, but startled awake. Took a minute to get her bearing. The lights were on. She was back at Ty's. She was safe. For the moment, Kelan was also safe.

But every time she shut her eyes, the satyr would slip into her dreams. The ordinary would become distorted. The floor would come alive like it did in King's rotunda. Things she thought were solid would change into something else.

She thought of the dead rose King had sent her and the threat it held. Sitting up in her bed, she folded her legs and began to rock. King had already killed three people in her life: her mom, Danny, Alan. He'd taken Lion and the watchers. He'd been playing this game for a long time. He knew its rules, its strategy.

Kelan and the guys were smart as hell, but nowhere near as devious as King. They weren't on equal footing. It was not going to end well. And she would be to blame.

Fiona got out of bed and began to pace about her room. Maybe she should pull her savings from her bank. She could buy a beater, drive as far as it took her, then buy another. She'd pay cash for everything, find a job that paid her under the table.

Did King already have eyes on her bank account? If she moved her money out, would he know she was getting ready to run? He'd known she was at the diner. What didn't he know about her?

Leaving meant losing everything. But staying meant that, too. Her friends here had taken her in when she had no home or family to turn to. How could she selfishly stay and be the cause of the terrible things King would do to them?

Fiona looked at her clock. It was late. She cracked her door and listened. The house was silent. She stepped out of her room, moving swiftly to Kelan's.

His door wasn't locked. She went inside and shut the door behind her. Peeking around the corner of the short hallway, she could see he was sleeping soundly, one big arm bent over a pillow covering his face.

How she wished she could crawl into bed with him, but that would probably scare the living hell out of him. Instead, she tiptoed over to the armchair in the corner of his room. Folding her feet in front of her, she stared at him, knowing he was warm and solid and everything that was not a satyr.

Kelan stirred. He might have sniffed the air…she wasn't sure, but he called her name, then lifted the pillow from his head. "Fiona?" A quick glance around the room, and he found her.

"I'm sorry," she whispered. "I tried to be quiet."

"Come here."

She didn't wait to be asked twice. She uncurled from her chair and crawled into bed with him. He pulled the blankets up over her, then moved his pillows so that she had what she needed to be comfortable.

"You warm?"

She nodded.

"I'm glad you came in." He rubbed her back.

"How did you know I was here?"

He smiled. "Unless a big pink strawberry sprouted legs and walked into my room, I knew it had to be you."

"My shower gel." She pushed up on her elbow. "Is it too strong?"

"No. Makes me want to eat you, though." He smoothed a bit of her short hair from her face. "Just thinking about it is making me very, very hungry."

She moved to lie on top of him and wrapped her hands around his shoulders. "I wish we'd been together last night."

"I wanted to. I'm trying to give you the room you need to heal." He cupped the back of her skull. "I just don't really know how to do it. I tend to tackle things head-on, but I think you need a softer approach. I was waiting for you to come to me. Like you did tonight."

She pushed up from his chest, still sitting on him, and pulled her tank top over her head. He sucked in a sharp breath as he looked at the skin she bared. He ran his hands up her belly, over her ribs. His hands on her breasts were warm. He flattened his palms and rubbed them over her tight nipples.

He moved his hands down her ribs, to her waist, then her hips, where they stopped at the fabric of her pink flannel pajama bottoms. "Can we get rid of these?"

Lifting up to her knees, she pushed them down her hips, then sat back between his legs to take them all the way off.

Kelan smiled as he sat up, then leaned over her, moving her back against the mattress. He braced himself over her. The soft light touched his face, letting her see the intensity in his dark eyes. She reached up and took hold of his silky hair as it fell forward; it was the only soft thing about him. She tugged it until he was close enough to kiss. And then his lips were against hers. She wrapped her hands around his neck.

He lowered his body over hers, holding some of his weight on his elbows. There was no sadness in his eyes, no hint he knew she was leaving.

This was the Kelan she wanted to remember always.

He touched her face with one of his hands as he kissed her again. His mouth opened. She held her palms against the hard line of his jaw as his tongue entered her mouth. His breath, warm and sweet, mingled with hers.

Her body felt so small under his. She moved her hands to stroke his wide shoulders, the muscles of his back that were so tense. She moved her hand lower, to his hip. He spread his legs, settling himself between hers. He wore a pair of black boxer briefs, and she resented that thin layer of fabric between them. Her hands made the return path up his back, over his shoulders, down his big arms as he kissed her chin, her neck.

He arched his back and kissed lower. Her collarbone. His beard pricked her sensitive skin. When he moved lower still, she almost complained, but his mouth was still on her, his breath still hot as he kissed and licked and nipped her.

His hand cupped a breast, and his mouth covered her nipple. She felt him flick it with his tongue, then roll it between his teeth. Shivers raised gooseflesh all over her body.

She looked at him as she forked her fingers into his dark, silky hair. He lifted his face, meeting her eyes. God, she loved this man. He lowered his head to her body, kissing just below her breast, then moving his mouth down her ribs. When he reached the skin just above her navel, it sort of tickled. She sucked in her breath. He smiled and bit her skin. Her mouth opened, but she couldn't utter an intelligible word, so she clamped down on her lip instead.

He moved lower, swirling his tongue around her belly button. Fiona braced herself on her elbows, fascinated at the feel of his face and lips and tongue as he went down her body. He kissed one hip, then opened his mouth and gently clamped down on her hipbone.

And then he was there. Between her legs. Dear God, the feeling of him spreading her legs, opening her for the stroke of his tongue. Fiona gasped at the soft, wet feel of him licking her.

"Kelan—"

"Mm-hmm?"

"I like that. A lot."

He looked up at her and grinned, his big white teeth glowing in the soft light from the window. "Good. Because I intend to do this a lot."

He eased his arms under her legs. One of his powerful hands rested against the soft flesh of her lower belly while his other reached up and fondled her breast.

Fiona settled back against the bed and gave herself over to the crazy sensations his tongue sent through her body. He mouthed her clit, flicking his tongue back and forth over it. He went lower, penetrating her. His thumb touched her clit. She felt a flood of heat and moisture. Her breathing was coming in ever faster and shallower gasps.

He owned her body. It responded to him as if he was its master, not she. Her legs were draped over his shoulders. She braced her heels against the bed, on either side of his ribs. Heat carried her straight into waves of release so fierce she cried out. His arms tightened on her. He kept his face there, riding her passion, teasing, touching, tasting.

When the storm eased a little, he straightened, pushed his briefs down. His erection was heavy and pointed toward her. She pulled a long, hissed breath. He kicked free of his briefs, holding himself, easing his hand back and forth over the wide crown of his penis.

And then he leaned over her, fitting himself to her. She spread her legs as she felt the tip enter her. Kelan held his weight on one straight arm. His free hand gripped her hip, holding her, positioning her as he eased inside, deeper, deeper.

She was wet, from his mouth, from her orgasm. The deeper he went, the more he stretched her. It was the most amazing sensation, but then, so was everything he did to her. When he was fully inside her, he lowered himself down to her body, then spread his legs and began pumping himself in and out of her.

She lifted her legs, wrapping them around his hips. His body, moving over and in hers, made her feel incredibly alive. No. Not alive. Infinite.

When she started to move against him, meeting his thrusts, he lifted his head and grinned at her. "Come for me, Mahasani. Let me feel you let go."

He moved so that he ground himself against her clit. She couldn't hold back any longer. Her release was violent, endless. She wrapped her arms around his neck as it happened, desperately needing an anchor in a world that had lost all gravity.

He buried his face in her neck as his release took him. He pounded in to her, hard, harder, so deep, then he went still, which sent her off again. It was like she opened her heart to him and let him walk right into her soul. The rawness of it made her cry.

This was what she was going to leave. God, it hurt.

Kelan pushed his hand up into her hair and kissed the side of her. "Aw, honey, are you going to cry every time we make love?"

She sniffled. "I might. I can't seem to help it." She held his face, looking into his eyes, trying to see if he understood. "You touch my soul every time."

He smiled and stroked her chin. "Good. I wouldn't have it any other way."

"I'm glad I didn't meet you when I was younger. The wait for this would have been unbearable."

He nodded. "I would have made us wait, years, if need be."

She smiled at that, but the warmth faded as cold reality intruded. "Hold me tonight."

"I will. Tonight and every night."

CHAPTER TWENTY-SIX

Angel went in search of Rocco, hoping to find him before Kit went looking for him. He'd removed his tracker necklace, leaving it in his room at Blade's. It was not a good time to go incommunicado. If Ryker hadn't seen him going in and out of the old barn at Mandy's, none of them would have found him until he decided to rejoin them.

Mandy's repeat client was in need of a sidewalker. She'd asked Angel to help again—and he was happy to, but it felt as if he was stepping on Rocco's toes. His friend was the one who should be there with his woman, helping her build her career, seeing her growing confidence and sense of self. This first cycle of Mandy's career only came once. And what a thing it was to see the way she helped her clients. Rocco was missing all of it, and Angel had had enough.

Angel climbed the groaning steps of the decrepit barn. The upper hay storage area was still fairly intact. Looked like someone had swept most of the old straw and mouse shit off the edge to the dirt below. There was a floor lamp, a worn ladder-back wooden chair, and a beat-up trunk. That was it. Rocco's hideaway was a Spartan nest.

Rocco himself stood at one of the broken windows under a shallow eave. The hot September wind spilled freely into the dusty timbers.

"This place is a death trap," Angel said, knowing full well that Rocco had heard him come up. Maybe Rocco had a death wish too.

"Go away," Rocco said without looking away from his window.

"What are you doing here?"

"There's nowhere at the house to have any solitude."

Angel clenched his jaw, biting back the anger that flashed to the surface. Rocco wasn't a whole man, in mind or spirit. Anger would mirror anger and serve little purpose in Angel's mission.

"Mandy has a repeat client today. That guy without legs."

Rocco turned halfway from the window. He sighed. "Forget it. I'll leave."

Angel should have let him go. Really, he should have. But the fact that Rocco was living freely, doing whatever the hell he wanted to do—everyone else be damned—stuck in Angel's craw. He reached out and grabbed Rocco's arm. "Not before we do a little talking."

Rocco laughed. "If I wanted to talk, I'd have fucking come to you."

"Yeah? Well, I came to you, so you're gonna hear

me out."

Rocco ripped his arm free.

"You're starting to really piss me off," Angel said.

"Get over it."

"I can't. Not when I see the hell you're putting your woman through."

"That ain't your business."

"It sure as fuck is. She's coming to me for the things you should be doing."

A muscle bunched in Rocco's cheeks. His eyes twitched as they narrowed. "You got a thing for her, don't you?"

"Oh yeah." Angel nodded. "Big time. She's first class, all the way. And I watch you spit on her every single day."

Rocco's eyes narrowed. "The hell I do."

"Every time she laughs, and you don't notice. Every time she reaches for you, but you walk away. Every time she steps forward in her career, and you don't see. In every little way that you can, you spit on her. You're hurting, so you find little ways to make her hurt, too." Angel paused and shoved a hand across his short hair. He lowered his voice, trying to calm things down a notch. "You gotta find a way to get your shit together or you're gonna lose her."

Rocco's nostrils flared. "She's having my baby."

Angel nodded. "Yeah. But any man can raise your kid. That's her choice."

Rocco threw a punch that caught him off guard. Angel ground his teeth. "Wanna do that again?"

"Yeah. I do," Rocco said. Before either of them knew it, they were sparring, moving back and forth across the creaking second floor of the barn.

Rocco realized, while his fist was lifted yet again, Angel had quit fighting a while ago. He pushed himself free and bent over. Jesus. Angel was his friend. He was hurting his friend. He was a sick motherfucker. He forced himself to breathe, though he wished he could just stop.

He felt Angel's hand on his shoulder. "Feel better?"

He lifted his head and met Angel's dark eyes. No. No, he did not. But at least he didn't feel numb—he hurt like the punching bag Angel had used him for.

"Look, I'll take your anger. I'll take your fists and your rage," Angel said, "but give your woman a little love. Please."

Rocco didn't answer. He wiped a dirty wrist across his face, watching as Angel walked away. He listened to the steps creak beneath Angel's weight, waiting to hear his SUV fire up and drive away.

He realized this was what it felt like to live long after life had lost all meaning. It was as if a demon had stepped inside of him in the Hindu Kush and was slowly devouring his soul.

He looked over at the trunk sitting next to the chair. Dragging himself to his feet, he stumbled over to it like an addict to his drug. He turned the skeleton key and stared at the locked box inside. He took a key from his pocket and unlocked that box, too. Inside was an old six-shooter he'd bought from a dealer in Cheyenne. He didn't want Mandy or the guys to know about it.

The relief that washed through him was heady. He lifted it out of the box, felt its weight in his hand. Opening the cylinder, he checked to be sure he hadn't left a bullet in it. It was unloaded. He had to check, because his mind wasn't his ally anymore. He might have brought another bullet out last time he came out. The single bullet was still standing in the box. It was all he would need, when the time came.

He spun the empty cylinder then held the gun in the palm of his hand. All he had to do was load up that bullet, pull the trigger, and kill the demon inside him. He drew a deep breath and leaned back in his chair.

It felt good to have an option. He sat there for a while, enjoying the freedom the cold steel in his hand gave him. After a while, he locked the gun up, then locked up the trunk, and headed back over to Blade's to get back to work.

* * *

Wynn rubbed a towel over Zavi's wet hair. She'd just washed him in the shower in the women's locker room. They'd spent a fun afternoon playing in the pool. The compound here had so much for them to do, it was like living at a sleep-away camp.

She changed Zavi into fresh clothes. "Why don't you shower too?" he asked.

She pulled her white terrycloth robe over her swimsuit. "I'm going to clean up in my room. All my things are there."

"What kind of things?"

"My blow-dryer. My makeup."

"I don't like using the girls' locker room. Why can't I use the boys'?"

"What difference does it make? They're exactly alike. They both have showers and towels." She combed his black hair with her fingers. He was such a pretty little boy. "Besides, this is the one that I use, and I like having you with me."

"How old do I have to be to use the boys' locker room?"

"Oh, I don't know. Seven?"

"Seven!" He fell back against the wall, deflated. "I'll never be that old."

Wynn laughed. "Come on. Let's go back to the house. Kathy said she would have an afternoon snack for us. And then maybe we can go watch Mandy work with her client when he comes out."

She was still smiling as they stepped into the hallway. The big house was a maze of halls and rooms, which she was trying diligently to commit to memory.

A door closed behind them. Wynn turned just enough to see one of the guys step into the hall.

Instantly she felt self-conscious. The unisex, uni-

314

size terry robe she wore wasn't exactly made for a woman of her height and weight. The top hung loose, exposing the cleavage her swimsuit revealed. The sides closed over her hips, but not down her legs. Most of one thigh flashed behind the terrycloth.

Clothed or not, it wasn't nice to pretend that the man behind them wasn't there. Zavi beat her to greeting him, though.

"Hi, Uncle Angel." The little boy stopped walking and faced the big man.

Wynn turned again and smiled, then gasped. The man was fresh from a shower, bleeding from the corner of his lip and his left cheekbone.

"Good heavens. What happened to you?"

"Nothing." He stopped just a few feet from her and Zavi.

Zavi took her hand. "They always look like that. Kathy said she'd have some cookies for us after our swim. And Casey will be home from school soon. Can I go see what kind Kathy made? I want to get one before Casey does."

Wynn tore her eyes from Angel. The man needed to be patched up. Zavi would be fine with Kathy. "Sure. Stay with Kathy. I'll catch up to you when I come in."

She watched Zavi run down the hall that connected the gym building with the rest of the house. She was alone with Angel. Being face to face with him was like staring down a grizzly. He wasn't as hairy, but he sure was intense.

"What happened?" she asked again.

"I was sparring."

"With a Mack truck?"

His lips thinned.

"You could use a couple of stitches."

"You sew?"

Wynn's brows flew up. "Yes, but not humans."

Angel shrugged. "Then leave it."

"No. It's actively bleeding. There's a first-aid kit in the locker room." She took his wrist and started back toward the women's locker room.

He didn't budge. "I'm not going in the girls' locker room."

She released his hand and shook her head. "You and Zavi. There's no one in there. And we won't be long."

"You want to play nurse, do it in the men's room."

"Fine. We'll go to yours." They started in that direction. "And I'm not playing nurse. I'm trying to save your pretty face from some ugly scars."

His demeanor changed. "You think I'm pretty?"

Wynn was surprised by that question. Her gaze swept over the hard lines of his face. He was many things…edgy, determined, fearsome…but pretty was definitely not among them.

"Of course not," she said, smiling. "Pretty men would use the women's locker room."

He laughed then winced.

Wynn was glad he hadn't been mistaken about the room being unoccupied. She had him sit on a bench

316

by the lockers while she accessed the white metal box with a big red cross on it. She retrieved some antiseptic spray, some gauze squares, and a few different bandages, then set them next to him. She washed her hands then straddled the bench.

"Turn so you're facing me," she directed.

He did. His legs were spread open, his knees touching hers. They were big knees, attached to muscular thighs that his cargo pants hugged. Not to mention they were long legs. She thought about trying to adjust her robe to cover more of her own legs, and wished for the millionth time in her life that she were different. Petite. Slim. Pretty. Like most of the other women in the household.

But she wasn't. She was what she was. And right now all that mattered was getting her boss' friend patched up. She sprayed the gauze pad with the antiseptic and dabbed it against his torn lip. She made the mistake of looking up into his eyes as she pressed the pad against his skin. His black eyes had darkened perceptibly. Her lips parted as she pulled a long breath. This wound would be hard to seal, as it opened every time his mouth moved.

"Be still," she admonished.

"I don't want to be still. You have beautiful eyes."

Again she met his look, then blinked and looked down at the pile of medical supplies between their legs. She took a butterfly bandage and taped the wound together.

She repeated the same steps with the cut on his

cheek, moving along quickly so that he wouldn't say anything else embarrassing and get her thinking about things that would never be. She wasn't the kind of woman men looked at lustfully. Maybe someday she would find someone who was a fit for her. Maybe not.

But whoever her man was, he sure wasn't going to be a friend of her employer's, working in a dangerous shadow industry like they did. There was a word for what he was, and it sent chills across her skin.

Mercenary.

* * *

"Blade, what have you been able to find in your mom's papers?" Kit asked as the team reconvened that afternoon. Kelan noticed that Rocco and Angel weren't back yet.

Blade shook his head. "We haven't gone through everything. We're only scratching the surface." He looked at the different piles of items filling the long conference table. "What's here is a hodgepodge of systems and beliefs from ancient secret societies. Don't know yet why they're important. We found a manual of ceremonies and a manifesto for them." He looked around at the team. "Some dark stuff here. Over the decades, they've developed a rich mythology, full of rituals and hierarchies and odd rules. Maybe they've co-opted the ancient societies' practices."

Rocco came in from the stairs. Kelan noticed his knuckles were banged up. He didn't remember those injuries from their fights in the tunnels. He wondered if he'd been pounding one of the punching bags with unprotected fists.

"This"—Blade waved his hand at the stacks of papers as he searched for the right word—"*cabal* is big and well organized. And it's old. Not as old as all the secret societies it's absorbed, but maybe a hundred and fifty or sixty years old. Seems to have started somewhere in the South, after the Civil War, instigated by wealthy Southerners stung by their losses in the war. They connected with disenfranchised aristocrats in the nineteenth century in Europe and powerbrokers in the Middle East in the twentieth century. It's now a global organization."

Kit exchanged a look with Owen.

Rocco joined the discussion. "The cabal's success is based on their shared interest in power—and the fact that they are a secular group. It appears they care nothing for other member's religions, only the resources they each bring to the table. Seems since the beginning, they knew their rise to power would come…in time, once their foundation was fully formed. They've worked assiduously for generations to make that happen. Each generation, and region, has a governor."

"Their reach appears to have its tendrils in every world government," Blade added as he nodded at the stack of papers. "At least, it did twenty-thirty years ago. Some of the ledgers show they absorb funds by any means possible, including sex trafficking; drug and weapons trade; antiquities theft; jewelry heists; blackmail; whatever. Once you're a cog in their wheel, you never get out. They roll over you if you cease to be of use. The structure they've set up lets the higher members of the cabal be exempt from persecution/prosecution. If someone has to take a fall for something the ruling class does, that fall guy can be found or bought."

Rocco's face tightened. "The journals seem to indicate that they foment war and disease. Their goal is to reduce world population to less than half a billion people."

Kit took a long minute to absorb their analysis. He looked at Owen. "The Armageddon Lion's been telling us about."

Owen nodded, then started a slow prowl around the conference table. "What are the regions you mentioned?"

Blade called out the list. "Region 1: North America; Region 2: Western Europe; Region 3: Pacific Union; Region 4: Latin America; Region 5: Eastern Europe; Region 6: Western Asia; Region 7: Eastern Asia; Region 8: Southern Asia; Region 9: Middle East; Region 10: Africa. They loosely correspond to focus areas identified by the United Nations, except these were compiled in an Omni World Order manifesto decades earlier."

"Each region has a governor," Rocco said.

"Where does King come into play?" Val asked.

Blade shook his head. "Don't know yet. But this stuff is full of hyped-up names that sound like they came straight from some massively multiplayer online role-playing game world."

"It's true," Rocco said. "The mythology they've constructed around their organization reads like a script for a game. The king's virgin daughter is supposed to marry a warrior who will be the king's hammer, forcing all the regions under the rule of one emperor."

"Maybe Bladen was scripting a game," Owen mused.

"Except that's what really happened with Fiona," Kelan reminded them. "It wasn't a game."

Rocco shook his head. "It does seem like a game, but there are real names here—many of them correspond to the names in the separate ledger that Bladen kept."

Blade looked at one of the ledgers. "One of the ledgers lists names of people, their country, region, crimes, and punishments. Bladen's list is a subset of them. Why or how he picked the subset that he did, we don't yet know. Perhaps he pulled out the pedophiles. Greer was able to identify payments Bladen was receiving from his subset, so maybe he was skimming off the top of this Omni organization, which might have been why one of his own men killed him."

"Lobo intercepted several key foreign nationals

from some of those regions you mentioned," Owen said. "We're trying to unravel how they're connected to this cabal. Not having much success—they've invoked diplomatic immunity or lawyered up."

"Get us their names so we can cross-reference them against these ledgers," Rocco said. "We still have a ton of records to get through. We're a long way from finished with our analysis. And we haven't even tackled the encrypted documents yet."

CHAPTER TWENTY-SEVEN

Fiona parked next to Rocco's just outside the old barn at Mandy's place. Hopefully, he'd heard her car, but just in case, she called out, "Rocco!" as she entered the dark, old barn. He didn't answer. "Hey, Rocco!" Still not a peep. Maybe he was somewhere else on Mandy's ranch?

She found stairs at the back of the barn, and started up them. One of the treads was missing. She climbed over it. The upper platform of the barn was not what she was expecting. It was wide open and empty, except for a few pieces of furniture.

Rocco was standing by an open dormer window. "Something I can do for you, Fiona?"

It was peaceful here; she could see why he came here for an escape. Maybe she needed to find herself a spot like this at Ty's. But, of course, she wasn't going to be staying long, so it probably didn't matter.

"I was wondering if we could talk."

"About what?"

She looked at him. "Darkness."

He turned from the window and looked at her. "I

don't want to talk about darkness with you. You shouldn't even see the darkness."

"I didn't until King took me. He had both my mom and stepdad killed. He kidnapped Lion—my brother—and still holds him somewhere. He killed a friend of mine the same week he killed my mom. He tried to have me raped. The more his noose closes around me, I see less and less of the light."

Rocco frowned. "Yeah. I guess fate fucked you over too."

"Kelan says fate's the life plan we write for ourselves before we come alive."

Rocco gave her a small smile and shook his head. "Kelan sees things in a different way. I don't know that he's right."

Fiona drew a long breath. "I wouldn't have written losing my mom the way she went. I wouldn't have wanted Lion kidnapped. I wouldn't have had my friend murdered. And I sure as hell wouldn't have picked King for my father." She took a step closer. "I don't want to live in this dark place. I want to go back to the sunshine, which I still believed in, until a few days ago."

Rocco nodded. "At least you can still remember the sunshine."

Fiona blinked at her sudden tears. "How do we get out of this, Rocco?"

He sent a look over her shoulder to the trunk. She looked where he was looking, but saw only the piece of furniture. "They say it's a choice."

"What is?" she asked.

"All of it. What we choose to see. What we choose to feel. Life, even."

"Will it pass on its own?"

Rocco's face tightened. His nostrils flared. "You ask me like I know the answer."

"You've been in this place longer than I have."

"It hasn't passed yet."

"Do you want it to?"

He stared at her, as if shocked at her question, then looked out the open window. "Maybe not."

She went to stand beside him and look out at the sunny September afternoon. "Is it guilt, then, that holds us here?"

He frowned. "What are you guilty of?"

"Being King's daughter."

"Lion's King's kid, too. Do you blame him for his parentage?"

"No."

"Then why blame yourself?"

"If I weren't here, if I went away, Kelan wouldn't be in danger from King anymore."

"Yes, he would. You've seen the ink on his arm, right?" She nodded. "Well, he would bring war to King, the likes of which have never been seen in this world if he lost you because of that bastard."

Fiona sighed. Maybe it was a choice. Maybe that was the secret cure. "I choose sunshine, Rocco." She said it, but she didn't feel it.

"Just like that?"

She nodded.

"Well, then. Good. Get out while you can."

"I choose sunshine for you, too."

"Don't work like that, kiddo."

"Maybe it does." Maybe she could will it to be so. She'd have to once she left Kelan.

* * *

Val leaned against the driver's door of his SUV while he waited for Ace. It was ten after one. He wondered if she was going to stand him up.

No sooner had he had that thought than her old beater pulled into the small parking lot of the trail.

Ace got out of her car, wearing the diner's apron. "I'm glad you're still here. We got slammed just as my shift was ending." She untied her apron and tossed it in the back of her car. Val took in her garb. It wasn't what he would have selected, but it worked on her. Her platform black-buckle knee-high boots looked like some futuristic girl vamp warrior gear.

Made him wonder how kinky she liked to get in the sack.

And that gave him an instant hard-on.

He grinned at her, then tried not to, which made his grin bigger. "Hi," was all he could manage. Of all the girls in the world, why did he get tongue-tied with this one?

She leaned over and braced a foot on the floor of her car so she could unbuckle her boot. Her hips had a gentle curve to them that her low-rise jeans emphasized. Especially with her butt sticking out toward him like that. Her shirt hiked up, revealing a thin strip of ink on her back, but he couldn't make out the pattern. God, he wanted to lift her shirt and have a good look at the art she'd covered herself with.

When she got her boots off, she sat on the driver's seat and started lacing up a pair of regular hiking boots. Far less exotic. Val missed the vamp boots.

"I've been looking forward to this hike for a week. It's why I only worked a half shift today. I saw some pics of the trail on the internet." She put her feet down and looked up at him.

For a second, he saw her kneeling in front of him, ready to take orders. *Sonofabitch.* It was going to be a whole lot of no fun climbing a mountain with a hard-on, but his had been persistent since she got out of her car, so he was just going to have to deal with it.

She tied a light jacket around her waist, grabbed a water bottle and a big camera, then locked her car. "Ready?" She smiled at him, flashing those sharp canines at him.

"Oh, yeah."

She held her camera up and snapped a pic of his face as they walked toward the trailhead. He smiled at her, and she snapped that pic too. Lowering the camera, she caught an image of his boots.

"Can you hike in those things?" she asked.

"I got around the Hindu Kush just fine in them."

"You fought in the war?"

"I did."

"What branch?"

She took a pic as he said, "Army."

"What was your MOS?"

It surprised him that she knew to ask what his specialty was using that term. Most civilians just asked what he did in the war. "Sniper."

They walked a few steps in silence. She seemed pensive now. Gone was her light mood. She was as changeable as a spring storm—and as beautiful to watch.

The path was wide and covered in gravel, making the hike an easy one. She caught a pic of the trailhead sign, then turned to look at him. "Are you a good guy, Val?"

He stopped walking. "I guess that depends on who you ask."

"I'm asking you."

"I try to be."

She watched him a long minute, then looked away and snapped a few more pics as they started up the trail. "There's a waterfall halfway up." That thought seemed to cheer her up.

About three miles up, after climbing over fallen logs and following the trail deep into a forest of ponderosa pines and aspen, they found the waterfall. It wasn't huge, but it was tall enough that the sound of roaring water eclipsed that of the aspen clattering in the breeze.

Ace snapped a dozen pictures, getting different

angles on the light, with him and without him. He took out his phone and grabbed a pic of her. The green of the forest and the late afternoon sun hitting the water made the glen seem magical. He could have sworn he saw a glow coming off her.

She set her camera down and sat on a rock to unlace her boots. In almost no time, she'd shucked her jeans, jacket, and tee, leaving her wearing only a pink and black eyelet bra and panty set. And Jesus Christ, how she filled out that bra.

He looked around to see if anyone else was near, but of course there wasn't. It was midweek on a school day. They had the trail to themselves.

She took his hand. An electrical current whispered like a breath up his arms and across his neck. "Come in with me."

"I can't."

"Of course you can."

He shook his head. "I'm carrying. Guns and water aren't friends."

She laughed. "Guns plural?"

He locked his mouth in a thin line and glared at her. She turned away and went for her camera. The panties she wore were high cut, baring the most enticing half-moons of her ass cheeks. She brought the camera over to him.

"Will you take a picture of me in the water?"

"I'm not a photographer."

"It's just like staring down a scope. Just point and shoot." She showed him the button. "Use this one."

Look at the camera, not her chest, asshole, he told himself. It was a hard argument to make when her breasts rose in generous mounds above their cups. She reached behind herself and unfastened the hooks of her bra. He focused on the camera's details so he wouldn't think about the girl.

He caught just a glimpse of her breasts before she turned, presenting him with her graceful back...and the most stunning body art he'd ever seen. Some incredible artist had etched a butterfly that covered her entire back. The bottom of the wings stroked her hips, and the upper tips of the wings hugged her shoulders.

Val went cold. Fucking ice cold.

"Why a butterfly, Ace?"

She arched her back and looked over her shoulder at him. "Do you like it? I just had it done recently."

"It's beautiful. But why a butterfly?" God, was she the one Jafaar had said he was sending to infiltrate the team?

"They are fragile and mystical and change the world with their paper-thin wings. They represent rebirth, transformation. They're powerful beings."

He lifted her camera shot a few images, then took some with his phone. Holy fuck. He hoped he wasn't going to have to pick between her and his team, because there was no choice to make. He never wanted to see her beautiful butterfly ruined by a bullet, but his team would always come first.

* * *

Kelan spent the evening in the bunker, working with Rocco on the cryptic documents from Bladen's library. Rocco quit about a half-hour ahead of him. When Kelan couldn't make sense of what he was reading anymore, he decided to call it a day. He had reached a collection of documents that talked about a War Bringer, but in these documents, the War Bringer was an enemy of the Omni World Order. This War Bringer was no unifier; he was a destroyer. The legends Kelan was reading pegged this guy as someone the Omnis feared and were ever on the lookout for.

"You're the War Bringer...the true one," the old man from the tunnel had said. Was he referring to this legend?

Kelan leaned back in his chair and rubbed his thumb and forefinger over the bridge of his nose. Nothing with this group made sense. Nothing the Omnis did was straightforward. Nothing meant what it meant.

He stood up and stretched. Tomorrow, he'd write up an analysis of the papers he read today. He checked his watch. It was almost midnight. Fiona was hopefully sound asleep. If she wasn't in his room, he'd join her in hers.

Max came out of the ops room, catching Kelan before he left. "Hey, bro."

"Night, Max."

Max shook his head. He looked troubled. Kelan frowned. "What is it?"

"Fiona bought a car online earlier today. A real piece of shit. Why would she do that when you just gave her the Acadia?" He lifted his shoulders. "I just got that alert…and the one that said she emptied out her bank account at an ATM in town."

"Fuck. Where is she now? She here?"

"Yeah. Her room, I think. I know she came back from town, but I don't know if she's being good about keeping her tracker on."

Kelan took the stairs to the den three at a time. He felt a wash of rage, such a foreign emotion to him. Even fighting an enemy never summoned anger. Lethal intent, yes. Rage, never.

His chest was expanding and contracting in rapid waves as he walked down the hallway to the living room stairs. He looked across Blade's stately living room and had the insane urge to tear it apart. He fisted his hands into tight balls and went up the stairs to the bridge.

Outside her room, he paused. Blood was pounding in his head. He was deaf to any sound and not certain he could even form words in his current state. Instead of making matters worse by confronting her now, he decided to wait and cool down a bit. He pivoted on his heel and went to his room, right next to hers.

God. Damn. He wanted to break something. He paced the length of his room. Spreading his fingers out wide, he focused on his breathing. Anything he broke out of sheer rage would never be whole again. Only he could dissipate his anger, and he had to do it before he saw her again. He forced his breathing to slow until his blood wasn't drumming in his ears anymore; it had returned to the source of his emotional explosion—his heart.

He ripped his tee over his head and rubbed his chest with the heel of his hand. It wasn't anger he'd been feeling, he realized, but fear, fear of a life without Fiona.

He heard her door close. He stepped into the hall. She was hurrying toward the stairs with her overnight bag and purse. He took the stairs two and three at a time, catching up with her between the living room and the wine cellar. He caught her arm and spun her around.

She was crying. She dropped her overnight bag. "Let me go, Kelan."

"I can't."

"You have to."

He released her and straightened. "Don't do this, Fiona." He rubbed his chest again. *Goddamn*, it hurt.

Fiona wiped her tears and resumed her trek toward the garage. Kelan heard the screams his soul made. None of them hit the air. She took the keys to her Acadia out of the basket, then walked into the garage. The lights popped on. He followed her.

* * *

Fiona opened her door and tossed her purse inside, then realized she'd left her overnight bag in the hallway. God, this would have been so much easier if Kelan had just let her go.

She turned to say a last goodbye. He was right there. He bent down and took a knife out of his ankle sheath. Her eyes widened. What was he going to do with that?

He held the tip of the wickedly sharp KA-BAR to his chest. "Don't leave me on the wayside of your life, struck but too crippled to get out of the road." He spoke through clenched teeth. "Show me mercy, Fiona. Kill me outright." The tip of his knife cut his skin.

"Kelan, stop!" She pulled at his hand, but her strength was no match for his, and wrestling for the knife widened the cut. She cried as she set her hands on either side of it, flattening them against his bare skin.

"Dig my heart out of my chest and take it with you, where it belongs. Because without you, I won't need it."

"Kelan—"

"Do it, Fiona. Or don't fucking go."

She quit struggling with him as a sob broke from her, which she tried to stop, but that first one was the start of an endless string of them. She leaned forward to kiss the small incision Kelan had made, relieved he'd lowered his knife. Her tears mingled with his blood.

His fingers dug into her hair and fisted it, lifting her head as his mouth smashed against hers. She didn't know if the blood she tasted was his or hers. At least he wasn't trying to stab himself any longer. She wrapped her arms around his neck and lifted herself into their kiss, opening for him, trying to let him see how deeply she loved him.

He slammed his fist on the hood of her SUV, releasing the knife, freeing his hand to hold her against him, to stroke her back, to cup her ass. The kiss ended and started again, in a sloppy, vicious twist of lips and tongues and teeth. The deeper the kiss, the more they both hungered.

He moved her just enough so that he could open the door to the back seat. Bracing his foot on the edge of the car, he lifted her up, over his knee, onto his thigh. Bending her backward, he kissed her chin, her throat, nuzzled the space between her breasts through her T-shirt.

Fiona arched her back, rolling forward on Kelan's hard thigh. The pressure against her clit sent waves of heat through her body. She whimpered. He gripped her hips, kissing her as he rocked her forward and back, grinding her core against his thigh.

Something broke free inside of her. She clamped her thighs around his big leg and gave herself over to the sensations rolling through her. When they eased somewhat, Kelan ordered in a gruff voice, "Put your legs around me."

She did as asked. He leaned into her SUV, one

knee on the seat as he brought her inside, setting her on the bench seat. She barely noticed the curves of the seat against her side. She just wanted Kelan in there with her.

Kelan unfastened her jeans and pulled them and her panties down to her ankles. He opened his zipper, then settled between her legs. Fee urgently wanted him inside her. She watched as he positioned himself, and then he entered her, filling her, stretching her.

Completing her.

Like this, they were one.

She reached for his face, holding him to her as she kissed him. Tears still spilled down her cheeks as she opened herself to all the sensations pummeling her— his dark, wounded eyes, the desperation in the way he took her, his hands so gentle on her.

Bracing her heels on the bench seat, she pushed up, meeting his thrusts. He held her hips, angling her a little differently. He pushed her shirt up, pulled her bra up over her breasts, then mouthed her hardened nipple. Heat speared her core. She cried out, feeling the beginning waves that would take her to her release. His thumb lightly brushed her clit, sending her headlong over the edge. She wrapped her arms around his waist and thrust against his body, spurring him to longer strokes that only deepened her passion. He was not far behind her. She felt his hot release shoot into her body, and took everything he gave her.

For a long moment afterward, neither of them moved nor spoke. They were both breathing hard.

Kelan stared into her eyes as he stroked her face. He withdrew, then pulled back and got out of the car to straighten himself. She did the same.

She took the hand he held out and let him help her from the car. He sheathed his knife, shut the door, then picked her up and carried her back into the house.

"When you can cut the heart out of my chest, then you can go." He bent when they reached the place where she'd dropped her bag and picked it up. "I have no doubt, none at all, that you're strong enough to do it. So until then, you stay with me. We'll spend every moment that we have left together."

Fiona felt herself crying again. She reached up and wrapped her arms around his neck. "I don't want to go."

"I don't want you to go."

* * *

"Max. The garage went dark. What the fuck's going on?" Kit barked into his comm unit.

"Um. K and Fiona are having...words."

"Oh. They okay?"

"Don't know, and I'm not about to interrupt them to ask. They'll either bring themselves inside, or we'll go clean up the blood after a while."

"Shit."

"S'all cool, boss. I'll get you if you're needed."

"Right. Copy that. Night, Max."

CHAPTER TWENTY-EIGHT

Kelan carried her to his room and kicked the door shut behind them. Like all the rooms in Ty's house, this one was furnished in typical western ranch decor, with rough aspen log furniture and deep greens, blues, and burgundy textiles. His room had a California king bed and the standard furniture—dresser, side chairs, small table, nightstands—that all the other bedrooms had. He'd simplified his room's decor by getting rid of the knickknacks. Still, it was a far cry from the streamlined simplicity of their condo in Fort Collins.

He set her on her feet by the edge of his bed, then put her bag down.

"I left my purse in the car," she said.

He stood before her, a great wall of a man. Uncompromising. Certain of himself and the world and their future.

"We'll get it tomorrow."

He moved into her space as he peeled off her jacket. She sat on the mattress. He put a knee down beside her. She scrambled backward, making room for him even as he crawled over her. His hair fell forward in a dark fringe.

There were no lights on in his room, but the blinds weren't drawn. Muted light from outside filtered in around them, giving his eyes an unholy glow.

His anger had not yet abated.

She moved farther onto the bed as he crouched over her. She ran her hands up his arms, over his corded muscles. He took her hands and lifted them above her head, then kissed the soft inside skin of her upper arm. He hadn't shaved since the morning—she loved the scrape of his face. She squirmed, but his one-handed grip was relentless.

He kissed his way across her almost bare shoulder to her throat. He drew a deep breath of her skin, then brushed his lips against her neck.

"Kelan—" she started. They needed to talk.

"Not yet." His warm mouth moved over her larynx, then down the center of her chest.

"Let me hold you."

"No," he whispered. She felt his hot breath on the inside curve of her breast. His free hand lifted the bottom of her tank top, baring her belly for his enjoyment. He nibbled at the curve of her ribs, the soft bend of her waist.

He straightened, getting off the bed. His dark eyes held hers as he set his foot on the bed. He removed his ankle sheath, putting his KA-BAR on his nightstand.

"Take off my boot."

She sat up and unlaced it, then pulled it off him.

His sock quickly followed. He set his other foot on the bed and had her remove that boot and sock, too. He lifted her leg and untied her sneaker, dropping it and her sock on the floor. He bared her other foot, then leaned forward. Taking hold of her tee, he pulled it over her head. He reached behind her and unfastened her bra. He pushed her shoulder back against the bed, straightening her so he could unfasten her jeans and drag them and her panties off.

He kissed her as he pulled her closer to the edge of the bed. Then he knelt between her legs to help himself to her sweet flesh. He slipped a finger inside her, just one finger, then added a second. She could feel how slick she was. She sat up and started to touch herself, but he moved her hand away and put his mouth where her fingers had been, while his slipped in and out of her.

Her hips thrust against his hand of their own accord. She was breathing in short huffs. Her body tensed...waiting...waiting. His fingers went still. He looked up at her. She blinked, her body easing back from the edge.

"Say you're not leaving."

"No."

"Fiona. Say it."

"I can't."

He withdrew from her. He went into the closet. She heard him open his safe, then heard the sound of something heavy being set in there before he locked it again.

He picked up his knife from his nightstand, then knelt by her feet again. She watched him warily as he fastened his KA-BAR sheath to her ankle.

"You have the tool you need so that you can do what you have to when you leave."

"Kelan—" She sighed and bent down to remove it.

"Leave it."

"I'm not going to hurt you."

"So you're not leaving."

She didn't answer that. His lips thinned. Even in the dim light, she could tell the tension about him deepened.

He lifted the corner of his blankets. "Get in."

She stood. His knife sheath was heavy, the leather hard. It felt like an ankle monitor. She slipped under his arm and scooted across the bed. Bending her knee, she tried to unbuckle the thing before he got in bed.

"Leave it," he ordered.

He rolled her over onto her belly. Catching her hands in one of his, he kneed her legs apart. His hand stroked her back. It was big and warm, and his light touch sent shivers through her.

He kissed her at the base of her neck. His mouth moved over her shoulder, then her spine, which he followed all the way down to her ass. He bit one cheek.

She gasped.

He moved his hand between her legs and slipped

two fingers in to her. It felt intoxicating to surrender so completely to him. She felt safe…and manipulated when he withdrew his fingers.

She pushed up to her knees. "Kelan Shiozski— don't you dare use sex to control me."

He was sucking her juices from his fingers. "Don't leave me."

"King will not stop."

"Neither will I." He put his finger in her mouth. "Taste yourself." He smiled and licked his lips. "You're like strawberries and cream. Just like I knew you would be."

She touched her tongue to his finger, tasting something sweet and tangy. She couldn't take much more. She pulled free of his hold, then straddled his thighs. Glaring at him, she unfastened his jeans.

The moon had shifted outside, throwing more light into the room. He was watching her. She stroked the wide ridge of him through his boxers. His cock tensed and jumped at her touch. She smiled at him as she pulled his briefs down, freeing him. "Two can play that game."

He arched his back and pushed his jeans and briefs down to his thighs, giving her full access to him. "Do your worst."

She caught him in both hands, then leaned down and kissed him, belatedly realizing she really didn't know what to do with him. He seemed to like the kiss, so she did that some more, up and down the length of him.

"Lick me."

She resettled herself lower between his legs so that she could get a better angle on him, and then did what he suggested, running her tongue up the hard length of him. His lips pulled back from his teeth as he hissed a breath.

She did it again, then wrapped her lips about him sideways and moved up and back. He took hold of himself and pushed his cock toward her mouth. "Take me in your mouth."

She moved up to kneel over him, then lowered her head, taking him in her mouth, flicking her tongue over him as if she was Frenching his mouth. She wrapped a hand around the base of him—he was too long and too wide to fit all of him in her mouth, so she focused her efforts on the swollen crown.

Kelan took as much of her virginal caresses as he could. He pulled her off him before it was too late. Coming in her mouth was a lesson for another day. Just the thought of that almost sent him over the edge.

He sat up fast, then lifted and turned her. She was still on her knees. He bent over her and entered her without prelude. She was wet and ready for him. He leaned over her, bracing his arms on either side of hers, pumping into her like a boy who had no control.

Because he didn't. He'd almost lost her tonight. Again.

He kissed her shoulder blade, buried his face in

her spine. And then he reached for her breasts, feeling them move with each thrust. As soon as he palmed one, she cried out, and her body banged against his.

He could feel her orgasm overtake her, the tremors, the squeezing of her inner muscles. He pushed up against her and slammed into her, then groaned as his own orgasm hit.

When it was over, he eased himself from her body then kicked off his jeans. He moved the covers and brought her back up to the top of the bed, settling her against him as he waited for her tears.

He was coming to love that emotional side of her. Maybe it was just arrogance that he was pleased he pleasured her to tears each time.

"I love you." He could feel how tightly she was wound. "Talk to me, Fiona. We are two parts of one whole. If you break, I break."

"Kelan." She wrapped her arms around his neck and pressed her face to his throat. "I never want to see you hurt."

He chuckled. "Says the woman who is going to cut my heart out of my chest while it still beats."

"You know I'm not going to do that."

"Then I'll never be hurt, because I'll never be without you."

"No, you'll be hurt because you're with me."

He caught her knee, then pulled her leg up so that he could take off the knife. "Let's get some sleep. We'll talk about it more in the morning."

* * *

Angel was in bed, trying to sleep, when there was a knock on his door. He checked the clock—it was late for any fun and games.

He threw the covers off and went to see whom it was. Rocco stood at his threshold. His hands were in his front pockets up to his thumbs. His shoulders were hunched. His eyes looked wrecked. *Goddamn.* Angel didn't ask any questions. He just went back into his room, pulled on a pair of jeans, then followed his friend down to the gym.

* * *

Val knocked on Owen's door. A thin line of light showed beneath it, so he knew his cousin was still up.

"Come." Owen's call was muffled through the door.

He was lying on his bed, watching some rerun on TV. Val plopped down next to him. Val took the controller and changed the channel.

Owen looked over at him, a slight grin on his face. "Have a bad dream?"

Val shrugged. "Maybe."

Owen took the controller back and returned to the channel he'd been watching. "You did good with Fiona's hair." He grinned. "I'll admit I was afraid you might start moonlighting there when you took her."

His grin became a smile. "We're too heavily invested in Blade's place to get run out of town now."

"Yeah, I wasn't run out of town back then."

"You sure as hell were. How do you think you got into West Point so easily?"

"You pulled strings to get me in."

"I had no leverage. Your dad did that."

"I thought you did."

Owen shrugged. "I got him to work it from his end with his connections. I wanted you away from him, before one or both of you ended up dead. You set some sniper records at West Point that still stand today."

Val grinned. "I think dad almost had an apoplexy when he heard I applied for an MOS of Barber."

Owen laughed. "There was no way the Army was going to let a sniper of your caliber cut hair."

"I knew that. And Dad should've known that too. He just never gave me much credit for anything."

"Maybe he would have if you hadn't tortured him so much."

"Maybe I wouldn't have tortured him so much if he'd ever tried to just accept me as I am."

Owen turned to look at him. "And maybe you've got to do that for yourself first before expecting him to. If you quit giving a shit what he thought, he'd figure you're ready to stand on your own."

Val shrugged. "Whatevs. I'm over it. The way I see it, the old man got the son he wanted, so it's all good." He looked at Owen. "I've been wondering something lately. You think our dads were involved in this Omni World Order shit?"

Owen hit mute and stared at Val. "Where the hell did that come from?"

"We know from Blade's mom that it was in full swing at least a generation before all of us. The progress Rocco's making with those docs she hid indicates it was well underway long before that, even. I'm just trying to make the pieces fit the puzzle."

Owen's face was like stone.

"Max was created for the Red Team—set up in a sting, then raised to be a warrior in prison. How do you get into the Army with a record like his...unless he was created by the Army? I don't see a connection with Selena or Angel, but Kit was Blade's handler before either of them even knew what a handler was. And Rocco—he was just a windfall. Best to grab him and use his skills than to let them fall to the enemy. But look at how Greer's grandfather trained him. He was taking out enemies long before his kills were sanctioned."

Val watched Owen, wanting to catch his carefully managed expression when he said this next bit. "And weren't Greer's grandpa and your dad instrumental in getting the Red Team started?"

"How did you know about Greer's grandfather?"

"Greer and Blade have been doing some digging."

"And they didn't bring it to the team?"

"It's only a fragment of info, which doesn't seem to be news to you." He held Owen's gaze. "Tell me

I'm wrong."

"You aren't wrong, but I don't know what any of it means. Yet. It's why I got out of the Army. I don't like dancing at the end of strings someone else is pulling."

"And you didn't think to fill us all in?"

"On what? A conspiracy theory I have about"—he made air quotes—"anarchists united who want to rule the world? Who the fuck would believe that?"

"Well, obviously your dad and Greer's grandpa did, else they wouldn't have started the Red Team. And they got buy-in from somewhere in the government, or the Red Team would have been a no-go."

Val went silent a minute as he processed the impact of that. He got up and started walking around Owen's room. "So what's the real nature of your relationship with the rogue Red Teamer you've been wanting us to find—Wendell Jacobs?"

"Our fathers were friends. His dad was—"

"U.S. Senator Dean Jacobs from Virginia, founder of the Red Team unit," Val finished for him. "Shit, O. You seriously didn't think we'd figure this out?"

"I knew you would. But I didn't want my theories to steer you. I want you to prove my suspicions wrong...or right. I don't want to influence you."

Val looked back at Owen. "Did you know, when you started Tremaine Industries, about the Omni World Order?"

"Yes."

"Did you know when you and Wendell joined the Red Team?"

"Yes." Owen stood. "I knew when we were boys. I knew the Order killed my dad."

"And you didn't tell me then?"

The stillness in Owen's face cut like a knife. "You were four years younger than me. You weren't afraid of anything. You were so busy being your sisters' darling little brother and the bane of your father's existence. Life was a game to you, a thing full of joy, a thing to laugh at. How could I tell you there were monsters out there? Monsters who'd killed my dad and might very well be after me?"

Owen blinked away the anger in his eyes. "I needed you to be normal. I needed you to be exactly like you were because it meant not everything was tainted. And yeah, I made sure you got into West Point, and I brought you into the Red Team." He walked over until he was almost nose to nose with Val. "I did it because in every sense that matters, you are my brother, and I couldn't stand losing you, too."

Val's jaw worked as he fought to calm his breathing. "Maybe you haven't worked this out yet, in your fear-frozen brain, but you've got a whole bunch of brothers now. And a sister. Don't blindfold them. Bring this to them. We all know the origins of the Red Team, but I doubt any of us have put together Wendell and his father the senator. Greer knows about his grandfather, but maybe not about your and Wendell's dads. We've all seen the banners and the extensive infrastructure the Omni World Order is building. Right about now, your conspiracy theory isn't sounding like random shit you made up."

Owen glared at him. "I'll bring it to the team when the time is right."

Val shook his head. "Fuck you." He pivoted on his heel and slammed out of Owen's room.

* * *

Val needed to work off some steam. He was halfway to the gym building before he realized that he'd gone to Owen's room to tell him about Ace's butterfly tattoo, which he still hadn't done.

He shoved through the doors to the weight room, then stopped short. Rocco and Angel were sparring, but it wasn't a friendly match. They hadn't even heard him come in, so intent were they on killing each other.

"What the hell, you guys?" He went to break them apart, which was easier said than done. When he finally separated them, he held a shoulder of each. "Wanna tell me what the fuck's going on?"

Both men continued to glare at each other. Val now knew the bruises he'd seen on them weren't left over from King's Warren. "Shake it off. We're on the same team, remember?"

Angel stepped back first. His bare back was a mass of knotted muscles. They wore boxing gloves, but no helmets or teeth guards. It was like they had a death wish. Val looked at Rocco. Maybe one of them really did.

"Fine." Val straightened. "You guys need to cool off. Let's go to Winchesters. We can talk things out over a couple of beers."

"We're good," Rocco said. "I'm gonna take a shower, then hit the sack."

Angel wiped a thin stream of blood from his nose with the back of his wrist. "I'll meet you upstairs in ten," he growled.

* * *

There wasn't a night that Winchesters wasn't busy. Tuesday night was no exception, but Val and Angel managed to find an empty table. They sprawled across the booth benches. When the waitress came, they put in their orders for beers. The dance floor was throbbing with the bass of country music and boots on wood floors. Val sent a look around the room.

There was a woman sitting at the bar. He recognized her slim shoulders and narrow waist, not to mention the purple, spiky hair. A man was sitting next to her at the bar. Val couldn't tell if they were together. He discovered his answer when Ace's posture changed to create more separation between her and the idiot next to her.

Angel turned to see what Val was watching. "That Ace?"

"Yep." Val was getting increasingly ticked off that

the guy couldn't take a cue. When he leaned over too closely to Ace, Val caught the quick movement she did with her foot that destabilized the stool he sat on, tossing him to the ground. Ace banged her beer bottle on the bar top then got up and walked out.

And damn if the bastard didn't follow her.

"I'll be right back," Val told Angel.

Angel leaned back in his seat. "You good? 'Cause I think I've had enough fighting tonight." He grinned at Val.

"Yeah, I got it."

"If you're not back in five, I'll come save your ass."

"Thanks. For nothing."

Val trailed the guy outside. He was lit up like a beer fountain. He was searching in his pocket for the key to his truck, leaning heavily against his driver's-side door while he did it. When he fished the keys out, Val swiped them from him.

"What 'er you doing, man? Those are mine."

"So they are. This your truck?" Val asked.

"Yeah. Gimme 'em. I got to follow that chick."

"No, you don't." Val pushed the guy's head against the side of his truck.

"Ouch! That hurt!" he complained.

"Whoa. Be careful where you step."

"I didn't do that, you did."

Val unlocked his door and opened it, managing to clip the guy in the nose.

Ace was watching them. "Do you have a crazy

need to ride a white horse or something?" she called from a couple of cars over.

Val grinned, thinking that was not what he wanted to ride.

A couple other guys came out of the bar—friends of the drunk who was now holding his face. Val tossed them his keys. "Glad he has friends here. Save him from rounding up a ride home. He's not too stable on his feet. Don't let him get behind that wheel."

"We got him."

Val walked over to Ace's beater, watching the guys out of the corner of his eye. They loaded their drunken friend into one of their cars and headed out.

"You think I couldn't have dealt with that shitpouch by myself?"

"Sure you could have. But what kind of a friend would I be if I saw trouble coming your way and did nothing about it?" He opened her door for her. "You got my number, right?" She nodded. "Call it if you need it."

He watched her drive off, then went back inside. Angel had just rebuffed a couple of women, if he were to judge from the disappointed looks on their faces as they turned away from the table.

Val slipped into the booth. Coming here hadn't really improved his mood. It didn't look like it had done anything for Angel's either. He nodded toward the women. "Didn't feel like company?"

"No."

Val made a circle around his face as he looked at Angel. "Maybe they dig all the bruises."

Angel shrugged.

"You got a beef with Rocco?"

"No."

"Hmm. That wasn't a regular sparring match I interrupted."

"Drop it, Val."

Val leaned against the seat back. "Fine. We'll just sit here and be miserable. Alone."

Angel nodded toward the girls. "Want me go get them for you?"

Val considered that and laughed. For a long time, it had been him getting the girls for Angel. A pair of lichen-green eyes flashed in his mind. There really was only one girl he wanted right then. And she had an agenda he couldn't quite figure out...that probably didn't include him.

"Nah. I'm good with the beer."

CHAPTER TWENTY-NINE

Kelan stepped into Fiona's room. They'd spent the whole night together. Though short, it was the most satisfying night of his life. Fiona had come back to her room to shower and dress this morning.

It was too early yet for breakfast, but he wanted to check on her state of mind. She'd left his ankle sheath on his nightstand. If she was at all waffly about staying, he was going to make her wear it.

He leaned on her dresser, waiting for her to come out of her closet. When she did, she was adjusting the two layers of tank tops she wore, one pink, one white. Over both of them, she wore a flower-print sweatshirt that was cut off at her midriff. Her tight blue jeans showed her skinny legs. Peach flip-flops were her sandals.

She lifted her head and looked at him. He could see the shadows were back in her eyes. He sighed, trying to figure out what to do about her persistent belief that her leaving would protect them all.

Like any of them needed an itty-bitty thing like her to stand between them and their enemies.

They could have another round of amazing sex to try and settle the matter…but maybe what she needed most was to hear it from the fighters who would put their lives in danger to retrieve her if she left.

She didn't say anything, so he broke the silence. "Can we sell the car you bought yesterday?"

Her jaw opened. "You know about that?"

"Yeah, and the bank account you cleaned out."

"Kelan—"

"If we knew about it, you don't think our enemies do too? We know they're watching you." He went to her door and held it for her. "Let's take a walk."

"Where?"

"Down to the bunker. I told you about Blade's stepdad's papers that his mom hid away. Maybe it would be a good thing if you helped us record and analyze them." He looked at her as they entered the foyer downstairs. "That would give you an important way to strike back at your father while we wait for this be over."

She put her hand in his. "You'd let me do that?"

"We could use the help. I'll mention it to Kit."

Kelan led her down the secret stairs from the den to the bunker. He chose that entry point because he knew it would put Fiona in mind of where she'd been held. Hair of the dog that bit you, sort of thing, he figured. She did not resist his lead. Her hand was tiny in his, soft, so goddamned tender, he didn't know how she existed in this world.

They walked out of the stairwell and into the long

conference room. The guys were all around the table, already at work. Greer killed the stuff on the big smart screen.

"Kelan, what the hell?" Kit asked.

He pulled Fiona in front of him and crossed his arms in front of her, holding her body fully against his. "Tell them. Say it to these men—and woman— who fought for you, the ones who will fight for you again and again. Tell them you're going to leave, and why."

Fiona's body tightened, like a great ball of rubber bands stretched too tight. Her hands held his forearms, her nails digging into his skin. He felt the splash of a tear on his skin. The sound of her swallow echoed in the silent room.

"I can't be with Kelan. I am to blame for everything my father's done, everything he might yet do. I cannot risk Kelan. Or you. Or anyone. I have to leave."

There. It was spoken aloud, into the burning light of these warriors' eyes, eyes that only knew truth and honor.

Owen was the first to speak. "Fiona, you're conscious of the mark your footprint makes in this world. That's extraordinarily rare." He bowed toward her from his place by the wall. "I honor that awareness. But you cannot bear the burden of others' footprints. You can only lead them with the integrity of your own."

Fiona sniffed.

"Who knows what will come of your time with Kelan?" Blade said. "Maybe that one small act of defiance against King will change the world."

Max stood. His face was tight with anger, his expression war-like. He marched over to them. Kelan narrowed his eyes in warning, but Max never looked at him as he touched Fiona's cheek. His thumb wiped a tear away. Kelan thought he was like Frankenstein's monster wiping dew from a flower.

"No." Max's nostrils flared. "You will not live your life in response to the madness of your father. You will not deny yourself, your heart, your future, all the fucking awesome experiences life has to offer."

When he stepped away, Rocco was there. He stared at her a long minute. "There is sunshine, Fee. I do believe it." He moved beside Max and folded his arms.

Then Kit was up. "You are a little sister to me. I reject your fear. I see only your courage." He took his place next to Rocco.

Angel was next. He smiled at her, in as gently a way as possible for him. "I will slay your dragons, if Kelan leaves any for me to fight."

Kelan felt more warm tears spill to his forearm as Fiona looked up at Greer. "Eight brothers and a warrior sister. We all veto your decision. If it backfires, we'll carry that burden, not you." He kissed her cheek, then took his place in the growing circle around her.

Blade lifted Fiona's chin. "I know how debilitating

a cage is." Fiona sniffled and drew a ragged breath. "I couldn't break free without Kit's help"—he looked around at the team—"without everyone's help. Kelan knew to bring you to us to bust you out of your cage. We will break those fucking bars, and break them again, and burn them down if we need to. You, Fiona, must be free, because if you aren't, no one is."

He moved aside, and Val stepped in front of them. For once, he had nothing to say, either sassy or serious. There was no humor in his eyes. Kelan had long suspected he'd never had much of a childhood, but that he'd chosen to see life from the joyful eyes of a kid in an unending effort to experience it. But now, looking at Fiona, there was no mask in place. He lowered his head and let it hang there a long moment. When he straightened, his eyes burned with an unholy blue heat.

"I will lay my life down for you, Fiona." He looked around at the team. "In the same way I would give my life for my warrior family." He looked at her again. "I don't do it in vain. I do it to give you the freedom to thrive in any choice you make. I do it selfishly to know that my life mattered."

Fiona nodded and sniffled, then broke from Kelan's hold to reach for Val. He hugged her a long time, rocking her a little. When he stepped to the side, Selena was there.

"Whatever you need to feel safe, Fee, ask me. Training. Weapon drills. Someone to stand at your door at night while you sleep. I'm here for you."

Fiona hugged her too.

Owen joined the circle, standing across from Fiona and Kelan. "King be damned. Your future is your own to make."

Fiona choked on a laugh. She sniffed and nodded. "Okay. I will."

Kelan grinned. A long sigh broke from him as he hugged her. He kissed her head. "I'll take you upstairs."

They went back up the way they'd come down. The symbolism was important to Kelan. Just as she'd been held in darkness—physical and mental—she also had the power to walk up out of it. He didn't let go of her hand until they'd crossed the room, the patio outside, and half the upper yard. When the sun poured down on them, he faced her.

Her life was her own, and what she chose to do with it mattered.

"You've heard from everyone. They care about you. They are your tribe. You're not alone. You don't exist in a vacuum. None of us does. You matter to the people who matter to you." He put his hand flat against her chest. "What does that feel like in your heart?"

She shook her head. Her eyes were wide and dilated. She didn't speak. She couldn't—Kelan knew there were no English words that approximated what she had to be feeling. He knew the words in Lakota, though, and he would teach them to her, in time.

He lifted her hands up above her head. His

thumbs opened her tight fists. "Feel the sun on your hands. Feel it pour down over you. Feel its cleansing heat. Give it your fear, your dread, your anger, your resentment. Then let the earth fill the newly empty space in you with hope, joy, possibilities of all that you are and wish to be."

Her image wavered before him as his eyes filled with liquid. "Feel your whole self. Your true self."

He let go of her. She kept her hands raised. Eventually, she drew a long, slow breath and let it out.

"The sun and the earth will always cleanse and replenish you. Infinitely."

She lowered her hands. Her eyes never left his. "Is it possible to be whole and to be a half at the same time?"

He didn't answer. Was she asking what he thought she was?

"I'm ready to join my life with yours, Kelan."

Kelan let out a whoop and swept her up into his arms, then swung her around a couple of times until her laughter broke through the wind in his ears. He took that sound into his heart, and knew he would hear it for lifetimes to come.

He set her on her feet then led her back to the house. At the patio, he let her go. "Pack what you need for an overnight stay. I have everything else we'll need. I'll bring Blade's Jeep out front."

He noticed that there were several faces watching them from the living room. Once spotted, the women dashed from the windows.

Fiona hurried across the patio, then slowly turned to look at him. "Is the claiming ceremony secret? Something I shouldn't talk about with the others?"

Kelan considered her question. "It isn't secret, but it's complex. Saying any part of it without giving the intentions behind the ceremony won't do it justice— and it may cause your friends to have bad feelings about it. There is no one it must please but you, so handle their curiosity as you wish."

She smiled, then came back over to kiss his cheek, which he bent to accept. He walked down the patio and into the house through the den, intending to find Kit to tell him he'd be out for a while.

The entire den was loaded to capacity with the team. To their credit, he couldn't remember seeing them at the window. They looked up at him, faking surprise. He grinned. "Fiona has agreed to the claiming ceremony."

"Hey, that's great, Kelan!" Selena said.

"So that wasn't the ceremony happening out there?" Val asked, only to get an elbow in the ribs from Blade. "What? I wasn't looking. Okay, well, I was a little curious."

Kelan's brows lowered. "The claiming ceremony is a sacred event, not entertainment for bored friends."

"Huh. Sacred like tantric sex?" Val looked hopeful.

Kelan took a step toward Val, but Kit stepped between. "Forget it. Forget him, us. Just go do your thing, feel me? I don't expect to see you again until you decide to come back."

Kelan held out his hand shook with Kit. "Thanks." He was almost to the door when he looked back.

Owen nodded at him, a faint smile on his lips.

"Hey—congrats, K," Blade said. "We love you, man."

Kelan shook his head and chuckled, as did the rest of the room before he shut the door.

CHAPTER THIRTY

Kelan loaded Blade's Jeep with the things they'd need: the trunk of ceremonial items, a cooler with food and drinks, camping gear, and his go-bag.

Fiona came out of the open garage bay. She put her stuff in the Jeep, then came over to him. She looked like a vision wearing a camp shirt over her tee, cargos, and hiking boots. Some sights just wrote themselves into your heart—this was one of them. Her face had none of the shadows that had darkened it in the last few days. She smiled at him. He lifted her hands and held them in his against his chest. He would never forget this moment.

"Ready?" he asked.

"Yes."

He leaned forward and kissed her forehead. "I already feel whole."

"Me too."

He opened the Jeep door for her. The soft-top was down, letting them enjoy the heat of the late summer day. When they returned in a day or two, fall will have started. It was an auspicious time for their ceremony.

Fiona pulled a baseball cap on as they left Blade's driveway. Her blond curls danced and bobbed in the wind. Took everything Kelan had to tear his eyes from her and focus on the road.

"Where are we going?"

"The place I selected is on the BLM land that Blade's estate leases."

"I can't wait to see it."

They drove away from Blade's for about a half-hour, then turned north onto a dirt road. The terrain was rough and the going was slow as they headed out onto the treeless, rolling hills of the open range. There was more grass than scrub brush. The green land rolled into the distant horizon, touching the blue, cloudless sky. To the west, large outcroppings of granite boulders became thicker and taller. They went down a hill, moving into switchbacks that seemed to come out of nowhere, over a wide creek, then back up the other side.

He looked at Fiona, curious about her reaction. Her eyes were big and awed. "I had no idea this was here."

He smiled. They hadn't even gotten to the best part yet. Another forty-five minutes of driving brought them to a narrow entrance into the huge rockface they'd been skirting. Soon the pass opened up to a small canyon. The road moved to the left, hugging the side of the cliff in what didn't seem like a man-made road.

Fiona took hold of the roll bar. "Is this safe?"

Kelan grinned. "You're strapped in, right?"

"Kelan!"

"It's safe. I've been out here a couple of times."

The road started to move away from the rockface, dropping down into a treed area. They drove through a grove of aspen and cottonwood, then came out into a clearing by a fast-moving creek. Willow shrubs grew up from the banks.

Kelan drove across the water and up the other side. A small pool had formed at the edge of the creek, its water steaming in the cool valley air. He pulled around the pool and stopped just past the wide entrance of a cave.

"What is this place?" Fiona asked as she got out of the Jeep. "How did you ever find it?"

"Finding you was harder than finding this place." He reached for her waist and pulled her close. Her hands moved up his chest to hold his neck. She took her hat off, and he kissed her lips. For a long minute, he lost himself in her eyes.

"You know, we are just like my grandfather and Bear Paw Woman." He brushed his hands over her pale curls. "But our coloring is opposite."

Fiona smiled. "Do you think they're happy for us?"

"I know they are. We're why they began the claiming ceremony."

"What happens now?"

"I'll prepare the cave."

"Can I help?"

"No, but you can watch. I'll explain as I go."

Fiona went to stand at the edge of the cave. It looked as if someone had already swept it out and cleared any debris. It wasn't a very large space, maybe ten by fifteen feet.

Kelan stood before the cave opening and lifted his hands, his arms spread wide. He said something in a language she didn't understand. He lowered his arms and smiled at her. "I asked my ancestors to bless and protect this space and us while we unite our lives."

Fiona smiled back at him. "It was beautiful."

"It's important, while our spirits are bare and our souls are open, to have their protection."

He lit his sage and set it to smoke in his abalone shell, then walked into the cave. Making a circuit about the space, he spread the smoke, saying something else she didn't understand. The hushed reverence in his words was mesmerizing.

He picked up a stick then drew a big circle in the dirt, and then a smaller one in the center. Checking the compass on his phone, he broke the circle into four quarters, then drew a line from each quarter to the inner circle.

He retrieved four small paint cans from the Jeep, along with four wide brushes. "This is the part of the ceremony Bear Paw Woman's father had my grandfather add." He gestured in the air. "We have the four elements represented already—air, water, earth, and the fire we'll set. This circle represents the four directions, the four seasons, the four stages of human life. Including them in this way shows we accept that we become one from separate parts, just as you and I will become one from two separate beings."

He painted the outer edge and one inside line for each color, explaining what he was doing as he went. "Yellow is for the east. It represents awareness, insights, and understanding. It's the color of our souls and of spring. Red is for the south. It represents the struggles we have in our lives, transmuting negative to positive. It's the color of our hearts and of summer. Black is for the west. It represents harvesting what we've sown, introspection, and life lessons. It's the color of our minds and of autumn. White is for the north. It represents the skills we use to survive, the positive behaviors that help us live long and healthy lives. It's the color of our bodies and of winter."

"What's the circle in the middle for?"

"That's where we'll sit during the ceremony, in the middle of these powerful energies." He brought in rocks and placed them in a smaller circle in the middle. He collected kindling and wood for a fire and set it in the ring of rocks, along with a box of matches.

Kelan went back to the trunk and retrieved the small iron brands. Fiona frowned looking at them. How she wished the branding wasn't part of the ceremony. He set them next to the fire ring. He must have noticed her concern when he came outside.

"Fiona, it will transform us both, uniting us. I'll have the scars on my body, but you'll have them in your heart. We'll each remember the vows we had seared into us during our claiming."

Fee blinked a tear away.

He went over to the Jeep and withdrew the last things from his trunk. His go-bag, which he set outside the cave entrance. And then two outfits—a white deerskin dress beautifully embellished with colorful beadwork, and a set of deerskin leggings and tunic. There was also a wide leather strip and what looked like a long, fringed scarf with more of the beadwork on the ends.

He went over to the cooler and pulled out two bottles of water. "Thirsty?"

"I am." She cracked hers open and took a long swallow. "What happens now?"

"I start the fire, and while we wait for the irons to heat up, we bathe in the spring. When they're hot, we begin."

"How do you know how to do this ceremony?"

"I read and memorized it long ago. When I told my parents about you, my mother reminded me again of all its parts."

"You told them about me?" Why that made her feel a bolt of dread, she didn't know.

"They love you already, because I do."

"Really?"

He came over and pulled her into his arms. "Absolutely. When things calm down, I'll have them out to meet you. Or we'll go see them."

"I'd like that. It's nice to have a family again."

"Have you selected your vows?"

Fee nodded. "Do we discuss them first? What if I chose bad ones and you have to sear them into your skin?"

Kelan smiled. "Are they tenets you'll live by?"

"Yes."

"Then you can surprise me with them in the ceremony. Ready to begin?"

She nodded then touched her hand to her chest. "My heart is beating so hard."

He kissed her, then went into the cave and lit the fire. Once the wood had begun to burn, he set the irons in the fire. His face was solemn when he returned. He met her eyes, then began undressing.

The air was cool in the ravine—she couldn't wait to get in the hot spring. She removed her boots, then the rest of her clothes, feeling the chilly breeze whisper about her. Kelan took her hand and led her into the steaming pool. It was shallow and hot. Big rocks, rounded from the water, lined the edges. Smaller ones were across the bottom. The pool was too hot for anything to grow. Minerals bubbled up from the sand and river gravel. The water had a pleasant scent—like heated dirt and rock.

Kelan picked up a handful of sand and rubbed it on her chest and arms. She did the same for him, then lifted his forearms and kissed the insides of both wrists. They didn't talk; their silence was tense. She splashed the water over her arms and body, listening to the nearby stream and the sound of the birds in the little valley.

After a while, Kelan took her hands. He led her from the pool. The cool air seemed much colder now. He handed her a big bath sheet. She dried herself then watched him dress. He tied the heavy strap about his hips, then pulled on the leggings and tied them to it. The leather framed his sex in a pleasing way. She smiled at him, but he didn't return it.

He tucked the leather scarf over the strap in back of him, then pulled it between his legs and tucked it in up front, leaving the decorative edge out. She realized what she'd thought was a scarf was really a breechclout. She'd never seen one on anyone before.

He didn't put the tunic on. He needed to keep his arms clear for the ceremony. She looked from his bare feet to his face, struck by his beauty and fierceness. She'd seen him in operational gear, casual wear, tuxedoes, and now this—and this was by far her favorite attire for him.

"If my heart wasn't already yours, it would be now." She couldn't do more than whisper. The smile he gave seemed sad. He must be feeling the same overwhelming emotions she was.

He picked up her dress. "Your turn."

Fiona removed her towel, which she'd been using as a blanket, and tossed it over the side of the Jeep. He lifted the dress over her head. It felt like heaven. Light, but warm and soft. "This is beautiful."

He took her hand and began leading her into the cave. "Wait!" She ran back to her purse and removed a piece of paper. "I wrote my vows down. I was afraid I would forget them in the heat of the moment." She bared her bottom teeth in a worried frown. "Is that allowed?"

"Of course. I've memorized mine, but I've also written them down."

"Good. I don't want to forget anything about this ceremony."

They went into the cave and sat beside the fire, facing each other. Kelan checked the irons. The tips were glowing red. "We'll do your vows then mine." In his beautiful Lakota language, he said something—a prayer, she supposed.

He looked at her. "I asked the spirits stand guard while we exchange our vows." He rearranged the irons in the oven. "We'll say them in this order: our bodies, our hearts, our minds, our spirits."

Fiona felt a knot in her stomach. She wanted to race through the next few moments as much as she wanted to move slowly so she could remember all of it.

"Let's begin." Kelan removed the first of her irons from the fire, the one that represented her body. He held it above the base of his left wrist, then nodded at her.

Her hands shook as she lifted her paper over her folded legs. She glanced at him, then said, "Kelan

Shiozski, I vow to ensure that our physical lives exist in a place of peace."

That was a good vow. He nodded at her, then set the iron to his skin and counted one...two...three...four. The pain was intense. His skin sizzled beneath the hot metal. He set the iron beside the fire, then focused on his breathing, dissipating the pain as he repeated her vow silently to himself, forever connecting its meaning with its symbol on his skin.

He took up the second iron, then looked at her. Tears were running down her face. "Your heart vow, now."

Her blue eyes caught his. "I vow to celebrate our similarities and differences with equal reverence."

He pressed the second iron just to the left of the first, counting the slow seconds. He lifted the iron away and repeated her vow to himself.

The marks were small. Not quite an inch each. He smiled as he looked at red welts that were rising. They would fit nicely under the wrist cuffs he'd had made. He'd lived thirty-four years, and only now did he feel he was becoming a man.

"Your mind's vow, now."

Fiona bit her lip then slowly said, "I vow to give your needs and opinions equal consideration whenever I make a life decision."

He nodded. Her vows were strong. He was proud of the mate she was becoming. The third iron went to the left of the second one. Again he took a deep breath, then repeated her intention.

"And now, your spirit's vow to me."

Her face was dangerously pale. She wept as she said, "I vow to participate in the lifelong transformation we'll make from being two separate individuals to a couple with one footprint."

Kelan placed the last brand on his left arm. He took a long breath then released it as he repeated her last vow. The shadows of the cave enhanced the reflection of the flames on her worried face. "You honor me well, Fiona."

She sniffled and nodded. "Are you all right?"

He smiled at her. "I'm better than all right. I'm becoming whole."

He set her irons to the side of the fire then removed the one representing his body. He looked at her. "I vow to provide the nourishment your body and your mind need to thrive." He set the first brand on his right arm.

"Say my body's vow back to me, Fiona. Look at the mark on my arm as you say it."

Her gaze dropped to his wrist. "You vow to provide the nourishment my mind and body need to thrive."

He nodded and smiled. "I do." He took the next iron out of the fire and held it above his right wrist, next to the first mark. "From my heart, I vow to practice patience and self-control when confronted with challenging situations in our union."

He set the second brand. When he looked up,

Fiona was holding her hands over her mouth. "Breathe, Fiona. Like this." He held her gaze as he took a long, slow pull of air. She did the same. "Repeat my heart's vow."

"You vow to practice patience and self-control when we face challenging situations."

He smiled. "I do." He held her gaze as he set the third iron. "From my mind, I vow to keep silence, action, and leadership in the proper balance in our interactions." He pressed the iron in the next place on his arm.

Fiona nodded, then breathed with him again. "From your mind, you vow to balance silence, action, and leadership in our interactions."

"The last one now, from my spirit. I vow to nurture and encourage you and our children." He set the final mark on his skin. When it was finished, Fiona repeated his vow as tears streamed down her face. "You honor me well, Kelan."

He smiled at her. "It's done." He rested his forearms on his thighs. His skin was red and angry.

"Is the pain terrible?"

"It's incredible, Fiona." He looked at his arms, then held his wrists for her to see. "Look at the marks that show us as one."

Fiona cupped her hands beneath his. "My heart will never be the same."

"Nor mine." He stood. "I'm going to close the ceremony now. I'll tell our ancestors of our claiming and thank the four directions for their protection."

He went to the opening of the cave. Holding up his arms with his wrists held out facing the world, he did just that, using the words of his Lakota ancestors in a singsongy chant that rumbled from his heart.

When he was finished, he looked at Fiona standing beside him. Tears spilled down his cheeks because his spirit was too full to contain them. Holding his arms out to the side, he leaned over and kissed her. "I love you."

She smiled against his mouth. "I love you."

"Will you get the salve and bandages from my bag? We'll cover these up and let them heal."

She fetched those two things, then they sat beside the fire. She dipped her fingers into a sweet smelling cream. "What is this?"

"It's a blend my mother uses for burns. It contains mock orange, aloe, coconut oil, and some other things."

Fiona took his right arm and gently smoothed the cream over his burns. When she'd wrapped his forearm, she smiled up at him. "I feel just like Bear Paw Woman."

"How so?"

"Tending the wounds of a fierce animal."

Kelan grinned. "I'm fierce?"

"Terrifying."

He smiled as she repeated her ministrations on his other arm.

"Will you wear your cuffs now?"

"Tomorrow, when we go back to the house.

There's something else in the bag that I need you to get."

Fiona frowned. "What is it?"

"Your birthday present."

She opened the bag and dug around, then lifted out a small jewelry box. She gave him a curious look, then unwrapped it. Lifting the lid, she took out a pair of silver earrings made from two dimes.

"Those dimes were minted the same year you were born. They're twenty-one years old. It's a small gift, but I had it made specifically to honor this birthday."

Fiona shut her eyes and squeezed the earrings in her hand. "I love them."

"I know you said you wanted to skip this year—"

Her eyes shot open, and she looked at him. "I don't anymore. You've made this an extraordinary one already. I want to remember everything about it." She put the earrings on, then leaned forward and kissed him as she said, "Thank you for my gift."

He spread his fingers in her hair and brought her close for another kiss. "I love you, Mahasani."

CHAPTER THIRTY-ONE

Wynn parked out front of her grandmother's current nursing home. She'd arranged everything for her move and made certain it would happen with the least disruption possible. She hadn't expected to be able to be here when she started her new job just days ago, but when she told Mandy what was happening, her new boss made certain she took the day off.

There wasn't anything she could do for her grandmother during the move, other than hold her hand before they took her and be there when they settled her in her new room. Still, she felt certain her presence would make her grandmother feel better about the change.

She looked at her watch. The move was planned for ten a.m. She had forty-five minutes yet, plenty of time to visit with Grams and help her understand what was happening.

Wynn waved to the nurses at the main desk. They looked at her in an odd way. She figured days like this were always a little awkward, when a family moved a resident to a different facility. The crew here was kind—she knew they'd miss her grandmother.

When she got to her room, it was empty. A man was mopping the floor. *Oh, God.* Had Grams passed? She covered her mouth, blocking a sob, and spun on her heel. One of the nurses who cared for her grandmother was there. "Where is she?" Wynn asked.

"She was moved a half-hour ago."

"They took her already?" She looked at her watch again, wondering if she'd gotten the times mixed up. Oh, but what a relief that she was fine, just already on her way to her new home. Wynn dragged in a big breath. "I thought that wasn't supposed to happen until ten."

"We thought so too." The nurse looked perturbed. "And I guess you changed your mind about where you wanted her moved to. It's risky moving a stroke victim to a private residence. I wish you had consulted with us about that. We could have helped ensure you were prepared for her intense needs."

"What are you talking about?"

The nurse handed her a clipboard. Wynn saw her signature on a change order, canceling her previous move request and changing the new address to one she didn't recognize.

"When did you get this?"

"This morning, when her care team came for her."

"I didn't do this change request."

"You signed it."

Wynn shook her head. She didn't have the time to argue. She had to go find her grandmother. "I'd like a copy of this, please."

The nurse pulled out a copy from the clipboard.

Wynn snatched it and hurried back to her car. The address was for a house in one of the upscale neighborhoods about twenty minutes away. It was a private residence, still in Cheyenne. How could a mix-up like this have happened? Did the ambulance crew mistake her grandmother for someone else? Was someone else's matriarch on the way to the other nursing home?

Wynn pulled up in front of a stately neo-Tudor mansion. She hurried up the long, tiered front walkway, then rang the doorbell several times.

A woman in a nurse's outfit opened the door. "Ms. Ratcliff?"

"Yes. Is my grandmother here? I think there's been some terrible mistake."

"She is. Let me take you to her."

The woman turned down a long hall to a bedroom. It looked, in every way, just like a room in a nursing home, with all the requisite equipment for a stroke patient. Her heart monitor had a steady beep.

Wynn pushed her hair behind her ears and hurried to the bed where her grandmother lay so peacefully. She grabbed her hand, relieved at its warmth, and was careful not to jostle her IV feed. "Grams, what happened? How did you get here?" she asked, knowing her elder couldn't answer.

A movement on the other side of the bed caught her attention. A man stood up from a chair and pushed the bed curtain back to the wall. "Hello, Ms. Ratcliff."

Wynn frowned at him, trying to remember if she'd ever met him. "Who are you?"

"I am Jafaar Majid."

"Why is my grandmother here?"

He looked down at Grams' peaceful face. "It is a difficult thing, is it not, to see one's beloved so vulnerable."

Wynn straightened. "I asked why she's here."

"She is—how do you say—leverage. You have something we want. And now we have something you want. The scales are balanced."

"Are you saying you kidnapped my grandmother?"

"Indeed."

Cold terror clamped Wynn's heart. "I'm calling the police." She scrabbled around in her purse for her phone. When she lifted it out, a woman was standing next to Gram's IV, holding a needle to it. What were they doing?

"What's that?"

"Nothing. Only a bubble. Sad that a little air, something so vital to us, could kill your grandmother."

"Why are you threatening her?"

"I told you. You have something we want. And yes, you can call the police, but before they can get here, your precious elder will be dead."

"What do you want?"

"It is my understanding you've taken a new job,

working for a delightful family a little ways up the road. In fact, you now live with them." The mask of affability he'd worn fell away. "They are enemies of mine. I need you to listen to their plans, let me know what they are up to."

"I don't have access to that. I work with their son. I have no idea what they're doing."

"Make it your business." He waved a hand around the room. "As you see, we've taken the utmost care to provide your grandmother with everything she might need as she recovers her faculties from the stroke." His eyes met hers. "But we also have everything we need to make her life a living hell. Fail us, and we will introduce terrible pain that she cannot fight. Help us, and we will assist her recovery process. Go to the authorities, or to your employer, and your sweet grandmother will be killed."

Wynn could barely breathe. This lunatic would kill her grandmother before Wynn could get any help to her. She looked at Grams, and noticed her eyes were blinking rapidly. Was she silently screaming for Wynn to help her? How could she do anything but that?

"What kind of info are you looking for?" she asked.

Mr. Majid smiled. "I knew we could come to terms."

OTHER BOOKS BY ELAINE LEVINE

~Red Team Series~

(This series must be read in order)

1 The Edge of Courage (2012)

2 Shattered Valor (2012)

3 Honor Unraveled (2013)

3.5 Kit & Ivy: A Red Team Wedding Novella (2014)

4 Twisted Mercy (2014)

4.5 Ty & Eden: A Red Team Wedding Novella (2015)

5 Assassin's Promise (2015)

6 War Bringer (2016)

~ Men of Defiance Series ~

(This series may be read in any order)

1 Rachel and the Hired Gun (2009)

2 Audrey and the Maverick (2010)

3 Leah and the Bounty Hunter (2011)

4 Logan's Outlaw (2012)

5 Agnes and the Renegade (2014)

ABOUT THE AUTHOR

Elaine Levine lives in the mountains of Colorado with her husband, a middle-aged parrot, and a rescued pit bull/bullmastiff mix. In addition to writing the Red Team romantic suspense series, she is the author of several books in the historical western series Men of Defiance.

Visit her online at ElaineLevine.com for more information about her upcoming books. She loves hearing from readers! Contact her at elevine@elainelevine.com or sign up for her new release announcements at http://eepurl.com/tJuy5.

If you enjoyed this book, please consider leaving a review at your favorite online retailer or at Goodreads.com to help other readers find it.

I'm excited to bring you an excerpt from Abbie Zanders' Dangerous Secrets (Callaghan Brothers, Book 1). Abbie is definitely an author to add to your reading list, so visit her website at AbbieZandersRomance.com when you get a chance to check out all her stories!

—Elaine

~*~ * ~*~

Taryn felt instantly at home in the Pub. She'd spent most of the last eight years working in one just like it. Unofficially, of course, but no one ever questioned it and that kind of thing had never really mattered to Charlie.

It gave her an idea.

It took some effort to get to the bar, but not all of it was unpleasant. With the level of noise and density of the ebullient crowd, Taryn quickly discovered the most effective method for making forward progress was a well-placed hand in a strategic location. By the time the men turned to see who had taken such liberties, Taryn had disappeared once again.

It was the younger guy who spotted her first. A brief raise of his eyebrows and a flickering glance toward the window was followed by a dazzling smile. "So she is courageous as well as beautiful," he said, handing two filled mugs to the man on her right. "What's your pleasure?"

Taryn returned his smile with one equally devastating. It was a skill she had mastered years earlier. She also let her eyes linger on his lips just a second longer than necessary as she ran her tongue lightly across her lip. Ian's eyes flashed. Gotcha.

God bless the male sex, they were so easily baited. "You're very busy tonight."

"Yeah," he agreed, leaning against the bar as if there weren't two dozen people around her vying for his attention. "A little."

"Looks like you could use another bartender."

Ian's grin widened. "You offering?"

"Oi, Ian," called Jake. "What the - " Jake stopped when he saw who had captured his brother's undivided attention.

"She says she can help out behind the bar," Ian informed him with a grin.

"Is that right?" Jake walked over, gathering a few orders along the way. "You tend?"

She nodded, her smile fading a little. This was the man who had pinned her with his gaze through the window. He was much bigger close-up. Definitely related to the younger guy, but infinitely more intense. Harder. She suppressed a shiver. Maybe this wasn't such a good idea after all.

* * *

The closer Jake got to her, the stranger he felt. He likened it to an electrical current flowing through his body, which, unfortunately, he had experienced. Comparatively speaking, this instance was much more pleasant.

Who had eyes like that? Layered, like a custom paint

job. If he had to guess, he'd say her eyes were purplish with a couple of clear coats of smoky gray on top, the exact hue of the sky moments before a summer thunderstorm. It had to be a trick of the lights, though, because no one could actually have eyes like that. Thankfully, there was no trace of the haunted look he'd seen earlier, making him think he might have imagined it.

"What was that last order?" he asked, locking his blue gaze with hers.

"Excuse me?"

"The last order I took. What was it?" He fixed her with a level gaze.

"Oh, come on, Jake," began Ian, but Jake ignored him.

The woman took a breath. He knew, because his eyes were drawn to the subtle rise and fall of the nicely-endowed chest peeking through that jacket.

"Two pints of Killian, one Irish coffee, a Baileys and cream no ice, and two fingers of Grey Goose with a splash of lime."

The corners of Jake's mouth twitched. "What's the secret to pulling a good draft?"

She appeared to consider his question for a moment, then leaned forward. Jake mimicked the movement, putting his ear within inches of her lips. Even with all the noise, Jake had no trouble hearing her low, quiet-toned answer. "Giving it just the right amount of head."

The twitch became a full-fledged grin.

It was a crazy idea. Jake didn't tolerate just anybody

behind his bar. But he was desperate. Plus, for some strange reason, he liked the idea of having her back with him instead of out in the rowdy crowd. Quite a few of the men were already looking at her as if she was a tasty snack. He rationalized the impulse by telling himself he wasn't doing it for her or even him, for that matter; having someone like that behind the bar was simply good for business.

"Right," he said. "You're hired. Get your ass back here."

The smile she gave him lit up the entire room, but it quickly faded when she tried to move. He understood the problem immediately: to get where he was, she would have to cross the length of the long bar and around the other end, which, given the current mob, would take about half an hour. She looked at him helplessly.

"Oi, Big John!" Jake barked. "A little help for my new barmaid, please."

A huge, bearded man shifted next to her; plate-sized hands circled her waist and she was suddenly suspended over the bar. A host of cheers and catcalls went up in the immediate vicinity as Jake grabbed her out of the air and brought her down on the other side.

Jake was stricken by yet another strange sensation as his hands closed around her waist. It was like hitting the sweet spot on a baseball bat, or releasing the perfect three-point shot, knowing it was going to be a total swish without even having to look. And his thumbs didn't skim the underside of her breasts. They didn't. Because if they did, he'd have to think about how full and firm they were against his fingers, and that would be bad...

—Excerpted from Dangerous Secrets (Callaghan Brothers, Book 1) by © Abbie Zanders. Reprinted with permission.

58225908R10243

Made in the USA
Charleston, SC
06 July 2016